A FINAL RECKONING

A Selection of Titles by Susan Moody

LOSING NICOLA *
DANCING IN THE DARK *
LOOSE ENDS *
A FINAL RECKONING *

DOUBLED IN SPADES
DUMMY HAND
FALLING ANGEL
KING OF HEARTS
RETURN TO THE SECRET GARDEN

* *available from Severn House*

A FINAL RECKONING

Susan Moody

Severn House Large Print
London & New York

This first large print edition published 2015
in Great Britain and the USA by
SEVERN HOUSE PUBLISHERS LTD of
19 Cedar Road, Sutton, Surrey, England, SM2 5DA.
First world regular print edition published 2013 by
Severn House Publishers Ltd., London and New York.

British Library Cataloguing in Publication Data

Moody, Susan author.
  A final reckoning.
  1. Murder–Investigation–England–Cotswold Hills–
  Fiction. 2. Detective and mystery stories. 3. Large type
  books.
  I. Title
  823.9'14-dc23

  ISBN-13: 9780727872906

Severn House Publishers support the Forest Stewardship Council™
[FSC™], the leading international forest certification organisation. All
our titles that are printed on FSC certified paper carry the FSC logo.

Typeset by Palimpsest Book Production Ltd.,
Falkirk, Stirlingshire, Scotland.
Printed and bound in Great Britain by
T J International, Padstow, Cornwall.

Until the screams began, the house was quiet, wrapped in an expectant pre-Christmas hush. A sharp ear could have picked up the trembling tinkle of a glass bauble on the decorated tree in the hall, water running, the slump of ash in the big fireplace, voices excited behind a closed door. An even more acute listener might have caught the skitter of mice behind the deep carved skirting, or the chew of beetles in the heavy beams of the ceiling. Even the most alert eavesdropper could not have heard the imperceptible fall of snowflakes drifting through the silent air outside though not yet beginning to settle on the frozen ground.

Otherwise, there was only silence.

Until the screams began.

Terrified, agonized, long-drawn-out and desperate, 'Mummeeeee,' as though the person screaming already knew that no help would be forthcoming. At first there were words, high-pitched, hysterical: 'Don't! Stop! Mum! Please, Mummeee, oh don't! Ouch! Owww! You're hurting me,' the voice rising to a scream until gradually the frantic syllables gave way to a thick-throated gurgle, 'Ah, aaah, ohhh,' and then an ominous silence.

At the same time, another voice joined in, a voice sure of itself, asking what the hell was going on, before a third voice sounded, low and menacing, 'You fucking interfering bitch, mind your own fucking business.'

More shouting, 'Oh, my God, what the hell are you . . .' before the words changed suddenly to a strident note of terror, 'No, no, have you gone crazy?' Then a further series of shrieks, a thud followed by two more, and further horrifying silence. Light footsteps, running, running.

The third voice again, a mad voice, whispering, whispering, 'You'd better look out, you little bastard. You can run but you can't hide, you fucking monster, I'll find you in the end, and when I do . . .'

More footsteps, more hideous shrieks, 'Stop, stop, I didn't mean to, honestly, I . . .' gradually dying away in a series of agonized whimpers. Then silence once more.

The sharp-eared listener might have heard the distant sound of bare-branched bushes being thrust aside, the inhalation of breath in the bitter air, the wincing run of bare feet on winter woodland. Until once again, silence returned, broken only by the tinkle of the coloured balls on the tree and the tiny sound of a pine needle dropping to the stone-flagged floor.

One

Where do you begin a story like this one?

Do you start with your characters, build up a portrait of them, small accretions added for the reader: who they are, what they do, where they're going, what they want? She likes Mahler, milk-chocolate, Marmite; he's afraid of heights, or broke his nose playing rugby when he was at university? That way, you make them known, you provide them with an identity which holds the attention even before you launch into your story.

Or do you begin *in medias res*, plunging slap, bang into the defining events from which your narrative springs? This has the advantage of an immediately dramatic situation, but then you have to trust your reader to stick with you while you use flashback to define character and conflict. In my own case, I was thrust into dramatic events long before this story began.

I was nearly thirteen when my sister died. Small for my age, red-headed, feisty and, like her, very intelligent. All qualities I still possess. (Sorry: I don't believe in false modesty.) We were living in California at the time, near the Berkeley campus, where my father, Alexander Monroe, was a professor of moral philosophy. That particular day, warmer than usual for the time of year, Dad was in his study, while Mom pottered in some undefined way. As for me, I lounged on the swing-seat in the garden, wrapped in a rug and relishing *Le Grand Meaulnes* for the fifth time. I was lost in the romantic ideal of searching for the unobtainable. Shrubs bloomed thickly round the garden: red bougainvillea, Ti trees, silk tassel. In my memory of that unforgettable day, the air was thick with the scent of lavender and lilac, cloves and thyme, though I know it could not have been, since it was just before Christmas. But the sky was an intense California blue, and I remember doves cooing somewhere, the vibrating flash of a hummingbird at the feeder, the harsh squawk and flare of the blue jays, three Canada geese picking in a ladylike way at some seed my mother had thrown down for them, though all of that might have been a subsumption of the many summers I'd spent in that garden.

I remember, too, experiencing one of those ecstatic flashes of happiness at the absolute rightness of things, like electricity exploding over and around me. To be aware of joy when young is a gift, I think, not given to everyone.

Inside the house, the telephone shrilled. I heard my mother's voice answering. I heard her give a couple of responses to questions from the other end. There followed a terrible silence. Even I, only dreamily half-attentive, could feel the intensity of that silence. And the sound of the denying shrieks which came after. They went on and on, filling the garden, the house, the quiet street, the neighbourhood, the world. By the time I had dropped my book and rushed into the sunroom, Mom was in my father's arms, moaning

4

incoherently, her forehead against his chest, her limbs shaking. It was so obvious that something too dreadful to bear had happened that I didn't even ask what, just threw my arms around them both, not really wanting to hear any more. Because I knew instinctively that this was the end of happiness, the end of childhood. When she drew back to press her wet face against my cheek, she looked as though she had aged twenty years. Her teeth chattered; her eyes had grown hollow. She was no longer my little French *maman*, she had become a ghost, all in the space of a few minutes.

To be explicit, as far as the police were able to reconstruct it, this is what appeared to have happened, though I only learned the details bit by bit. It was two days before Christmas, and my sister Sabine was working for an English family who resided in a small country house called Weston Lodge, about forty minutes into Oxfordshire from London. The other staff had all gone home for Christmas, leaving just one all-purpose employee in place. Also in the house at the time of the atrocity were the owner of the Lodge, the Honourable Clio Palliser, her two sons – Edward and George – and a third boy, a school friend for whom the Pallisers acted as a guardian, his own parents living and working abroad. All three boys were upstairs. Overexcited by the approach of Christmas, and with their father, Harry Redmayne, not yet home from his work in London, they'd apparently behaved pretty badly, had acted up, been disobedient and cheeky.

The third boy was absent for the earlier part of the evening, having been invited out for supper with some nearby friends of his parents; on his return, the sons of the house had joined him for half an hour or so at the grand piano in the front hall to practise the carols they were to sing to the family on Christmas Day. Apparently, while he'd been gone, the other two had not only scrawled rude words (FUCK YOU, to be precise) on a valuable painting in the drawing room, they had then tried to burn the manuscript of their mother's latest book (or article, I was never sure which) in the big fireplace in the hall.

They were twelve and thirteen; their friend was also thirteen, like me: all three of them were old enough to know better, old enough to be aware of the maliciousness of the damage they were causing. Eventually, they'd been persuaded to get ready for bed. George, the younger son, got into the bath, while the older two played with Lego in their shared bedroom, awaiting their own turn for the tub.

Sometime after that, the mother (the Honourable Clio) had emerged from her study, discovered the damage to the picture and the manuscript, and had come raging upstairs, brandishing a knife. Before anyone was really aware of what she intended (and how could they possibly have been?), she'd gone into the bathroom, grabbed twelve-year-old George by the hair and slit his throat.

The sheer horror that boy must have felt, the disbelief as his own mother killed him, is almost too much to contemplate. The temporary

6

mother's help had come out of her room two doors down from the bathroom to see what on earth was going on, and the mother, by now (one presumes) totally off her head with manic fury, had flown at her, plunging the bloodied knife into her eye, and then into her heart, leaving her lying dead or dying in the passage. Meanwhile, the two elder boys, hearing the screams, had come out of their room and into the passage, and seeing the carnage, had run literally for their lives. The Honourable Clio had gone after them, and found thirteen-year-old Edward hiding in the broom cupboard under the back stairs, had dragged him out, cut off three of his fingers and slit his throat, too. This gave the third boy time to escape, which he did by squeezing through a ventilation gap – a short-cut exit the boys had often used before – in the cold-pantry off the kitchen, and out into the snow, where he took to his heels and ran as far as he could away from the house.

Later that evening, Harry Redmayne, the father, had arrived home, ready to enjoy the Christmas holidays with his family, only to discover the house splattered with gore, his blood-drenched wife silent in front of the hall fire, three dead and mutilated bodies, and a boy missing.

Redmayne called the police, and a search was immediately organized, but the third boy wasn't discovered until early the next day. He had managed to find his way in the dark to a disused shed hidden in undergrowth in the nearby woods where the boys sometimes used to play, and had holed up there. No one knew how he could have survived the cold, but somehow he did – luckily, he had not yet taken all his clothes off when the carnage began. As far as he could, he had given the police an account of what he'd heard.

There was no difficulty in determining who was responsible for the bloodbath. The Honourable Clio Palliser, who had retreated into what they termed 'elective mutism', did not speak or write a single word in her own defence (as if you could defend the indefensible). She was arrested, tried and sent to Broadmoor, to spend the rest of her life under lock and key.

And what, you might wonder, did any of this have to do with my family in sunny California? Why had my mother collapsed? How had my childhood been destroyed by a single telephone call?

Because, quite simply, the murdered mother's help was my sister Sabine.

Until then, we had been a close-knit and loving family, but Sabine's death broke us up. She was my elder by seven years (my fragile French mother had lost two babies between Sabine and me) and, in many ways, she, rather than my parents, was the strong core around which we all revolved. Our essence, if you like. That she was away in Europe at all had left us depleted, especially at Christmas, but after obtaining a first degree at Pomona, a small liberal arts college, she had chosen to take a fine arts course at my father's *Alma Mater*, the University of Edinburgh. At the end of her first semester, she called to say that rather than come home, she was planning to stay in Europe for the vacation, in order to earn some money. University life was proving more

8

expensive than she'd bargained for, so she'd applied for a job she'd seen advertised in one of the student newspapers, spending a month *au pair*ing in a country house owned by a well-known art dealer and his wife, somewhere in the middle of the Cotswolds.

'You don't have to do this,' my father told her over the phone. 'You know I'd be happy to pay your fare out here. Call it your Christmas present, if you like.'

'Thanks, Dad,' Sabine said, 'but this could be a real opportunity for me. Not just a good experience, but with this guy being so big in the art world, it might even open doors later, when I've got my Master's.'

'Who is he again?'

'He's called Harry Redmayne. You can check him out, if you're worried. He paid for me to go down to his London office for an interview. Very nice, very charming. And obviously a man with good judgement, since he gave me the job.'

'Quite right too,' my mother said. 'But I really wish you would come 'ome for Christmas.' Her French accent was stronger than usual, a sure sign that she was agitated.

'So do I, Mom,' soothed Sabine. 'But I'll come over at Easter, maybe, instead. The thing is, from what he told me, there are masses of marvellous paintings all over his house – I might even find a good subject for my thesis.'

'But what exactly are you going to be doing, *chérie*?'

'I'm going to be a general factotum.'

'What's that when it's at home?' asked Dad.

9

'That's what Mr Redmayne called it: general factotum. Basically, it means a dogsbody,' my sister said cheerfully. 'A bit of this, a bit of that. Driving people around, doing the shopping, keeping an eye on two or three kids, which I can do standing on my head after babysitting Chantal all these years. The mother is some kind of expert on Nordic languages or something, and I got a strong impression from Mr Redmayne that she's a little short on the mothering gene, which is why he wants me around.'

'Sounds a bit dodgy, sis,' I said.

'No, she's trying to get a book finished, so basically they're looking for an extra pair of hands.'

'Well, *chérie*, if zat is your decision, we must accept it,' said my mother. 'But I am not 'appy about it.'

'We're really going to miss you over Christmas, hon,' Dad said.

'And I you.' Her voice wavered slightly. 'Turn down an empty glass, won't you?'

'It won't be Christmas if you're not there, Sabine,' I complained. It would be my first Christmas without my big sister.

'*Chérie*, please . . .' It was my mother again, suddenly sounding agitated. 'You *must* come 'ome. I want you to, *please*.'

'Don't worry, *maman*, I'll write,' she promised. 'I'll call . . .'

But she never did. And that was it, until the phone call from England and the brutal realization that we would never see Sabine again.

* * *

10

You can never get over something like that. But then you shouldn't expect to. My mother tried, she really did. Remembering her distress during Sabine's last phone call, I've often wondered if she'd had some premonition that things would end badly. Looking back, I think it was not just grief but also guilt that gnawed at her soul. She knew as well as Dad and I did that life moved on and you with it, that time passed, that anguish faded. It was the natural order of things, after all, and to be honest, a lot of the time you didn't think about it until something came up to remind you, and once again the sharp pain bit at your heart and the tears began to fall in that helpless hopeless way. Oh God . . . Why Sabine? Why us? *Why*?

There was no answer to that. How could there be?

Whatever age I was when Sabine died, I would have been deeply scarred, but I believe that on that adolescent cusp, no longer a child, not yet an adult, hormones rampant, skin several layers thinner than usual, acutely sensitive to everything and everybody around me, I was more susceptible than I might otherwise have been. With the result that the gash in my personality remained unhealed.

Time passed. We moved on – or tried to. But my mother couldn't handle it. She faded away, almost literally, until one day, two years later, Christmas time again, Dad and I came home to find her sitting on the sofa, staring at nothing, holding a little woolly bear in her hand. She turned her head towards us as we came in through the patio door, smiling faintly, said, 'Sorry, my darlings,' and fell slowly back against the cushions, while we both watched, astonished and uncomprehending. Dad called an ambulance while we tried to resuscitate her, but she was gone. They called in a verdict of Accidental Death, but Dad and I knew that the cause was, quite simply, a broken heart. My personal opinion? Sounds weird but I think she was more or less dead when we arrived back and had only waited for one last look at us, one final word, before she let go.

Dad and I tried to take up our lives again. He took early retirement, and began turning his love of book-collecting from a hobby into a serious profession. Together we decided to sell up and move to Rome, where I finished my schooling at the Lycée.

I didn't get any taller after that year: I've often wondered if the sudden shock inhibited my growth. After taking a first degree (at Pomona, of course, like my sister) and consulting with my father (*'It won't bring her back again,'* he said, looking at me over the tops of his half-moon glasses), I applied for the same courses at Edinburgh University as Sabine had been taking. Scotland was the coldest place I'd ever been, but even so, I enjoyed my years in the chilly city. There was a kind of melancholy about the country's history and culture which perfectly harmonized with my own deep-rooted sadness. And I made some good friends, particularly Brigid Frazer and her brothers Douglas and Hamilton.

After graduating, I spent a year at the Institute in Rome, to be near Dad again, then eighteen months in Copenhagen, at one of their art schools, concentrating on Nordic painters. During that time, I had a short-lived but passionate affair with a handsome Danish guy I met at a party at the American Embassy. Magnus Jenssen (or possibly Jens Magnussen – I can't now remember which) was blond and tall and very social; although he spent most of his time in London working for an architectural company, he came over to Denmark almost every weekend and seemed to know everyone in that small country who was worth knowing.

Back in Rome in my father's apartment, I began casting around for jobs in a leisurely way, enjoying doing nothing after so many years of study. One evening, while Dad and I sat reading in peaceful silence, there came a call via the entryphone. A strange tinny voice, at first incomprehensible until I realized he was speaking with a rich Scottish accent, announced that it was Hamilton Frazer, the elder of Brigid's brothers. I buzzed him up, suddenly gladder than I had felt for some time, Magnus (or Jens) notwithstanding. He stood in our apartment, tall as a tree, smiling a Cheshire cat smile, while my father poured him a whisky and watched benignly as he and I took up more or less where we'd left off more than two years before.

'It's so *good* to see you again, Chantal,' he said, holding both my hands in his, and the possibility of love shifted weightily inside my heart. Not the fiery kind of passion which had Magnus and me tearing each other's clothes off (consuming each other, drinking champagne at three o'clock in the morning while standing naked on the balcony of his flat, both aware that together we were going nowhere, that this was a strictly here-and-now affair, to be enjoyed like an ice-cream on a hot day or champagne in the early morning) but something far more valuable. In that moment, as I looked into Ham's good face, his honest brown eyes, I knew that we would be happy together.

As, indeed, we were. After our wedding, we moved to London, where Ham worked for a large legal company dealing mainly with maritime law. We did all the newly married things: had friends round for supper, were invited out in our turn, haunted the flea markets and second-hand shops, putting together an eclectic mix of junk and genuine finds, going to the theatre and the pub and – very occasionally, when we could afford it – the opera. We were young and in love, in a quiet comforting way. Sometimes it occurred to me that *quiet* and *comforting* was somewhat staid for people of our age, but I only had to see Ham smiling at me to know that it was exactly right. We spent Christmases in Rome or with Ham's parents in Scotland.

The years passed happily, despite the fact that there were no children. But we told ourselves there was plenty of time. Ham was left a substantial inheritance by a godmother and we bought a large three-bedroomed flat in South Kensington. I interviewed for a job at Chauncey's, a small but prestigious auction house in Bond Street. My sister had always envisaged working for Sotheby's or Christie's: in a way, I felt that I was taking over the life she had been deprived of. It would be quite a while before I began to question just how healthy that was. As my father pointed out,

I ought to be forging my own pathway, not stepping along hers. My new job was very poorly paid but was excellent experience – or so Ham and I told ourselves – for the future. I don't know what we envisaged this future consisting of: me taking the art world by storm, I think, maybe fronting some arty TV programme and wearing significant spectacles, or writing a book to be hailed worldwide by the cognoscenti of the art world, while Ham made potfuls of money in the background.

But the future never materialized. At least, not the particular one we had in mind.

On his thirty-second birthday, after we'd been out to celebrate at our favourite little restaurant round the corner from the flat, Ham complained of stomach pains.

'I ate too much,' he said ruefully. 'I feel completely bloated.'

I wasn't as sympathetic as I should have been. 'You're always moaning about stomach ache,' I said. 'Take a couple of antacid tablets. You'll be fine in the morning.'

And so he was. Until about a week later when he began vomiting blood. We went immediately to the A&E department at our nearest hospital. A few days after that, he was diagnosed with advanced and inoperable stomach cancer. They did the usual things, chemo and radio and so on, but not with much success. When he could no longer work, when he finally had to retire to bed, I took extended leave from Chauncey's to stay at home with him, forced to watch my darling Hamilton growing ever more yellow and shrunken.

His family came down from Scotland as often as they could, and we had some wild parties around his bed, pretending to be enjoying ourselves, every now and then leaving the room to mop up tears or swallow the lumps in our throats. Within three months, Ham was dead.

Standing with his parents and his siblings in a windy graveyard in the little village outside Edinburgh, where he'd grown up, I reflected that for a woman so young, I'd had more than my fair share of death. My sister, my mother, and now my husband and dearest friend. There I was, an only child, a widow and still only thirty-three. Squeezing Brigid's hand tightly in my own, I wondered what dark angel had presided over my birth.

So here I am, back – in one sense – at the beginning of my story. Ready to take it up again where it left off. Since Sabine's death, twenty-three years had slipped by and I had barely noticed the passing of time. Ham had died two years ago and I had spent most of my time since then either at work, or thinking about work.

It was a Friday, a cold grey afternoon in Bond Street, and I had begun to consider the idea of going home to my empty flat, and beyond that to the weekend. I had no real plans. The possibility of an exhibition at Tate Modern, a film I wanted to see playing at one of the arts cinemas, maybe meet up with Lorna, my closest friend and colleague, who worked in Chauncey's manuscript department. Dull stuff, I suppose – but then I *was* dull. Or had become so in recent years.

Thinking that even for a Friday, two thirty-five

was possibly a little too early to be making tracks, I idly flipped open a glossy art magazine, one of a pile I wanted to look through, just in case something germane to my job should show up. And there was an advertisement for a new country hotel.

My eyes passed over it, barely taking it in.

WESTON LODGE HOTEL

After extensive refurbishment, historic Weston Lodge, set in the heart of the Cotswolds, is launching itself as England's most luxurious premier boutique hotel.

GIVE IN TO TEMPTATION!

A new concept in luxury. Take advantage of our not-to-be-repeated

Special Introductory Offer

to celebrate the three-day Bank Holiday Weekend at extremely favourable rates.

GO ON, SPOIL YOURSELF!

and enjoy gorgeous views, gourmet meals, vintage wines, salt-water swimming pool, spa, massage, aromatherapy gym, squash and tennis courts, or stroll through our extensive gardens, or simply relax in the comfort of our well-stocked library.

EVERY COMFORT

is yours for as long as you wish to stay with us. Hurry to make your booking as numbers are limited. A weekly rate is also available.

At first the name didn't register. What caught my attention was the idea of complete freedom from responsibility. The spring bank holiday was still three weeks away and so far I had no plans beyond a vague thought of flying over to see my father. I imagined myself ploughing up and down the salt-water swimming pool. I thought of vintage wines and gourmet meals, of a masseuse easing the knots of tension from my shoulders, of strolling through the extensive gardens as dusk fell and the moon began to rise, of relaxing in the library.

And then, as though a fist in a boxing glove had suddenly burst from the page and caught me between the eyes, I looked again. Weston Lodge. *Weston* . . . It *had* to be the same place. Faced with the name, offered this bolt-from-the-blue opportunity, without further thought, I called the numbers provided at the bottom of the advertisement and booked myself in for the Special Introductory Weekend.

After that, I telephoned my father and told him what I had done. He was silent for a beat longer than he needed to be. I could so easily imagine him looking over the top of his half-moon specs, which he didn't need since he had better sight than an eagle, but which he believed enhanced his *gravitas*.

'Whether it's antiquarian books, business deals, or men, always hold back a bit,' he said finally.

'Thanks for the advice, Dad, but what's it got to do with anything?'

'You're being too hasty.'

'Too late now: I've paid.'

Another pause. Then he added, as he had many years earlier, 'It won't bring her back, Chantal.'

'I know that. I'm well aware. But actually going there, to the place where she . . . where she died – it's a sort of *homage*, if you know what I mean.'

'I know precisely what you mean, honey. But I'm afraid that it could all be too much for you.'

'Why?'

'You can't possibly know what effect it might have.'

'I'm not the heroine of one of your Victorian novels,' I protested. 'I shan't faint or have a fit of the vapours.'

'I'm not suggesting you will. I'm just warning you that you could find yourself in a very bad place, Chantal, a place you really don't need to go.' He sighed. 'It's long gone, darling. Much as we wish none of it had happened, it was a long time ago and it's *over*.'

'Not for me,' I said.

'What do you expect to come out of this?'

I didn't know. Possibly, there was more to my decision than a connection to my lost sister. Ever since her death, I had speculated obsessively about her murderer. What kind of person, however enraged, could possibly butcher her own children and slaughter an innocent bystander? What circumstances in that person's life could have led to such an unjustifiable deed? Maybe by going to the place where it all happened, I might be able to get some kind of a handle on an otherwise incomprehensible act of violence.

Perhaps, more importantly, I might somehow begin to understand and, by understanding, loosen the black tar-ball of hatred which lay inside me like a consuming cancer. I did not say any of this to my father. I think he believed I had got over it and was leading a more or less normal (what is normal?) life. I had never disillusioned him on that score. That afternoon, we argued it back and forth for a while, before moving on to discuss a convention he'd just attended in Oslo, and the cruise he and the forcible *contessa* – a rich Swedish widow with whom he was keeping company, the owner of an antiquarian bookshop near the Spanish Steps in Rome – were planning to take round the Mediterranean.

When we finally finished chatting, I sat in my office staring out of the window at London's Friday afternoon bustle, seeing nothing. Dad might be elderly now, but he was still on the ball. And maybe he was right. Even though more than twenty-three years had gone by since Sabine's death, it was possible that the shock of being right there where it happened could hit me so hard that I would break down, as I had done in the past. In one sense, I had no wish to explore the minefields of my memory, never knowing when something would detonate and send me into explosive mode. Nor did I want to relive those terrible years. And yet . . . to be where Sabine had been, where she had ended her life . . .

Back in my flat, I opened a bottle of white wine and poured myself a glass. I sat down at my desk, dealt with bills, answered some email (I said I was dull). Out of my windows I could see part of the red-brick frontage of the Science Museum and, further away, the glass tower of the Royal College of Art and the trees of the park. Above my desk was a cork-board on which I pinned items of interest: snippets from the newspapers, amusing cartoons, invitations, gallery openings. There were a couple of snapshots of the four of us, Mom, Dad, Sabine and me, before she went to Edinburgh. My favourite pic of Hamilton, in a white Argyle sweater and a kilt. A photograph of Sabine laughing in Californian sunshine, her long red hair blowing about her face.

Now, contemplating my impetuous hotel booking, I felt snails of unease, even of fear, slowly slithering around my gut. However much I wished to escape it, that sunny California afternoon, and the phone call which had unequivocally changed my life forever, were still with me, welded on to my memory, merged with my DNA. And gazing down at the bustle of the street below me – groups of foreign students, girls in horizontally striped stockings, couples heading for the nearby Italian restaurants or something more upmarket in the King's Road – I found myself wondering, as so often before, at what point Sabine had realized that there was no escape, that she was going to die, and what her last thoughts might have been as the murderer came at her with a knife. Did she think of Dad, of Mom, of me? Or of the guy she'd told me about – Malc, she called him – met through a university drama group?

Dad was right. It was an insane decision on my part to go to the place where she'd died, when I'd already shed so many tears over her, all the bright promise of her life ended, all her plans done for, her stories finished, the lovely things broken, the colours and the music, the babies who now would never be born, all that once had been, all that now would never be.

Two

Damn, damn, damn! I stood beside the car and kicked at the front tyre. Luckily I'd had time to pull over as close to the hedge as was possible before the engine stopped. Stupid damn thing. Like everybody who had grown up in the States, I'd been driving since I was fifteen or sixteen, but I knew absolutely nothing about the interior workings of a car. What was I supposed to do now, stuck miles out here in the country, surrounded by sheep and cows with not a building or another human being in sight? I could lift the bonnet and peer at the car's innards, but even if I did, they wouldn't mean anything. I'd just have to wait until someone came by. Some *man* . . .

I ought to be able to fend better for myself; I had learned very early not to depend on other people. Not for the first time, I thought about enrolling in an evening class on car maintenance, but I knew I would never get round to it. For a start, fingernails full of immovable black grease was not a good look when showing Edwardian watercolours or cut-glass claret-jugs to prospective clients.

How far was I from Weston Lodge? Close enough to walk? Near enough to telephone, see if they'd send someone to pick me up? I sighed. I'd been regretting this trip ever since leaving London. I feared Dad was right and it was all going to be more than I could cope with. Even now, Sabine's death was still too painful to contemplate with any degree of intensity; it had been easier to lock it into some box inside my head and get on with the here and now.

Standing in the spring air with trees budding all around me, and willows marking the line of a distant river, their spindly yellow branches strung with delicate green, I asked myself why I would want to go back, when I'd spent so much of my life struggling to go forward. What impulse urged me to visit the scene of the crime? Was it because I knew that mental images could be far worse than reality? Was it precisely because I wanted to make real that which I'd previously left to the imagination? Or was it because I felt Sabine was due at least this much, that because the Fates had intervened in the form of the advertisement for the Weston Lodge Hotel, I owed her this . . . pilgrimage?

I'd often visualized the house as it might have looked the night she died, decorated with piney boughs, great swags of holly, the mantel at one end of the drawing room a mass of ivy and greenery with tall church candles embedded among the leaves, mistletoe hanging from a central light-fixture, and candelabra blazing on the embrasured window-sills. From Sabine's letters home, I knew there'd have been a Christmas tree in the big hall, presents piled underneath, a turkey sitting in its enamelled pan in the stone-shelved larder, brandy butter for the plum pudding waiting in the icebox, the pudding itself tied up in a muslin cloth, like someone in the olden days

24

with a bad toothache. I'd added further details gleaned from my eclectic reading, from Dickens and Thackeray, from historic accounts written by diarists, plus an amalgam of all the Christmases I'd seen featured in *Style & Living*-type magazines. It was springtime now, and everything would look very different when – *if* – I got there.

A car was coming slowly down the lane. I stepped forward and held up my hand. The approaching car looked to be in even worse shape than my own, but at least it was moving. And there was a man behind the wheel! As he came nearer, I could see that he was on the elderly side and looked as though a puff of wind might blow him away. Still, white knights don't have to be wearing shining armour and carrying a sword. He slowed down when he saw me and wound down the window.

'Need a hand?' His voice was that of another era.

'Yes, *please*. Could you possibly—'

'Can't help, I'm afraid. Don't know the first thing about cars. But I know a man who does . . . Gerry, at the garage. I'll give him a call when I get home.'

'Oh . . . well, thank you very much.'

'Don't thank me too soon. I might easily forget. Memory's not what it used to be. M'nephew says I'm slipping. But then who isn't?' Briefly, he leaned an elbow on the window edge, seemingly about to settle into a discussion of this question, but then obviously thought better of it. 'I'd better go and talk to my hens. Bye.' He waved a tweed-covered arm and lurched off.

So much for that, I thought. The chances of Gerry-from-the-garage showing up any time soon seemed fairly slim. Opening the door of the car, I rootled around in my bag for my mobile, then for the piece of paper which had Weston Lodge's details on it. I dialled the telephone number and listened with irritation to the beeps which indicated that there was no reception in this area. Blast! Nothing to do but wait it out.

Luckily, I'd brought a book with me. After twenty minutes or so, when it seemed fairly clear that Gerry wasn't going to turn up, I heard the chug of another car coming towards me. Again I marched into the middle of the lane and held up a traffic-cop hand. Again a car pulled up in front of me – a low-slung sports car in silver grey – and a man climbed out. 'Can I help you?' he asked.

'I do hope so.' I gave him my best 100-megawatt smile. 'Are you Gerry from the garage?'

He raised his eyebrows. 'Not as far as I'm aware.'

'Do you know anything about cars?'

'Almost nothing.'

'Thing is, my car just gave up and died.'

'They do that sort of thing, don't they?' he said, lifting my bonnet. He stuck a bit of metal he'd found into some kind of hole. 'Especially when they're out of petrol.'

'What?'

'You've run out of gas.'

'But that's ridiculous. I filled up only a few miles out of London.'

'Perhaps your tank's sprung a leak.'

26

'Or my petrol gauge is faulty.'

'Or maybe you should buy a new car.'

'What a very brilliant idea,' I said. 'Meanwhile, how do I get to where I'm going?'

'You hope that the guy who has just stopped to help has a full petrol can in the back of his car.'

'And does he?' I examined him more closely, noted the cashmere sweater, the Tattersall shirt, the good flannels, and knew that the answer was unquestionably in the affirmative. This was a man who would always have a full petrol can in the back of his car. As Hamilton had. And, like Hamilton, he was nice-looking, if a bit solemn. Big, with a rugby player's neck, short brown hair, darkish eyes, good hands. My mother had always maintained that good hands meant a good man.

'As it happens, yes, he does.'

'So we're all sorted.'

'Looks like it.'

'Obviously, I'll pay for however much I need to get to my destination.'

'And where's that, if you don't mind me asking?' Good smile, to go with the hands.

'A place called Weston Lodge.'

'Ah.' He stared at me searchingly, and I saw that the darkish eyes held something I could not quite interpret. 'Are you going for any particular reason?'

'Uh . . . not really, no,' I lied. 'I saw an advertisement for this special weekend, and all in all, it seemed like a good idea. You know how it is.'

'Absolutely.' He finished pouring petrol out of his can into a funnel he'd inserted into my petrol tank. 'There, that should see you right. You're only about fifteen miles away from the Lodge.'

'You're from round here, are you?'

'Not at all. But as it happens – and I hope this won't spoil your weekend – I'm also taking advantage of the special offer. So I'll be around too.' He smiled again, and the sombre contours of his face changed as though a lamp had been switched on.

'Excellent,' I said. 'I'll see you there.' I wondered whether I should wait a bit longer for Gerry-from-the-garage, but given the length of time I'd already waited, plus the faulty memory of my first rescuer, I gave up after a while, and set off for Weston Lodge.

When I had driven up the long poplar avenue to the gravelled space in front of the house, the Lodge looked exactly as I had expected: small country mansion, a bit of Perpendicular, with early-Victorian 'improvements', battlements here and there, a couple of miniature towers.

Half a dozen cars were parked on the gravelled drive, with people milling about hefting suitcases or climbing the lichened stone steps up to the big oaken front door. I inched in between a gleaming black Jaguar and a sports car in racing green, praying that I wouldn't make some terrible driving error and scratch their paintwork.

Bags extracted from the boot, I took a deep breath. Beneath the anticipation of massages and aromatherapy, darker thoughts churned; I felt as though I was standing on the lip of a precipice and any moment now might fall over the edge. Was I going to make it through the weekend, and in any case, whether I did or didn't, what would I have achieved by coming? I had visions of myself being carted out on a stretcher, a screaming hysterical mess. Perhaps I should get back into the car and drive away again. No one would miss me: they could keep the deposit, even take the cost of the weekend off my credit card if they wanted.

But I knew I was being silly. I could leave at any time, if I wanted to, so I might just as well give the weekend a chance. Another deep breath before I climbed up the curved stone steps and walked through the door into a large circular hall, while my head thundered the phrase *I shouldn't have come, I shouldn't have come.*

A young woman sat at a round rosewood table in the middle of the space, surrounded by receptionist-type apparatus, a big bouquet of beautifully arranged flowers in a heavy Daum crystal vase sitting in front of her. The effect was nothing like the usual hotel reception-desk and created an immediate air of welcome. Light spilled in through tall windows, and I could smell lilac on the air which wafted in through the open front door. It was very different from my expectations. But what had I antici-pated? Bloodstains on the walls? Vampire bats flitting about? Guttering candles and intermittent bursts of lightning and thunder?

I laughed to myself as I was shown to my spacious room, which contained not just one but two double beds, both spread with gorgeous quilts and cushions. It was handsomely furnished with an eclectic mix of vintage pieces and state-of-the-art chic. Either the new owner had lots of money and superb taste, or he had lots of money and a really good interior designer. I ran my fingers across the polished surface of an antique side-table, then stared at my reflection in a beautiful carved and gilded fruitwood mirror, thinking that my auction-house employers would love to put some of this stuff under the hammer.

Dumping my suitcase on the webbing-and-mahogany stand provided, I stood for a moment in the middle of the hand-woven oriental rug which covered half the floor, before walking over to the French windows and stepping out on to a small balcony. A rural landscape spread before me: grass, trees, a narrow winding river, the glossy beige of cows, white clumps of sheep. There was a line of poplars in the distance, leaves shaking in the breeze, the silver undersides shining like coins.

For an eye-blink, Sabine swam into my head. She had lived in this house – for all I knew had slept in this very room. I closed my eyes, seeing the oft-reproduced face of her killer, as a familiar rage shifted inside me. The newspapers had called it a brainstorm, an aberration. That was no comfort whatsoever. While Dad and I had to spend the rest of our lives mourning and bereaved, the murderer was being cared for at taxpayers' expense, even being encouraged from behind the prison walls to continue what had been a promising academic career.

I forced myself to think of something – anything – else. That beautiful art deco cabinet, for instance. The stunning satin throws across the beds. The Victorian ewer and pitcher. My heart-beat gradually slowed.

A notice propped against a bowl of hyacinths informed me that at six p.m., David Charteris, the owner, invited me to a pre-dinner Mingle in the Large Drawing Room. I stared at this for some time. Mingle: what kind of a word was that to describe a meeting of independent adults? And how many of the hotel guests would attend it? I thought of the guy who'd come to my rescue – if he was there, I could at least pay him back for the two litres of gas he'd poured into my tank.

I felt slightly cheered.

I had forty minutes before I had to show up in the 'Large Drawing Room'. I took ice cubes and tonic from the minibar and dropped them into the glass provided, poured gin from the half-bottle I'd brought with me and listened to the satisfying crack they made as the spirit hit them, then cut off a strip of peel from the lemon I had also put into my bag before leaving London. I sat down in the comfortable armchair, finally feeling the sense of ease which I'd hoped for when I first read the advertisement for this weekend. Maybe I'd stay in this comfortable room for my whole stay, having my meals sent up, being cosseted. Since Ham had died, cosseting had not been high on the list of things I was getting a lot of. How strange, then, how quirky of me, to feel it here, of all places.

On the leather-topped table-desk was my computer case; inside it were the letters Sabine had sent from this very house. I hadn't read them for years, but I had known I'd have to do so if I was to make any sense of this weekend.

Make a start now? Or wait until later? *Now*, I decided. Don't put it off any longer. I really should have read them before I left home. Nerving myself, I swallowed more of my drink, opened my case and brought out an envelope.

Hi, Baby:

I can hardly believe it but I've been here for over a week and only now have found time to write to you. There's so much to tell you – and you did *ask to be told absolutely everything.*

Anyway, the house first. Gorgeous! Never thought I'd be living in something so grand, all towers and turrets and stained glass windows and the like. Rolling lawns, ancient trees, a small lake, terraces all round: they've even got their own little chapel set in the middle of yew-trees and gravestones, with all the ancestors buried there.

The parents are unlike anyone I've ever met. He – Harry Redmayne – is a tall handsome man, with black brushed-back hair, blue eyes, olive skin. Very very charming, very smiley, a lovely speaking voice. He wears beautiful suits – Savile Row, of course! – and shirts, handmade in London. The shoes are also handmade, with leather soles. (Some shoe-shop called Lobbs. I happened to see a bill for his latest pair and nearly fell over on my nose!) I didn't think people bothered with such expensive clothes any more . . . maybe it's because he's an art dealer in the West End and he has to dress like that for business purposes. Also, I heard him talking on the phone the other day, and I had the impression he's got political ambitions. I can imagine he'd be a real orator, with that voice.

She . . . the Honourable Clio Palliser (or Redmayne, I suppose, since she's married to Harry) . . . now she is really interesting, much more so, I think, than he is. She's as thin as a toothpick, unlike him (Harry really likes his food and his wine). She's very pale, etiolated (look it up!), kind of awkward, terribly academic and clever – she has a doctorate in some sort of language studies – Scandinavian or Nordic – and writes articles for learned journals and contributes to books on her subject, attends conferences, etc. Big parcels of books come for her all the time, sent down from London: art books and books on history and music and drama, biography, plus all kinds of fiction from highbrow literary fiction to cheap thrillers. Not to mention numerous literary and historical magazines. I love being able to sit in the library and just wallow in books! She's told me to feel free to take whatever I want off the shelves, which is marvellous.

But she is a bit weird. Finds it hard to

look me in the eye when she's talking to me, kind of blank-looking and not very smiley, obviously very nervy and shy, which is odd in someone who's a successful academic writer. And let's face it, I'm not exactly intimidating, am I? (No, I'm not!)

Must dash, more later, your loving sis,
Sabine

Swallowing the last of my gin and tonic, I laid the letter on my knee and stared out of the window. *A bit strange* . . . What an understatement that had proved to be. Most of us don't expect evil to be lurking at our elbow; we accept the peculiarities and eccentricities of our fellow humans without thinking too much about them. Like my sister, we tend not to experience any unease in the face of them. How ironic . . . but what difference would it have made if she had? None at all.

I looked around me. There was a small bookcase, stuffed with books, and I got up to see what David Charteris felt was suitable reading material for his guests. Most of the books were current paperbacks, but there were several nicely bound classics: some Dickens, some Jane Austen, a copy of *Peter Rabbit*, an *Alice In Wonderland*, the Collected Poems of Walter de la Mare, still in its original dust-jacket. We'd had a similar copy at home. I pulled it out to look for favourite childhood poems.

As I skimmed through the volume, the front half of the dust-jacket fell away and I saw a dedication, written in tiny script high in one

34

corner of the cover where it would normally be hidden by the front flap. *For my darling Clio, hoping you will enjoy these poems as much as I did when I was your age, with love from Mummy.* The *Alice In Wonderland* had a similarly concealed inscription, also hidden by the front flap: *For Clio Palliser on her 8th birthday, with all love, Mummy.*

In my hands was a book which had belonged to a vicious killer. Yet for some reason, I found these two inscriptions unbearably moving. They threw a new light on my sister's murderess, one I felt incompetent to absorb; she'd been a little girl once, she'd read the same books as Sabine and I, she'd had a loving caring mother. Grief swelled inside me like a balloon and moved unstoppably into my throat, while tears filled my eyes. It was years since I had cried over my lost sister but suddenly I was weeping not just for Sabine but also for myself and for the child who'd grown up to become a perverted slayer.

At six o'clock, I showered and changed into black velvet trousers and a rose-pink chiffon shirt, refurbished my make-up and brushed my GI-short red hair, then made my way down the grand central staircase to the big drawing room, which was already full of anticipatory chatter. Our host, if that was the right term, given that we were paying for this weekend, was standing at the door smiling in a suit that must have cost a small fortune. He was a good-looking man in his early forties, and very well-maintained: good skin, healthy hair, no spare flesh beneath his jaw.

'Hello, I'm David Charteris,' he said, shaking my hand and launching into a well-rehearsed patter of welcome. 'I'm so glad to see you, do hope you enjoy the weekend, plenty of nice people here, feel free to wander round the house, do go on in.'

I did, wondering if this whole thing was a good idea. How appropriate was it to be knocking back cocktails in the house where my sister had died a violent death? Since the alternative was to stay in my room (not an entirely unpleasant one, as I've already noted), I decided the answer was yes to both questions and took a glass from one of the circulating waitresses. The guy who'd come to my rescue with his gas-can was standing by the window looking glum and apprehensive. A number of couples stood chatting together, the husbands tall and tanned, the wives blonde. An interesting-looking woman stood fingering some kind of ebony and ivory bibelot, a man with an angry expression watching while she did so. My heart sank as I saw someone approaching me with a smile obviously intended to charm. Somebody ought to tell him that it needed quite a lot more work. Was it because I was short that men like him always made a beeline for me? Even more incomprehensibly, why did they always think they were God's gift to women, when ninety-nine times out of a hundred they very obviously weren't?

'So what's *your* name?' he said. Nice approach, guaranteed to irritate. Well-bellied, in a striped shirt under a tweed jacket, freshly shaven cheeks, slicked-back thinning hair, he seemed to be exactly the kind of self-important twerp I hated. And a prime candidate for a heart attack, judging by his cherry-red complexion.

'Chantal Frazer,' I said.

'I'm Charlie Leeming.' He spoke as if I ought to have heard of him. 'Chantal . . . that's some kind of a French name, isn't it?'

'It *is* a French name,' I said. 'Not some kind of one. My mother was French.'

'Ah . . .'

I looked round, hoping someone would rescue me. Like the petrol-can guy – who now was staring at my companion, mouth half-open, looking as though he'd just been landed by an incompetent angler.

'You seem like an interesting lady,' the Leeming man said, his would-be seductive smile morphing into a leer as though he expected that any minute, unable to resist his allure, I'd start tearing off my clothes.

'Why?' I don't suffer fools particularly gladly, and self-satisfied fools like this one were the worst.

'Uh, well . . .' He coughed. 'Wearing pink with your red hair: it kind of clashes, doesn't it? But it's very striking.'

'Do you work for *Vogue* or something?' I asked coldly.

'*Vogue*?'

'Or perhaps some other women's magazine?'

'No-o!' He gave a snuffling sort of laugh. 'Why do you ask?'

'All these fashion tips . . .'

He was obviously unsure whether he'd been insulted or not, but recovered quickly. 'I can tell

37

a woman who knows what she's about, if you see what I mean,' he said.

I raised my eyebrows at this moronic remark. 'Actually, I don't.' I saw with relief that Petrol-Can Man was shouldering his way through the crowd towards us. He reached my side and stood there, giving Charlie Leeming's clothes a supercilious glance. 'So . . . what brings you here tonight, Leemers, old man?' he said heartily.

Leeming turned to him. 'And you are?'

'Probably the same thing that brings the rest of us,' I said, sensing that, for reasons I was unaware of, horns were about to be locked.

'Well . . .' Leeming's tone was oily. 'Actually, I *do* have a connection with the Lodge, from way back. A strong one.' He nodded importantly. 'Just wanted to see the old place again.' Ignoring the other man, he gazed at me with anticipation, waiting for me to ask questions.

'Really?' I said.

'Yes, indeed. You see, I was very good friends with the two—'

'I see it obviously didn't happen for you,' Petrol-Can Man said quickly.

Deflected, Leeming stared at him. 'What do you mean?

'I mean that if you can only afford to come to a place like this on a cut-price offer, you can't exactly be making it hand over fist, after all.'

'Making what?'

'Money, old boy. Money. Isn't that what you were always going to do?'

'Who the hell do you think you are?' The Leeming character snorted unattractively through his nostrils and made a fist while his plump tomato face reddened even further.

'I don't *think*, I know.' Petrol-Can Man smiled at me. 'This man's not bothering you, is he?'

'I can handle it,' I said. 'And thank you again. Without you I might not have made it to this . . . occasion.'

'This *Mingle*. Stupid name, isn't it?'

'Do you two know each other?' asked Leeming.

'Only in a manner of speaking,' I said.

Petrol-Can Man glanced at him. 'Are you still here?'

Leeming glowered. 'I'll sort you out later,' he said over his shoulder as he moved off.

'You and whose army?' my rescuer childishly called after him.

I raised my eyebrows. 'What was *that* all about?'

'Goes back a long way. He doesn't recognize me, but I spent a term at the same school as that fat bastard. I can't imagine what he's doing here. I know for a fact that he never met any of the family, and at school, everyone loathed him. I remember him as a hulking great bully, shoving the heads of the smaller boys down the school lavatories, or hiding people's games kit so they ended up with detentions.'

'I wonder what his previous connection with this place was,' I said.

'Like I just said, he has none. Have you been crying?' he said.

'As a matter of fact, yes.'

He touched my shoulder. 'Anything I can help with?'

'I'm a big girl,' I said.

'But not a very *big* big girl, as far as I can see.'

He had a point. Like my sister, I was a tad over five foot two. 'True,' I said.

He grinned at me. 'So what do you think of the place so far?'

'Very choice.'

'It's been in the Palliser family for centuries, gifted to the Palliser of the time by a grateful monarch for services rendered during the Third Crusade. And later, it was briefly the stopping place for Ann Boleyn on her way to be married.'

'How do you know all that?'

'I read it in the brochure someone thoughtfully placed in my rather smart bedroom.'

'I see.' I wanted to say more, but we were joined by a couple from Liverpool who told us they'd visited the gardens last year, while the place was still being renovated, and were thrilled to be actually staying in the house this time round.

Eventually the circulating waitresses slipped away. There was a clapping of hands, a request for silence and David Charteris started to address us.

'My Lord, ladies and gentlemen,' he started, as everyone began eyeing everyone else, wondering which of them was titled. 'I'm David Charteris, your host, and I'm delighted to welcome you here tonight, at the start of this introductory weekend to what I hope will become one of the most sought-after small hotels in the country. If you enjoy your stay with us, please tell everyone you know. And if you *don't* enjoy yourself . . .' He looked round at us and shook his head. 'Nah, that'll never happen.'

There were appreciative titters from his audience.

'But if for some reason you *do* find yourself displeased, let us know immediately. Now, I won't detain you long, but I'd like to give you a brief history of the house, for those of you who haven't discovered the folder in their rooms, or haven't had time to read it . . .'

He proceeded to repeat what I already knew, plus quite a bit more. 'As to how it came into my hands . . . uh . . . the . . . uh . . . previous owners found it difficult to keep the place going, and turned to me, as a distant member of the family to whom it originally belonged. I was offered the opportunity to buy it at a knock-down price . . . and believe me, by then the poor old Lodge was just about ready to be knocked down itself.' He paused for another appreciative chuckle. 'As you can see, thanks to seven years, much thought and love, and a great deal of money, which I was fortunate enough to possess after some careful invest-ments and a lot of luck, my partner and I have finally turned it into the place we always knew it could be. So, if you enjoy being here half as much as we do, you'll have a very good weekend. Enjoy yourselves. Thank you!' He raised his glass in a toast to his guests, and they responded with a mild cheer.

A heavily edited version of the past, I thought. Not that one could blame Charteris for suppressing part of it. What did surprise me was that no one appeared to be aware of the tragedy which had taken place here twenty-three years ago.

41

A man of about fifty joined us. 'What do you think, then?' he said, addressing Petrol-Can Man.

'About what?' he asked cautiously.

'This place.'

'Very nice.'

The guy put out a hand. 'I'm Brian Stonor. You'll no doubt have appreciated mine host's sanitized-for-your-protection account.' He put his head on one side. 'Any particular reason why you're both here today?'

I shook my head firmly.

'None at all,' said my companion. 'I'd . . . uh . . . I'd heard that Weston Lodge was a fine old house, and I'm interested in country houses. Member of the National Trust and all that sort of thing. And the price was pretty reasonable so I thought I'd indulge myself.' He laughed uneasily. He must have known he sounded unconvincing. Bogus, even. 'What's *your* excuse?'

'Pretty much the same as you.' Stonor smiled at me. 'What about you?'

'Oh,' I said vaguely. I had a strong feeling that all three of us were hiding something. 'Same as you, really. An interest in old buildings, needed a break, that sort of thing. '

'I used to live hereabouts, when I was much younger,' Stonor said, giving me a piercing look. 'My mother sometimes worked here, as a matter of fact, when they needed extra staff for big occasions. They were great entertainers in their day, the Pallisers. Just thought I'd take the opportunity to look round the place again, see how much it'd changed since my time.'

'Mmm,' I murmured.

'I'll leave you two to get to know each other.' As he started to walk away, he added, staring at Petrol-Can Man, whose name I still hadn't discovered, 'You're a brave man, coming back here.'

My companion's face flushed. He'd seemed disconcerted by the other man's name, which was vaguely familiar to me too: had he been in the news recently? Appeared on some ridiculous reality TV show? Been had up on terrorism charges? None of these possibilities struck a bell.

I longed to know why Stonor should consider him brave to attend this weekend.

'I'm sorry,' he said eventually. 'I'm not being very polite. The truth is, I'm suffering from jet-lag: I just flew in from Singapore the night before last. And for various reasons, coming on this weekend is a bit traumatic for me.'

Trying to lighten the atmosphere, I asked, 'Which of them do you suppose is the lord?'

He made a visible effort. 'The tall thin bad-tempered one?'

'I'm guessing it's the elderly gent over there.' I indicated a man in thornproof tweeds which had probably belonged to his great-grandfather, teamed with a brilliant silk tie of green, blue and yellow swirls. I'd recognized him as the old boy who had told me he would send Gerry-from-the-garage to my rescue – if he remembered. 'And I also can tell you,' I added, 'that he knows nothing whatsoever about the combustion engine. And that his memory isn't what it was. And that he likes talking to chickens.'

'All that just by looking at him?'

'Pretty much.'

'Look, will you sit next to me at dinner?' he said. 'I hate having to make small talk to strangers.'

'Aren't I a stranger?'

'Not really. Surely you're aware that a damsel rescued from distress automatically becomes a friend. It's a universal law.'

'All right, then,' I said. 'Meanwhile, since that's what we're here for, I think we ought to do some mingling.'

We both moved around, meeting some of the other guests and, in my case, avoiding the Leeming man. The tall woman in the leather jacket introduced herself as Dr Maggie Fields, brought in by David Charteris to produce an inventory of the contents of the house.

'It's amazing that so much of it is still intact,' she said. 'Apart from a couple of cursory lists drawn up by the insurance company, it hasn't been catalogued for centuries.'

'I see it all the time,' I said. 'I go to a lot of these big houses through my job . . . I'm with Chauncey's.'

'We ought to keep in touch,' she said.

We exchanged business cards, and I moved on to speak to a nice couple from Liverpool, and two golf players with almost identical blonde wives. A man with thick blond eyebrows and the grizzled complexion of someone who spent most of his time out-of-doors came over and told me his name was Trevor Barnard. It was a name I knew well, both from reading my sister's letters and also from evidence produced at the trial of Clio Palliser. The third boy had stated that having squeezed out into the open via the pantry, he was too terrified to run down to Farmer Barnard's house in case she followed him and slaughtered the farmer and his wife as well as himself.

'It's good to see the house open again,' Barnard said. 'It's stood empty for years.' Looking round the big room, he added, 'Charteris has certainly made a good fist of doing it up.'

'These big places weren't intended to be locked up and left.'

'Which is why I always cheer when these football stars and pop singers, even the Russian oligarchs, buy them up. They don't seem to mind spending millions on houses that would otherwise fall into disrepair.'

'And if you know any history,' I said, 'the families who originally built them, or were gifted them by the reigning monarch of the time, were no more distinguished – or undistinguished, depending on your point of view – than the new owners today.'

'Very true. It only takes a villain three generations to become respectable – or so I read somewhere. But I can tell you the local community is really pleased that, in this instance, it's David Charteris who has taken over the Lodge. As a member of the Palliser family, he provides a continuity that's much appreciated.'

We chatted further until a gong sounded. At the far end of the room, Charteris tapped the side of his glass with a spoon until we were all quiet. 'I know we're all here to relax and enjoy ourselves,' he said. 'But I'd like to think of this more as a house-party than a collection of strangers. So just for tonight, I've taken the liberty of

45

telling you where to sit so that you can get to know each other. I hope you won't mind.'

'Good idea,' called the man from Liverpool. 'I have to sit next to the wife every day – it'll be good to get away from the old bat.'

'Darling, really,' said his wife. 'People will think you mean it.'

'How do you know I don't?' Darling put his arm around her and squeezed her affectionately while everyone laughed.

Petrol-Can Man rejoined me. 'So much for sitting next to distressed damsels,' he said. Smiling, he put out his hand. 'We really ought to introduce ourselves, don't you think? I'm Gavin Metcalfe-Vaughn. Widely known as Gavin Vaughn.'

'Hello, Gavin Vaughn.' I shook his hand. 'I'm Chantal Frazer. With a *z*.' I hoped he couldn't feel the tremble of my fingers. I hoped I sounded normal, though beneath my shirt, I could feel my heart pounding against my chest. His name was so familiar to me that once I had known it almost as well as my own. In the terrible aftermath of Sabine's murder, when I still pored over whatever information I could find about it, I'd read his name dozens of times: in reports of the trial, in the inevitable true-crime book which had followed immediately after, in the 'think' pieces and articles about the case. Over the years I had thought about him obsessively.

And now, almost unbelievably, he was standing here in front of me.

Gavin Vaughn. The third boy.

Three

'So how are your hens?' I asked my neighbour at the dinner table. 'Did you have an interesting chat with them?'

The elderly man in the thornproof tweeds bent tangled white eyebrows in my direction. 'They tend to bang on a bit about their various health problems, arthritis and slipped discs, that sort of thing, but otherwise, yes, I did.'

I laughed. 'Does talking to them help them lay?'

'Absolutely. They're so productive that I'm able to supply all the local restaurants and grocers round here. Nice little earner, actually. Keep hens yourself, do you?'

'No. Though I do like eggs.'

He frowned. 'Don't I know you?'

'My name's Chantal Frazer. You stopped in the lane this afternoon, promised to send Gerry from the garage out to help me.'

'Good Lord, did I really? I think I must have forgotten. So sorry, mind like a sieve these days. I'm Desmond Forshawe, by the way.'

'Presumably you're not staying here.'

'No. Couldn't afford it, frankly. I'm one of young David's neighbours, and when he came up with the idea of bringing in the locals to mix with his guests, I was first in line to sign up. Suits me, I must say; means a night off from

47

wrestling with the baked-bean tin.' He laughed, showing large yellow teeth. 'And what is your profession, may I ask?'

'I work for Chauncey's.'

'Ah, yes. I don't know them awfully well, but Julian Gardner's an old school chum.'

Sir Julian Gardner was the chairman, a formidable gentleman renowned for his large nose as much as for his encyclopedic knowledge of medieval armour.

'Usually use one of the other lot when I have to raise a bit of cash,' Forshawe was saying. 'To be frank, it's not much fun, owning a biggish house. Shocking problems with the roof, for a start. Attics full of plastic buckets when it rains. Used to drive m'wife mad, poor old girl.' He coughed, then gazed around the beautiful dining room. 'Pity you didn't know this place in its heyday. There were some pictures here then, I can tell you.'

Trying to remember some of the details Sabine had provided, I said, 'There was a Hockney, wasn't there? Um . . . a Gainsborough—'

'Gainsboroughs?' he interrupted dismissively. 'Two a penny in their day. No home was without a couple of the things.'

'—a collection of miniatures, a Peter Lely. Lots of other stuff.'

Again he antlered his eyebrows at me. 'Now where did you hear that?'

I was evasive. 'I can't remember, really.'

'Interesting. Because a significant number of the pictures – and other things, I may say – were removed after . . . when things . . . erm . . . fell

48

apart.' He paused. 'I imagine Harry Redmayne disposed of some of them. Not suggesting any hanky-panky in that quarter, mind. Probably had a perfectly legal right . . . or a lien, or one of those things, some of it probably his in the first place. Look, if you're interested in pictures, you ought to pop over and see my place. I've got some rather fine stuff myself. My late wife was something of a collector.'

'Thank you very much. I'd like that.' Quite apart from his genial charm, I could see the possibility of a business opportunity looming ahead.

'Come for coffee tomorrow.' He fiddled about in a pocket. 'Let me write that down in m'diary so I don't forget. Though I'll probably forget to look.'

'How do I get to you?'

'Ask young David. He'll tell you.'

Before turning to the man on my other side, I stared round the big room. Glazed on three sides, it must once have been the orangery. A small fountain played in the middle, and goldfish swam beneath flat leaves. There were three tables of ten; white candles everywhere, each separate flame reflected in the tall windows. Beautiful. This is what it would have looked like when the Hon Clio and her husband gave the dinner party which I remembered Sabine describing in one of her letters.

'Nice, isn't it?' said my new neighbour. He was thinning on top, and wore glasses, but was rather dashing, in a kilt with one of those Hamlet-sleeved shirts that tie at the neck with a leather thong.

'Stunning,' I said. 'Have you ever been here before?'

'Once.' He sighed. 'Yes, just the once. Years ago. And then only briefly. I–I knew someone who was spending Christmas here. Popped down from Edinburgh to visit her. And then . . .' He stopped.

'Then what?'

'Then life moved on. The way it does. Things happen, unexpected things, and you find yourself taking an entirely different path from the one you had planned to follow.' There were long grooves on either side of his mouth.

'That's very true. So why did you come on this weekend?'

'Partly for auld lang syne, I suppose.' His accent deepened. 'Or as the poet has it, *Ae fond kiss, and then we sever; Ae fareweel, alas, for ever!*'

'Sounds kind of sad.'

He smiled at me, the grooves showing in his cheeks like elongated dimples. 'Believe me, it was. Anyway, enough of that. One of my interests is orreries and such like, and there are three here in the grounds. Know what they are?'

'A sort of astrolabe, isn't it?'

'That kind of thing. Sundials, astrolabes and armillary spheres: I've been fascinated by them since I was at university. The drama group I belonged to put on an outdoor version of *A Midsummer Night's Dream* in the grounds of Castle Finnbreck. There were two or three there and I was completely hooked.'

'What part did you play?'

'I was Lysander.'

'Which university were you at?'

'Edinburgh.'

I could feel light-bulbs blinking on. If I had come here for a special reason, why shouldn't others have done the same? 'What did you study?'

'Engineering, as it happens. Why do you ask?'

'Nosy-parkering, I guess.' Once again I was struck by a frisson of *déjà vu*. Was it possible that this was the very man my sister had mentioned in one of her letters home, the man my sister had fallen for at university, the man who might even have become my brother-in-law?

I met this really nice guy, she had written. *Malcolm Macdonald, he's called. That's Mahhhlcolm, by the way, with a long 'a', not a short one. He's studying engineering. We were in a play together and it was fatal attraction at first sight, not that I'm about to boil any bunnies. You should just see him in his kilt: to die for! Could this be luuuurve? We've been out quite a bit now . . . getting closer every day – and (blush, blush) night. DON'T TELL DAD.*

'Sorry,' I said. 'I'm Chantal Frazer. I'm afraid I didn't catch your last name.'

'Malcolm Macdonald.' His kind blue eyes were sharply alert as he stared at me. 'Chantal, eh?'

'That's right.' It *had* to be him. I couldn't resist another question. 'So the orreries, astrolabes, whatever, are the main reason you came on this weekend?'

He looked uncomfortable. 'Yes, mostly, I suppose.' He fiddled with the leather tie at his throat, his eyes sad behind his glasses. 'To be honest, I . . .' He shook his head. 'It's all a long time ago now.'

'And have you had time yet to go and see the armillaries?' I asked. His accent reminded me of my dead husband.

'I went down this afternoon. There's a Serpent, and a beautiful Globe, though that one's purely decorative. I could take you down tomorrow and show you them, if you'd like.'

'I very much would like,' I said. It would give me a good opportunity to talk to him, to ask him to fill in the blanks of my sister's life at Edinburgh, to confide in him. No one knew how much I wanted to confide in somebody. Anybody. I had always been constrained from talking to my father, not confessing to the pain I carried – and the anger – for fear of reopening for him the wounds of Sabine's death.

'So where do you work, Chantal? What do you do?'

I gave him a potted version of Chantal Frazer's life and times.

'I often have to come down to London. Maybe one of these days . . .' There were unspoken invitations in his eyes.

'Mmm . . .' I said. Very non-committal. I wasn't quite sure why, but I felt a need to keep my own connection with the house to myself, at least for the moment. I wondered how many of the other diners also had some kind of link to those distant murders. And even if they had none, surely at least some of them must have been aware of what had happened here. Perhaps independently they had decided they didn't want their short holiday break tainted by the remembered blood of slaughtered innocents.

The noise of laughter, of cutlery against plates, the ring of crystal, the bouquet of well-cooked food which filled the air suddenly made me uncomfortable. I found myself fighting the urge to leap to my feet and scream, 'Do none of you realize that my beautiful sister was knifed to death in this very house, that she died within feet of where you're sitting drinking wine and *laughing*?'

I didn't give way to it, of course. One never does. One never would. And would I feel any better if I did so? Of course not. Besides, these oblivious people had a perfect right to be here, enjoying themselves.

Across the table from me, Brian Stonor was engaged in what looked like an extremely one-sided conversation with a woman wearing a pale green dress with a low-cut cowl neck, a great mistake at her age, in my opinion, since the throat it highlighted was more turkey than swan. He sat semi-sideways on his chair, nodding every now and then as his companion talked, while he gazed thoughtfully at Gavin Vaughn, who was sitting on another table, chatting to one of the blonde wives. He met my eye and winked.

By the time we were all drinking coffee, music could be heard, coming from the small salon where we had pre-prandially Mingled. When I stood up to leave the dining room, I found Gavin Metcalfe-Vaughn at my side. 'How about a saraband?' he said. 'Or a stately minuet?'

'I can't do either of those.'

'But there's some kind of troupe on hand to show us. Didn't you read the literature in your room?'

'After the trauma of being a damsel in distress, I'm afraid I didn't.'

We reached the salon, and there indeed were a dozen or so people dressed in elaborate costume, bowing and curtsying to each other, while six periwigged young men in silver-buttoned breeches played flutes, flageolets and a small drum. It was a delightful end to the evening, and I was perfectly content to watch when the dancers peeled away from each other and took hold of guests, bringing them into the circle. Gavin was commandeered by a tiny grey-haired woman in a silk dress, and started hopping around the floor, bowing elaborately whenever she cued him. I saw Farmer Barnard mopping and mowing with a laughing fancy-dressed girl, and even kilted Malcolm was moving about in a stately fashion, flourishing a lace handkerchief someone must have given him. After a while, I slipped away, stopping to thank David Charteris and compliment him on the food. I waved a hand at Gavin, who stopped dead when he saw me leaving, causing something of a pileup among the dancers; I managed to suppress my laughter until I was out into the hall.

Halfway along the passage to my room, light was spilling from a partly open door. While I'm not given to prying, everything about this house resonated for me; I wanted to know it as well as Sabine must have done. Peering through the crack, I saw uncarpeted wooden stairs leading up to what must be attics. On impulse, and because nobody else was around, I ran quickly to the top, ignoring the 'PRIVATE' sign on the

54

door. One of the treads creaked as loudly as a fired gun, and I winced. If anyone had heard . . .

I found myself in a large wood-lined room, only just high enough for me to stand upright, which looked as though it extended most of the length of the house. Windows were set at intervals along one side: I had seen many similar attics in the various houses I'd been sent to in order to assess and catalogue things that the owners wished to sell. It was one of the more exciting aspects of my job: the archaeological search involved in sifting through accumulations of possessions and finding the nugget of pure gold in the shape of some priceless painting or precious piece of Chinese porcelain which the family had not even been aware they owned. All along the length of one side, underneath the windows, were small brass handles, implying that at some point the whole length had been converted into additional under-the-eaves storage.

Surveying the long space, my mouth watered. The place was a treasure house, crammed with trunks and suitcases, boxes and cartons. Antique furniture, some of it covered in dust-sheets, had been pushed higgledy-piggledy together. I could see box after box of heavy cut-glass crystal glasses, epergnes, silver teapots, Limoges plates. An entire Spode dinner-service in dark blue and rose with gilded edges was set out on a *pietra dura* table. A painted *vitrine* held small silver objects: snuffboxes, bon-bon dishes, cigar-cases, carved birds and match-holders. There were several stuffed birds under glass. A rocking horse with flared red nostrils stood at the far end, next to an elaborate doll's house and an original boxed Hornby train-set.

Here and there were clothes-rails holding gowns and frocks; striped hatboxes lay piled on top of one another. For a brief moment, I contemplated sneaking one of the dresses down to my room: that chartreuse velvet looked as though it were exactly my size. As did a fabulous chiffon frock in shades of blue and lilac. But then I shuddered. I might be putting on the clothes which had once belonged to my sister's murderer . . .

I opened a box and lifted out a beautiful Ascot-style hat. Crushed velvet roses, peacock feathers: I put it on and posed in front of the mirror. Clothes maketh the man, they say. How much more do they make the woman? Looking at my reflection, I saw not my dull workaday self, but a marvellous creature made for drifting over hallowed turf, delicate manicured fingers clutching some little bag of silk containing a lipstick and a twenty-pound note. What more could such a being need?

Did David Charteris have any idea of the value of all this stuff – or even of what was up here? Probably not, which would explain why Maggie Fields had been hired to produce a complete inventory. Fleetingly, I wondered how long it was going to take her: just the attic alone looked like a month's work. Rather surprisingly, there were no dust balls, no spiderwebs, no errant beetles or mummified flies: everything was clean, dusted, obviously still cared for.

I replaced the hat and, lifting the lid of an old-fashioned steamer trunk, found it was stuffed

56

with photograph albums. Was Sabine in there somewhere, caught between the padded red covers like a pressed flower? Were the dead boys?

About to lift out the top album, I heard footsteps climbing the uncarpeted wooden stairs and then the pistol-shot crack of the rogue tread. Quickly, I tiptoed across the floor and hid behind a rack of evening clothes covered in a dust sheet. Velvet, silk, taffeta, chiffon, all of them still smelling faintly of some distant perfume – Molyneux No 5, Chypre? I recognized a Dior design, a Thierry Mugler, a Givenchy, and more *avant-garde* stuff, too: Herrera, Alaïa and even a Yamamoto. Couture as a form of art . . .

My view was very restricted, but peeping between the dresses, I could see a figure standing stock-still. A black-clad woman with her back to me. Was it one of the guests? Dr Fields, perhaps, or the wife from Liverpool? Or someone brought in to help for the weekend? A lot of the women had been wearing black that evening . . . My friend Lorna kept telling me that black was the new pink. Or was it the other way round? Perhaps this woman was one of the regular staff. It was hard to tell. Earlier in the evening, I had noticed a Mrs Danvers figure hovering in the background; she had looked too imposing to be doing mundane housework. I'd taken her to be in charge of the catering staff but perhaps it was her specialized job to look after this stuff, and she came in regularly to check that none of the guests – such as me – were up there, nicking or breaking precious items. And of course it would be especially important to do so with the house full of strangers.

I scarcely breathed, trying not to imagine the humiliation of being slung out on my ear for invading the private quarters of the house. Or was she herself a thief, casing the joint, either on her own behalf, or for someone else? This was, after all, the first time the house had been open for years. I'd read quite recently that thieves like to familiarize themselves with a place before they raid it: perhaps these were the normal precautions that any sophisticated thief might take.

After a moment, she turned towards a stack of pictures leaning again the wall, faces inward. She pulled out one and then another, and another, leaning them against the legs of one of the tables, and stepping back to view them. I nearly gasped aloud. Even from my hiding place I could see that one was a Hockney, another a Howard Hodgkin. Sabine had mentioned both of them. And there were several important Scandinavians I recognized, after my time in Copenhagen: Krøyer, Anna Ancher, Hammershøi. There were even more treasures up here than I'd realized. I held my breath. If there was the slightest possibility of my being taken for a would-be thief . . .

But finally the woman sighed, replaced the paintings and picked up the Howard Hodgkin by curling her fingers under its stretcher. She looked around, pulled at the door of the *vitrine* full of silver, which proved to be locked, picked up one of the Spode plates and examined its underside before replacing it, then walked to the top of the stairs and went carefully down, still carrying the painting. My God! Was I correct in imagining that I had just witnessed a blatant art theft? Should I report it to David Charteris? But then I'd have to explain what I myself had been doing up in the attics: naturally, he would think that I too was a would-be thief; I might have a hard time persuading him otherwise.

I waited for another ten minutes or so, to make sure the coast was clear, then pushed out through the frocks and once again approached the steamer trunk. Some of the albums had dates on them: I found one for the same year that Sabine had been here. But it must have dated from the summer before she arrived. These boys would have been the sons of the house – George and Edward, I remembered. Most of the time they were in shorts and T-shirts, posing in front of a tree, or playing tennis, or leaping into the river I'd seen from my bedroom window. There was a dog in some of the snaps, a brown and white spaniel with floppy ears. Sometimes there were just the two boys, loose-limbed lads with slicks of fair hair falling over their eyes, and crooked smiles. Sometimes there were three, and with a faint catch of the breath I realized that the third boy must be Gavin Vaughn as he'd been twenty-three years before, already taller than his friends, knee-deep in summer grass, hanging upside down from a low-branched tree, seated at a picnic table with his hand poised over a bowl of strawberries, grinning at the camera.

I stared down at their fresh young faces: Edward and George and Gavin. Carefree and happy, two of them never to know anything beyond the Christmas which lay only a few months ahead.

And the third to be haunted ever after – for even from our short acquaintance, it seemed obvious that Gavin Vaughn was troubled, just as I was. The poignancy of those photographs caught at my throat. Like my sister's, their bright promise had been snuffed out far too soon by the self-obsessed rage of a monster.

Drifting up from the landing below came the sound of voices as people began retiring for the night. I wondered if anyone else would make a secret visit to the attic, but though I waited a full fifteen minutes, no one showed up, and eventually I too crept back down the wooden stairs, careful to leave the light on and the door at the bottom of the stairs open the same width as when I first saw it.

All along the passage, my sister's presence was strong. Sabine must have trodden these same corridors, turned these door handles, looked from these windows to see the thin starlight throw shadows across the pearly lawns. Tomorrow, I told myself, I would make a more determined assault on the house, try to establish my surroundings based on the words she had sent me long ago. I wanted to see everything she'd written about, orientate myself in the past.

In my room, I made myself a cup of green tea from the selection on the table under the window, admiring the silky little bag it came in, and sat down with another of Sabine's letters. When we first heard of her death, I had read them over and over again, howling into my pillow so that my parents, mourning the loss of their first daughter, would not hear the anguish of their second. The last two or three of them had reached me much later, when Sabine had already been dead for a month; those I had never even opened. Since then, they had all lain undisturbed in their envelopes.

I paused over my sister's almost-forgotten script, recalling her idiosyncratic way of forming the downstrokes of her Ys and her Gs. The envelopes were soft and pliable with age now, as were the letters themselves. I sipped at my tea, unfolded the first one, closed my eyes for a moment in an effort to calm myself, and started to read.

Darling Sis,

Here's Chapter 2 of the great Weston Lodge saga.

It's absolutely freezing, and I'm wearing three sweaters with my thickest tights under my jeans, just to keep lukewarm. It's even colder than Scotland. Because it's so huge, the house is really difficult to heat, so you have run everywhere, just to keep the blood moving!

I was recently given the Grand Tour of the place by Harry, as he's asked me to call him. There's masses of beautiful antique furniture handed down from generation to generation, much more than they can accommodate, actually, because he told me the attics were full as well. Plus more marble statuary, vaulted ceilings, parquet floors, orangeries and morning rooms and shimmery silk carpets, Venetian mirrors and chandeliers and enamelled snuffboxes than you could shake a stick at. What's nice about it is that even though it's so grand, a lot of the fabrics are worn, the curtains are faded and if you look closely you can see the delicate little darns in the silk rugs – 'shabby chic', I think they call it. Harry absolutely revels in his beautiful collections: he says he's always on the lookout for things to add to it.

(And in case you're wondering, no, I don't fancy him. He's a bit of a dish, but not my type – and much too old for me. So don't worry, I'm not going to be seduced by the master of the house! Besides, there's my darling Malcolm waiting for me back in Edinburgh. Oh, I wish you could meet him. I wish you could see the way his kilt swings when he walks, and the dear little sealskin purse thing (a sporran) which sits so suggestively over his balls!)

As for the paintings here, it's like living in an art gallery. So many of them, especially portraits, and they're all over the house, beautiful women in white dresses and blue sashes, holding straw hats with more ribbons, or handsome men clutching guns and wearing buff-coloured waistcoats and red jackets with silver buttons. There's a George Romney, a Peter Lely, two Gainsboroughs, Raeburn, Lawrence, Stubbs – you name it, they've got one. Plus two fabulous John Laverys, one a seascape, and a portrait of a young girl. And if you don't recognize the names, you jolly well (as they say over here) ought to, seeing as how you want to do Art History at uni.

But my favourites are his collection of exquisite miniatures, painted on ivory or enamel. A couple of Nicholas Hilliard, which is exciting enough, but do the names Henry Bone or Richard Cosway mean anything to you? (No, they didn't to me either, but Dad might possibly know of them.) There's the usual yearning swains – Harry told me they were used as tokens exchanged between lovers (can't say a moony wimp leaning against a tree or standing by a sundial would have turned me on, but I guess things were different back then) – a couple of girls, some cheeky little lads, a lovesick young man in a ruffled shirt, holding a guitar, and several more. I really like the one on show in the morning room, which is a portrait of Clio's great-great-grandmother. Harry said they were worth a fortune, which I can well believe.

As for the Hon Clio, I've never seen anyone read so much as her, not even you. You can see sometimes that she's absolutely lost on another planet, and it's hard for her to shift her focus back into this one. If I need to ask her a question (which I try not to do as I hate interrupting her), she very politely puts her finger in the page she's at and closes the book on it, but her eyes are still glazed for a second or two, while she readjusts back to the ordinary world. Poor woman: I feel sorry for her. She's obviously not at ease with herself – or anyone else for that matter. Most of the time she's perfectly nice, but sometimes I think she can hardly bear to have me in the same room as her, she kind of simmers with repressed rage! Actually, in my opinion, she's severely paranoid. It's a bit frightening, actually.

There's other staff as well as me, it's like Upstairs, Downstairs *or something: a gardener (Neil), under-gardener (Roy), odd-job-man (Phil), plus two bad-tempered cleaning-women who come in three times a week (Linda and Leslie – the 'L's from Hell!) plus a housekeeper, Jill, who occupies a bedsit in the basement. Not so much a housekeeper, I suppose, as a cook-general, I think it's called. She and I handle most of the cooking between us, though Jill told me that when they have important dinner parties, a catering organization comes in and deals with it. She's nice.*

Give Mom and Dad my love, as always. And to you too, Sweet Pea.

Sabby.

Oh, Sabine, I thought, my funny, lively sister, I have missed you for so long. What could have been in the killer's mind? After all these years, it was still impossible to grasp. Did the families of victims always feel this way? Such questions were unanswerable now, and always would be. It had seemed incomprehensible to me then, and still seemed so now, that anyone could have been enraged enough to murder her own children, like some latter-day Medea. When it came out that the murderer had had previous psychiatric episodes, and had even been confined to a mental hospital two or three times, I had demanded bitterly of my father why it was OK for employers to require all kinds of references from prospective employees, but nobody expected employers to offer the same assurances.

Now, up in my room, I drew back the curtains and gazed out at the night sky. The stars were so much brighter here than in London, the darkness more velvety. I could hear the whisper of wind in the poplars which lined the edge of the meadow below the house, and the sound of sheep tearing at the grass.

Peaceful, idyllic.

Below me, a door opened and light streamed out of the French windows on to the old stone flags of the terrace. A man stepped out and moved to the balustrade, looking into the black night beyond the wide terrace.

Seconds later, he was joined by a woman, who said, 'So, Fingal Adair, what are you doing with yourself these days?' I recognized Maggie Fields' voice.

The man gave a start. 'Sorry?' he said coldly. 'Have we met?'

'Don't be pompous, Fin. First of all, here's a

whisky for you. Caol Ila; your favourite, if I remember rightly. And, second of all, have the thirty-something years since our university days changed me that much?' There was laughter in Maggie's voice, and I drew further back into my room, wondering whether I should close the windows. No way did I want to eavesdrop on what might turn out to be a romantic reunion between two old university friends. On the other hand, I might learn something interesting.

'Univer—' He stopped. 'It's not . . . not Maggie, is it?'

'It is indeed.'

'Good God above! I thought I'd seen you before though I couldn't for the life of me remember where.' He stepped back, away from her.

Again there was the gurgle of laughter in her voice as she said, 'Relax, Fin. I'm not going to bite you. And take this whisky. Better still, drink it.'

He sipped at it. 'What on earth are you *doing* here?' he said.

'I'm working here. I'm a freelance cataloguer, archivist, inventorist, call it what you like. Amazing, isn't it? I never thought I'd be back in this house again.'

'But how did you—'

'I heard via a colleague that they were looking for someone, so I rang David Charteris and convinced him that I was the best person for the job.' She tilted her glass to her mouth. 'So what are *you* doing here, Fin?'

He hesitated. Sipped again at his whisky. 'I saw an advertisement for this weekend and I . . .' Even in the dark, I could see how he stiffened up. 'Thing is, Mags, I really felt I ought to come as a kind of farewell to the Clio I knew.'

'And loved.'

'That too.' He sighed heavily. 'I never properly grieved when she left me. Not that I ever understood why she *did* leave.'

'I thought you two split up fairly amicably.'

'*She* split up. I didn't. You must have realized that.'

'I didn't.'

There was a pause, in which I distinctly heard him swallow. 'When she ended it, I seriously thought I might die,' he said, his voice low.

'I don't know what was going on in her head. She adored you.'

'*I* thought so. Just as I adored her. But she showed up at my rooms one afternoon, middle of the summer term, and said it was over. Just like that. She said she was difficult—'

'You already knew that.'

'We all did.' He gave a kind of choked laugh. 'She said that nobody could be expected to live with her, that she would never inflict herself and her problems on anyone, it was better to end it now, right now. And then she was gone, like a . . . a blown snowflake. Oh God, I was so . . . so . . . I was totally devastated. I *loved* her, Mags.'

'I know you did. That's more or less what she did to me, her supposed best friend.'

'I watched her out of my window as she walked away down the High Street. And that was that. I never saw her again. She left me a present, and when I opened it, I found an illustrated edition of *The Snow Queen*.'

'And what did you make of that?'

'I looked at the drawings of this tall figure in her sparkling robes of frost and ice, and her blonde-white hair, and I thought I knew what she was trying to say.'

'The splinter of ice at the heart?'

'Precisely. Except I didn't believe it for a single minute. When we were . . . together, there were no splinters of ice, I can assure you. As for what . . . well, what happened later, it didn't make the slightest difference to how I felt about her. Not that I could believe what she did, either. How about you?'

Maggie hesitated. 'Well . . . she could get pretty damned enraged sometimes. If those boys really tried to burn her manuscript, I can see how she just might have snapped. *Almost* see.'

'What,' Fingal said, 'did you make of her marrying that art student after she left?' Behind his voice, I could hear owls hooting out in the fields.

'I was flabbergasted, to put it mildly. About the whole thing. Who was he? Where did he come from? Where did she meet him? Was it here, at the house, or somewhere else?'

'So many questions to which we never got the answers,' said Fingal.

'Actually, her father was such a nasty piece of work that I've often wondered if he'd bribed the man to marry her, though I can't imagine why he would want to.'

'*I* wouldn't have needed bribing.'

'Did you ever meet him? This art student, I mean.'

'No reason why I should have.'

'He didn't show up at her trial. With his two sons murdered in that grisly way, you'd think the very least he'd do would be to attend.'

'Maybe he didn't know. I understood that he buggered off to Australia when the boys were still quite small.'

'Just walked out on her? Poor Clio.' Maggie took a deep sip of the whisky in her glass and sighed. 'She was never a happy bunny, was she? I remember asking her once at Oxford if everything was OK. She was pretty aggressive, actually. Snappy. Said of course it was, why shouldn't it be? So I said that lately she hadn't seemed as happy as she usually was.'

'What did she say to that?'

'She gave this terrible smile, almost like a rictus, and said, and I quote: "Happy? I don't think I know what that means." So I asked if it was something to do with Fin . . . with you, and she said, no, it wasn't – and anyway, that was over.'

Fin heaved a gusty breath. 'Oh, God.'

'Which was complete news to me, as you can imagine. Over?' I said. 'But the two of you always seem so – so completely together. So she gives that ghastly smile again and starts mumbling on about the ethical aspect . . . you were a tutor, and she was a student. You could get into terrible trouble if the authorities found out.'

'Rubbish!'

'That's exactly what I said. Rubbish and bollocks.'

'Bollocks describes it precisely,' said Fin.

'So then she said that, anyway, she didn't love you any more.And then she walked off, leaving me with my mouth hanging open.'Another strong slug of the whisky and Maggie added, 'It was absolutely obvious that she was lying.'

'Oh dear,' Adair said. He covered his eyes with his hand. 'What in God's name could have caused her to behave like that?'

'Oh, Fin . . .' Maggie put her arms around him. Her voice shook. 'It was the last time I saw her, too. When I got up the next morning, she'd gone. And then nothing . . . until this dreadful, dreadful thing with her boys.'

'I've gone over and over it in my head, and I still find it impossible to see her wielding a knife. Her own children . . . killing them . . .' Fingal choked on the words.

'So,' Maggie said, after a pause. 'Moving on, as one must, what's your life like these days?'

I had eavesdropped enough. They hadn't even mentioned Sabine, but I could understand that. The thing which struck me about their conversation was that clearly, like Gavin Vaughn and myself, they were still carrying the burden of that terrible evening.

Later, I lay in bed with the lights out. I had left the curtains open and the room was filled with glimmering light. A small night-breeze rustled the leaves of the poplars, and somewhere a mournful bird sang. There were tears in my eyes. I had hoped that by coming here I would find some kind of release, but so far the fact of walking in my sister's steps was bearing down on me even more heavily than before, rather than

70

setting me free. The initial searing pain of Sabine's death had long since subsided, but I was conscious now of something new, less immediate, perhaps, yet at the same time more intense. I wanted confrontation with the person responsible, wanted to hurt as I myself had been hurt. But that would never happen, and even if it did, I was not the kind to resort to such primitive action. Much more important was my need to be released from the hatred which blackened the edges of my soul, and had done so for two and a half decades.

But perhaps the killer already suffered every torture imaginable. I'd like to think so. After all, insane or not, what must it be like to wake each morning knowing that you had hacked your own children to death?

Tomorrow I would speak to Malcolm Macdonald, explain who I was. The same with Gavin Vaughn. Their faces flitted through my head.

And suddenly I sat up. I remembered now who Brian Stonor was! He'd been one of the policemen in charge of the case. I frowned into the darkness. It was becoming clear to me that if I could build up for myself a picture of Sabine's killer, a kind of truth might emerge. And if so, then perhaps I could put her death behind me. Not forget it.

Never that. But at least accept it.

I got up early the next morning and made myself a cup of tea which I took back to bed with me, along with another of Sabine's letters.

Hi, Chantal:

Just got time to write you a further instalment. Jill – the housekeeper – was driving in to do some shopping, so I took the opportunity to go into the local town this morning. The boys arrive the day after tomorrow so I shan't have much time after that. It was market day, so I mooched around, dropped into the local museum to gaze upon some shards of Roman pottery, a couple of trilobites and what might or might not be a fragment of the True Cross, given to a Saxon King, possibly by St Augustine himself. Or so the leaflet said. Who is ever going to know if it's true, or just a splinter chipped off the nearest tree?

I was walking past the pens full of sheep and cows, and the farmers' wives selling home-made jams and cakes, when a man accosted me. He said he was called Trevor Barnard and stated in a way that brooked no argument that I was the new Help up at the Lodge. 'General factotum, if you please,' I said, 'not at all the same thing.' Straight out of Cold Comfort Farm, *he was: all tweeds and checked shirts, and, if I'm not just dreaming this up, a moleskin waistcoat. I mean* really *– actually made out of dead* moles! *Can you imagine? Not to mention a penetrating blue gaze and outdoor tan. And extremely handsome with it, I may say. If it wasn't for Malc . . .*

'Let me buy you a cuppa,' he said, and because I thought he might be an interesting source of information about the Redmayne/Palliser family, I accepted his offer. You can't believe how much I learned. First of all, the Hall is from Clio's side of the family, not Harry's, which I hadn't realized from the possessive way Harry showed me round when I first came.

Secondly, Clio's family seem like a bunch of weirdos from way, way back. There are more eccentric aunts and mad uncles in her family tree than you can shake a stick at, not to mention daughters running away and never being heard of again, sons cut off without a shilling, sisters getting pregnant by the gamekeeper or the groom, heirs gambling away the family fortune, heirs being banished to Brazil, mental problems, even murders.

And thirdly, Harry is not the boys' father, which I hadn't realized. Apparently Clio was married when she was still very young, a shotgun wedding, according to Trevor, to some art student doing some work for her father. And then he disappeared (no details offered or asked for), leaving her with two young boys to bring up and the Lodge to maintain. Trevor said she was struck dumb, literally; didn't utter a word for three years! and easy prey for the lusty Harry (which is exactly how he put it), though it was apparently the house

73

he lusted after, rather than Clio. Sounds rather sad, doesn't it?

The Lodge passed to her in trust for her sons because the next in line, her two older brothers, both died quite a few years ago. First Clio and the younger brother went skiing in Switzerland, and he fell off a mountain. Went off-piste, or something. Then the elder one – in London, this is – went out for the evening, came back, and disturbed an intruder who bashed him on the head and killed him before making made good his escape, along with some family silver and some paintings worth a fortune which have never been heard of since. And they never got anyone for it. So eventually everything passed to Clio and the boys.

Intriguing, isn't it? Like living in one of those crime novels you're so keen on!

Much love from your Big Sis

I cried for a while before I finally got up. I missed her so badly. I always would.

By the time I got downstairs for breakfast, the dining room was already half-full. Over by the window, Brian Stonor sat alone, and I made my way over to him.

'May I join you?' I asked.

He looked at me, face astonished, then shook his head, as though to clear it. He half-rose: an old-fashioned gesture, and oddly pleasing. 'Sorry,' he said, 'I was miles away. Yes, do please sit here.'

A waitress took my order for a big pot of tea and showed me a menu. Despite having eaten well the night before, I ordered the full English breakfast without the slightest guilt. There was always the gym, and later in the morning I would be walking over to see Desmond Forshawe.

'So,' I said. 'You seemed surprised to see me.'

'Not surprised, so much as . . . startled.'

'Startled?'

'You look so like . . . like someone I . . . er . . . met years ago.'

I knew he must be talking about Sabine. Our likeness had often been remarked upon. I put down my knife and fork, drank some orange juice. Nodded. 'I think you mean my sister,' I said quietly.

It was his turn to nod. 'It crossed my mind,' he said. 'Last night . . . especially seeing you with Gavin Vaugn.'

'You sound as if you saw her . . . when she was alive.'

'I did. Just the once. Lovely red hair, she had. She was with the three kids one market day when I was visiting my father. I already knew the Palliser boys because, as I said last night, my mother used to work here occasionally and I'd seen them around.' He looked around for the waitress and ordered more coffee. 'Is that why you're here? Because of your sister?'

'Yes.' There was wholemeal toast and what looked like home-made marmalade. I buttered a slice. 'I'm not exaggerating when I say my sister's murder killed my mother. As you can

75

probably imagine, the whole family was damaged. Still is, really.'

He nodded sympathetically. 'I can understand that.'

Looking at him, I thought he probably could. 'Thing is,' I said, 'if I hadn't seen the ad for this weekend, it would never have occurred to me to come back here. Not for a moment. But I turned the page in some magazine at my work, and there it was. I told myself it was meant.'

'What, are you looking for "closure", as they say these days?'

'Not entirely. I just . . .' Through the window to my left I could see the stone terrace which ran along the back of the house, daffodils bright as lemons, interspersed with urns planted with miniature narcissi, grape hyacinths, tiny crimson tulips. 'I wanted to see where she spent her last days, I suppose.' Tears came into my eyes. 'I miss her so much, you see. It would be like having a bit extra, a bit more of her than we've so far been allowed.'

Stonor put his hand over mine but didn't speak.

I cleared my throat. 'Why do you call them the Palliser boys? I seem to remember reading somewhere that their mother had married an art student called – um – Jarvis, I believe it was, who was their father.'

'That's right, she did. But he left for parts unknown while the youngest child was still in nappies, never to be seen or heard of again. And since she was a Palliser, and the Palliser family had owned the house for generations, I suppose we all just went on referring to them as Pallisers.'

He waved across the room at Gavin Vaughn, who had just come in, beckoning him over. He began shifting butter dishes and sugar bowls around to make room. 'You know who *he* is, don't you?'

'I recognized his name when he introduced himself.'

'You talked about being haunted,' he said in a low voice. 'There's a man battling demons, if ever I've seen one.'

'Don't tell him who I am,' I said urgently. 'I'll do it myself later.'

Then Gavin was beside us, pulling out a chair, asking for coffee and going through the business of ordering his breakfast, while Stonor and I watched him in silence. There were shadows under his eyes, and his hair seemed dulled this morning. He looked like a man who had slept badly. Not surprising. I couldn't help wondering what could possibly have brought him back to this place where he'd experienced so much horror.

He took a piece of toast, then reached for the butter, over which his hand hovered for several seconds. He seemed slightly disorientated.

I leaned forward, smiling. I said, '"*Marmalade is tasty if it's very thickly spread.*"'

His reaction surprised me. He stared at me, the blood draining from his face. 'What did you say?' he managed, after a moment. His expression was a mixture of shock and belligerence.

I held up both hands as though to ward him off. 'Hey,' I said. 'No offence. It's from A.A. Milne. *When We Were Very Young.*'

'I *know* where it's from.' He drained his cup

of coffee and refilled it from the pot provided, his hand shaking slightly. 'Sorry,' he muttered shamefacedly to the tablecloth, after a moment. 'I'm a bit on edge.'

Over his bent head, Stonor and I looked at each other. He raised significant eyebrows. 'All right, son?' he said.

'Fine, thanks.'

I wondered just how much of an emotional toll it was taking on him, being back here. After all, he'd been right there when the Honourable Clio went berserk. How could you ever forget something like that? I'd not been able to, and I hadn't even been present.

Stonor pushed away from the table and stood up. 'I'm booked for a sauna and then a massage,' he said. 'I'll leave you to it. By the way, I'm off home after supper tonight.' Keeping his eyes on me, he reached into his breast pocket and brought out a wallet. 'In case I don't catch up with you again, you might like to have my card.'

'Might I?' I tried to hide my surprise. Why should he think I'd want his card?

'You, too.' Stonor handed out another one to Gavin. 'I'll be happy to talk to either of you – or both, of course – any time you feel the need.'

'You sound as though you think I *will* feel the need,' I said.

'You know what, Mrs Frazer?' He bent closer. 'I'm absolutely certain of it.'

Gavin and I stared after him. 'Enigmatic or what?' Gavin said.

'Both, I think,' I said.

When Stonor had left the dining room, I said

quietly, 'Gavin, I know who you are, your connection with this place. I know quite a lot about what happened back then, the murders and everything. That the Honourable Clio was your guardian, while your parents were abroad. That the Palliser boys were like your brothers.'

He didn't seem surprised. 'How did you know that?' His fingers nervously worried a teaspoon.

'I've read the books and the articles.'

Again, he nodded. Then he said, in a low voice, 'I was absolutely mad to come back.' He drank fiercely from his coffee cup. 'You know how it is when you return to a place you knew when you were a child? Everything seems so much smaller than you remembered it?'

It was my turn to nod.

'Somehow I thought it would all take on a different perspective, now that I'm an adult. Be less . . . less *looming*.'

'And it hasn't.'

'Not in the least.' He let the spoon go and looked at me. 'I don't think I'm going to make it through the weekend, quite honestly.'

'There's no reason why you should. Nobody made you come, and nobody can make you stay. On the other hand, maybe if you give it more of a chance, you'll find things easing up a little inside your head.'

'Do you really think so?'

'What do I know? But it's possible.' I smiled brightly. Little Miss Sunshine. Not, I should say, my usual mode. 'I'm going to walk over and see Desmond Forshawe this morning. I'm sure he wouldn't mind if you came along.'

'No, thanks.'

'You might enjoy it.' I looked out at the pale sunlight. 'Might clear your head a bit.'

'I'm sure it would, but I'm afraid I have things to do.'

I'd love to have known what they were. 'OK. Maybe see you at lunchtime.'

'Maybe.' As I left, he gave a kind of grimace which, rather charitably perhaps, I interpreted as an apologetic smile.

Four

Having asked David Charteris for directions, I set off across the fields towards Byfield Hall, which for many generations had been the seat of this particular branch of the Forshawe family. The going was quite easy. It hadn't rained for some time, and the narrow footpath bordering the sloping fields was dry. Down below me lay a huddle of farm buildings with fox-coloured roofs, the morning sunshine turning their walls a rich shade of honey.

Except for birdsong, the swish of grass, the occasional drone of an aeroplane high in the sky, it was quiet. But once into the woods that I'd seen from my windows, there was no sound at all, except the faint pad of my footsteps on the soft leaf-moulded track which ran from one end of the coppice to the other. At first I could see sunshine between the trees, but as I went in deeper, the trunks grew thicker together, blocking out the light. These were mostly coniferous woods, and the green light which filtered through the branches began to strike me as faintly sinister. Anyone losing their way in here could quite easily grow dis-orientated: very soon I found myself looking up for the faint lightening of the green that indicated the sun, which I knew to keep on my right. It hadn't occurred to me that I might need a compass, even if I'd thought to bring one with me. Even if I'd owned one.

I came across an overgrown clearing where the remains of a tumbledown old outhouse stood. It was built of rounded stones, roughly put together. The roof had long ago fallen in: nettles sentinelled the doorway, where the planks of a disintegrated door lay scattered. A square hole had been cut into one wall to let in the light. It was difficult to discern its original function, since it couldn't have been a shepherd's hut, nor a hide for shooters of pheasant or duck. Peering above the nettles, I could just make out in the gloom a piece of heavily rusted farm equipment and a pile of something mouldering in one corner.

Behind me, a twig cracked. For a moment I stood rigid, my pulse beating like a drum. Then common-sense asserted itself. It was broad daylight – at least, beyond this wood it was. Murderers, rapists, mad axemen usually plied their trade at night, among concealing shadows. I was perfectly safe. Refusing to turn round and survey the path behind me, I walked on. Impossible for me not to remember my Dante: *In the middle of the journey of our life, I found myself lost in a dark wood where the straight road had been lost sight of . . .* How apposite. I was thirty-five years old, astray in a dark wood, and certainly I had long ago lost sight of the straight road.

Another crack, a rustle of leaves. Someone – or something – was definitely following me. I whipped round and caught movement. I told myself it could be a deer, or a bird, a wild boar, a rabbit. I also told myself it could be a

82

drug-crazed terrorist or a rabid tiger escaped from a local circus, even though I knew I was being ridiculous. I quickened my pace, lengthened my stride. The hell with pride – the sooner I was out of these trees, the better. Ahead of me spread the rutted track, and as I walked, a fox emerged from the undergrowth and trotted across the rutted path, his bushy tail with its distinctive white tip held straight out behind. He turned his head to stare at me incuriously with shiny black eyes, then trundled on into the bushes on the other side of the track. Had I really been reduced to jumping out of my skin because of an animal?

At the same time, the trees ahead began to thin out and show daylight between their trunks. Thankfully, I reached the edge of the wood and emerged into sunlight. Fields spread away on every side. Ahead, there was an unmade track, and to my right, over a long stretch of drystone wall, I could see a fine house, very like Weston Lodge, but more elaborate. A gravelled drive led up to the front door, and sheep grazed in the pasture on either side. Even from here I could see a carved escutcheon over the front doors which stood at the top of a flight of steps flanked by urn-topped pillars. It had to be Byfield Hall. I strode along the track, reached a road and then, after about a hundred yards, some tall iron gates.

The sun was shining. Feeler safer, I turned and surveyed the woods behind me. Nothing, of course. No drooling man carrying a chainsaw. No saliva-dripping rabid dog. Just burgeoning leaf, bramble bushes, lightly swaying branches. In front of me, two enormous Cedars of Lebanon stood on either side of the house, drooping like green curtains across tightly mown lawns. As I approached, Desmond Forshawe appeared at the top of the steps and waved.

'I actually remembered you were coming,' he called. 'I even asked Mrs Derridge to make one of her lemon sponges for elevenses.'

Elevenses! What could be less menacing than a word so redolent of indulgent nannies, safe childhoods, welcoming servants' halls? It was a word you rarely heard any more, superseded by coffee-time or tea-breaks.

'Sounds fabulous,' I said as I came up the steps to shake his hand. 'Good morning, how are you? How are the hens?'

His old eyes brightened. 'In fine fettle,' he said. 'Keep hens yourself, do you?'

'Just eat their eggs,' I said, more or less as I'd replied when he asked the same question at dinner the night before.

'And you are . . . you're—' I could see him racking his ancient brains for my name.

'Chantal Frazer,' I said.

'Of course you are. Come on in.'

He led the way into a hall almost as grand as the one at Weston Lodge, but much less kempt. A huge and very beautiful chandelier hung in the centre, its swags and garlands of cut crystal half-hidden beneath swathing cobwebs. Three shabby sofas surrounded the big hearth where a fire of smouldering logs burned. Dogs lay here and there, their tails thumping lazily as their master came in. One big old Golden Labrador creaked to its feet and came over to inspect me. The others didn't bother. In dog years, I reckoned they were at least as old as Desmond Forshawe. *Lord* Forshawe, as it happened. Something I'd learned from David Charteris when asking how to get to Byfield Hall.

'Nice old boy,' he had said. 'The memory banks occasionally get overdrawn, but otherwise he's very much with it. And he owns some marvellous pictures.'

'That's why I'm going to see him,' I said. 'We talked about it last night.'

'Interested in pictures?'

'Very much so. I work for an auction house in London.'

'You should have a word with Maggie Fields; the woman who's inventorying, if that's the word, the house.'

Now Forshawe pressed a bell in the wall. 'We'll have coffee first, shall we?' He ushered me into a large drawing room, where another fire was burning. Huge windows at one end opened on to a terrace above unkempt back lawns and over-crowded flower beds. Forshawe walked across to look out. 'All got a bit neglected since m'wife died,' he said, waving a hand at the garden. 'She took care of all that sort of thing. M'nephews fly over from New York every now and then and organize a gardener to come in. Trouble is, old Cotter died last year, and I haven't got round to finding a replacement.' He looked at me ruefully, the eyebrow thickets moving up and down his forehead. 'Roses are in a dreadful state, poor old things.'

'They are rather, aren't they?'

85

A portrait hung above the fireplace, showing a tall slim woman in ceremonial robes, a necklace sparkling at her throat, one slim hand resting on a plinth of some kind. Two dogs lay at her feet, muzzles resting on paws.

As he led the way to the comfortable chairs in front of the fire, I said, 'Is that your wife?'

'Yes. A fine-looking woman, she was, too. And formidable. By God, when she came storming in, you didn't wait to find out what she was complaining about, just got as far away from the danger zone as you could.' He sighed. 'Miss her like the devil, actually.'

I looked more closely. Fine-looking indeed. And steely as a hatpin. She had the face of a woman not to be trifled with.

Mrs Derridge appeared with coffee things on a tarnished silver tray. 'Here you are, then,' she said. 'Now don't you go making a pig of yourself with that cake, My Lord. There's a nice bit of salmon for your lunch, sent over fresh this morning from Sir Michael.'

Forshawe winked at me. 'Right you are, Mrs D.'

It all sounded charmingly feudal, straight out of a play by Noel Coward, or a lightweight novel of the 1920s.

While Forshawe poured coffee from a silver pot, I walked over to look at a painting hanging between two of the long windows giving on to a terrace very similar to that at Weston Lodge.

'Is that really a Balthus?' I said. 'That is amazing.'

'Isn't it, though? *Jeune Fille Avec Papillon.*

One of our favourites, that is. We were advised to buy it by our neighbour, Clio Palliser. Lent it to her once.' He coughed loudly. Once again he turned the bushy eyebrows in my direction, obviously wondering if I recognized the name. 'She was very knowledgeable about contemporary art.'

'It's marvellous.' I looked again at the painting, with its trademark saucy nymphet seemingly unaware of the provocative pose she was striking, her little white knickers showing as she bent over a gaudy butterfly perched on the edge of a glass dish, while a sinister character lurked halfway behind a green drape, watching her. 'It's not one of his works I'm familiar with.' Hoping he didn't notice what I was doing, I peered more closely at the canvas and could clearly see where the words FUCK YOU had been deleted and the patch of canvas restored.

'Wonderful stuff, isn't it? A trifle perverted, to my way of thinking, but I don't hold that against the old boy.' Forshawe seemed a different person, the vagueness gone, his speech much crisper than previously. 'Actually, Clio was knowledgeable about so many things. Never could believe what they said she'd . . .' He shook his head. 'Sit down, my dear. Then I'll take you round the museum, as I call it. Show you some of the family heirlooms as well as the stuff m'wife acquired.' He laughed. 'M'nephews always used to accuse the old girl of liking her artworks and her dogs more than she liked me!'

'Your nephews? No children of your own?'

'None. Rather sad, really, but my wife didn't care for children, so there it was.'

87

I balanced a piece of the Derridge sponge on the edge of my saucer, gold-rimmed bone china so delicate that I could see the outline of my finger through it. Should I come clean? Confess who I was?

While I was deciding, my host put his head on one side. 'I'm not yet so gaga that I assume nobody else knows what took place across the way there, at Weston Lodge, twenty-three years ago. Are you one of them, hmm?'

I put down my coffee cup. Swallowed. Looked him in the eye. 'I know exactly what happened,' I said. 'Or is supposed to have—'

He interrupted me. 'I knew I'd seen you before. Or someone very like. You're that poor girl's sister, aren't you? She told me she had one, back home in California.'

'Yes.' I barely got the word out.

He laid his gnarled old hand on mine. 'I'm so very sorry. She was a really nice girl. And the boys adored her. What happened to her was . . . well, it was unconscionable.'

'Why did it happen? That's what we could never figure out. It was such an . . . *extreme* thing to do.'

'Poor Clio came from an extreme family,' Forshawe said. 'What m'nephews call dysfunctional. I've known the Pallisers since I was a child. And m'wife was actually related to them, second cousin sort of thing.'

Another piece of information, though I had no idea how useful it might be. 'Really?'

'Clio's mother died young, do you see? And I'm afraid that after she'd gone, Gerald Palliser let his sons run wild. Clio was basically brought up by the nanny, who was *not* a nice woman. My own parents always suspected she was one of those suppressed – or even overt, when you think about it – sadists. A lot of locking in coal-holes and whippings with a belt buckle, that sort of thing. And then her two brothers . . . Bad lots, the pair of them.' He shook his head. 'No one knows what goes on behind closed doors, do they? My sainted mama did try to talk to Gerald about it, but he didn't want to know.'

'Nasty.'

'I'll say. She stopped speaking at one point. This is Clio I'm talking about, not that wretched nanny. Went completely silent for about five years. I think getting away to university was the making of her . . .' His face was sympathetic as he replaced his cup on the tray. 'Actually, if you ask me, a lot of those so-called posh families were barmy, back then. Probably still are. Totally bonkers. M'wife's was a case in point.' There was a pause, during which I hoped he was going to expand on the subject, but instead, he said, 'More cake, m'dear?'

'No, thank you.'

'Well, I'm going to have another piece. I hardly ever get cake any more: m'nephews have told La Derridge to keep me off that sort of thing.'

'Tell me more about the Palliser family,' I said, while crumbs dropped on to his ancient tweed jacket. 'My sister wrote that the eldest son was murdered in his own flat by an intruder, and they never found who did it.'

'Bastard,' said Forshawe. 'Excuse my language,

m'dear. I mean the victim, not the burglar. Piers was an absolute bounder. Whoever bumped him off ought to get a medal for ridding the world of an unmitigated scoundrel and rogue.'

'The thief stole some pictures, as well as silver, didn't he?' I said.

'That's right.'

'I wonder what they were.'

'I can tell you some of them. There was certainly a Modigliani, and an early Lucian Freud: *Blue Nude*, I believe it was called. And there were quite a few of poor Clio's Scandinavian painters, four or even five. At least, she always said Piers had stolen them from her, and I know they weren't in the man's flat when they found him.'

'That's interesting. I've studied the Scandinavians myself.' I wasn't sure what I felt about the fact that Clio had too.

'I'm entirely ignorant on the subject, I'm afraid. All bloody Vikings, far as I'm concerned. But Piers . . . He'd been dead for over a week by the time anyone thought to break in. No friends, d'you see? It was the smell that alerted someone else in the block.'

There wasn't a lot I could say to that. 'The people who were there last night . . .' I said. 'Did you recognize any of them from the old days?'

'Possibly. Of course, I knew that the Fields woman was a close friend of poor Clio's, when they were both up at Oxford. She's some kind of archivist, I believe. When she applied for the job, young David asked me if I knew anything about her. I made a few enquiries, friends of mine who might be in the know, and they said she was

90

very sound. So he took her on. Good idea in my opinion. It's about time someone catalogued all the stuff in that house. It's been packed away for years.'

'Just left in the house, do you mean?'

'Some of the more valuable stuff was put into storage, I believe. Good thing too: there've been several attempted break-ins, people lurking round the property, that sort of thing.'

I resolved to talk to Maggie Fields again the minute an opportunity came up.

'And I'm not sure,' he went on, 'but I believe one of the people from last night was some kind of a policeman fellow who was around at the time. Investigated it, actually.' His look was shrewd. 'Forgive me for saying this, my dear, but it was a long time ago, now. You sound a little bit obsessed with the whole awful affair – not that one could blame you, losing your sister and so forth. It doesn't do any good to dwell on these things.'

'My husband used to say that too.' I remembered evenings sitting on the tiny balcony of our flat in London as the sun went down over Kensington Gardens, Ham twining my long red hair around his fingers, blackbirds warbling. 'You have to put it behind you, darling,' he would say. 'You mustn't let it fester.'

'Did he, now?' His eyes were kind. 'You do realize that there's no reason at all why any of the people now staying at the Lodge should have had anything to do with what happened.'

'You're absolutely right.' I gave a silly little laugh. On the other hand, so far four of them had a direct link, and two others (himself and Leeming) were indirectly involved. It couldn't all be coincidence.

'Look, if you've finished your coffee, why don't we go and look at pictures? That's what you've come for, after all.'

That – although I didn't say so – and a chance to talk about the woman who'd killed my sister.

He walked towards the door leading out into the handsome hall, then stopped. 'Last night you mentioned some miniatures,' he said casually. 'How did you know about them?'

'My sister wrote to me about them. She mentioned a Henry Bone, a Richard Cosway. And even a Nicholas Hilliard.'

'It was an early one,' he said. 'Nothing like the charming masterpieces he produced later in his career.'

'Even so, you said last night that you wondered where they had gone.'

'Indeed. I suppose anyone could have removed them from the house in the aftermath of what happened. Stick half a dozen in one pocket, half a dozen in another. Who's to know? The place was full of people in the days following the . . . er . . . what happened.'

'You think someone stole them?'

'I think it's very possible. As long as the police weren't watching, or hadn't impounded them or whatever policemen do in a case like that. On the other hand . . .' Forshawe looked thoughtful. 'They could equally have been hidden, while someone waited for an opportunity to retrieve them.'

'Like this weekend, for example?' That could explain the visit to the attic last night.

'Goodness me, that never occurred to me. But of course you're right.' He led the way down a long corridor. 'And I'll tell you something which you doubtless already know, given your line of work,' he said as he turned a corner into yet another passage, lined with indifferent portraits of what I assumed were long-dead Forshawes. 'I keep a close eye on the sales and so on, and they haven't come up for sale in the years since they disappeared.'

'Not in England, at any rate,' I said, the thought only just striking me.

'Good point.' He nodded. '*Very* good point. And they'll always be collectable, having been just about wiped out by the invention of the camera. Eighteen thirtyish, that was, as far as I remember. Of course an artist could always flatter his subject better than a photographer.'

'True. And in the last twenty years or so, some of the more well-known miniatures have quadrupled in value.'

'Indeed they have.'

I'd completely revised my opinion of Desmond Forshawe. Far from the bumbling persona he liked to project, it was obvious that, like my father, he was as sharp as a needle.

The following hour or so passed in pleasant contemplation of the collections of paintings and *objets* that his wife and he had put together. As I was leaving, I gave him my business card. 'I hope it never comes to it, but if you ever need to . . . to put anything up for sale, do give me a ring. We're not as well-known as the bigger auction houses, but we have a pretty good reputation nonetheless and produce excellent results for our clients.'

'I know.' He nodded. 'Chantal Frazer, right?'

'Right.'

'I'll try to remember the name.'

I had absolutely no doubt that he would do so.

Five

In order to get back to Weston Lodge, I skirted the dark wood, instead of taking the path through it. I was almost back at the house when I found myself passing a small stone building surrounded by yew trees, holly bushes and bedraggled philadelphus shrubs in desperate need of pruning. The door was arched and a small stone cupola above the entrance supported a verdigrised bell. Was this the chapel which Sabine had mentioned, where she'd heard someone playing?

Above the doorway, incised into the keystone, was a carving of a frowning male head, surrounded by acanthus leaves. I took it to be a Green Man, pagan symbol of fertility. Vine leaves emerged from his lips, together with what looked like tiny limbs, and grapes encircled his head. While I knew that the early Christian fathers had subsumed pagan images into the more benign religious God of Christianity – and Rosslyn Chapel notwithstanding – I had always found something too overtly sinister about the Green Man images. Not that this carving was. It reminded me very much of the hieratic work of someone like Eric Gill or some artist whose work I'd been scanning only the other day. Paul Somebody. Or Somebody Paul. Something to do with fairgrounds . . . What did it matter? He had nothing to do with this.

And then, astonishingly, delightfully, through

95

the open door came the sound of organ music, just as Sabine had described so long ago, a prelude by Buxtehude, a favourite composer of mine. I crept in and sat down in the last of the ten pews which faced the front of the chapel. The organ was set into an alcove and hidden from the congregation, if there had been one, by a carved screen. Shields hung from the ceiling, and marble memorial tablets proclaimed the heroism of various Pallisers and Charterises over the centuries. I'd expected cobwebs and dust, a scatter of owl pellets, mummified flies and small feathers, but, like the attic in which I'd trespassed the previous night, the chapel was immaculate. It was very small, not much bigger than a tool shed, panelled in wood and vaulted with rough timber beams. Above the lace-topped table which did duty as an altar was a small stained glass window, arched and leaded: its design was defiantly pagan, another Green Man, this time with grapes and vines crawling over his face and three green *putti* lining the bottom frame. In the background were things which must have had some kind of esoteric meaning: a crucifix, a scythe, a snow-white lamb, an earthenware pitcher pouring golden coins. The whole thing was strangely unsettling, and I wondered who had created it. And why.

The unseen organist came to the end of the piece, then began again, Bach this time, freeing me to move silently from my pew, up the aisle and out into the sunshine. All the way back to the house, I wondered who had been playing.

When I came in through the front door, David Charteris was standing in front of the hearth,

96

looking very much at ease. The receptionist had gone.

'Ah,' he said. 'Chantal Frazer. How are you doing? Are you enjoying yourself?'

'Very much,' I said. 'You've created a marvellous ambience here. You must have spent a great deal of time getting it right.'

He smiled. 'Thank you. I bought it from the Palliser Trust that had been set up after . . . Well, my partner and I thought about it for years before actually starting on the renovations. How we wanted the rooms to be, what modifications were needed, installing central heating, planning the garden and so on. Mind you, it wasn't really all that difficult: the place was like a beautiful woman who was losing her looks. It still had wonderful bones. We only had to give it a facelift here, some Botox there.'

'I've just seen the chapel.'

'Nice, isn't it? A real sense of history about it. It's supposed to be haunted, you know.'

'Really? I didn't see any ghosts.'

'Aural ghosts,' he said. 'They say that some long dead Palliser plays Bach on the organ, mourning for his son who died in the Crusades.'

'As a matter of fact, I did hear someone playing, but I don't think it was a ghost.' I gave him a smile. 'I was intrigued by the Green Man above the lintel. And that decidedly weird window above the altar.'

'Very strange pieces of work, I agree. And you will probably be surprised to hear that they're not Green Men at all. At least, not the window. It's Cronus.' He looked at his watch. 'Look, we've got time, come into the bar, and we'll have a pre-prandial sherry. I'll explain it to you then.'

Since I was here to immerse myself in Weston Lodge – I doubted I would ever come here again – and because Dad always liked to have a glass of sherry before lunch, I happily followed him into the bar, which was furnished, gentleman's club style, with deep, soft leather sofas and armchairs.

'Happy days!' He tapped his glass against mine. 'And many of them.'

'Hear, hear.' How fervently I hoped that happiness lay ahead.

'Now, that chapel.' He leaned back. 'As you noticed, both the lintel carving and the altar window are rather unusual, to say the least.'

'They certainly are.'

'As I'm sure you're aware, Cronus is the god who was encouraged by his mother to scythe off his own father's . . . erm . . . family jewels. And later in his narrative, he devoured his own children. Notice those little green kids at the bottom?'

'Yes.'

'Three of them, right? Two boys, one girl: the story goes that the artist was a young art student who supposedly was madly in love with Cl . . . erm . . . the daughter of the house. Forty years ago this was, or thereabouts. He did both the window and the carving. He based the features of Cronus on old Sir Gerald Palliser, a bastard of the very finest vintage, even if he was a relative of mine. A drunk, a philanderer and, so rumour has it, a wife-killer.'

'Not to mention an offspring-devourer.'

'Oh, he did plenty of that as well. Metaphorically speaking.'

I sipped my sherry. 'Did Sir Gerald realize that the artist's portrait of him was hardly flattering?'

'One of his vile sons – one of my second cousins – pointed it out later. As so often, the old boy flew into an apoplectic rage. By this time Clio, his daughter –' using the name was an oversight, I felt sure; I kept my face neutral – 'had married the art student and that was that. When the student, by now the father of two sons, left for parts unknown, Gerald was all for having the window smashed, until his legal adviser pointed out that the young man was considered to be a very promising sculptor. In which case, as this sage gentleman (my father, as it happens) pointed out, his early work was likely to fetch a pretty penny one of these days.'

'So whatever happened to Sir Gerald? And why did you call him a wife-killer?'

'Poor old Aunt Jane, as we called her . . . He was an absolute brute. Browbeat her unmercifully. He bullied her into her grave, in my opinion. She had the two boys – Piers and Miles – who took their attitudes from their father. Handsome devils, all three of them, and absolute sods into the bargain, if you'll excuse my language. And then some years later, she produced Clio. We all watched her . . . well, deflate is the only word. Even though I was a child then too, I could see it. And then she fell out of a window – though my father was always convinced she couldn't take any more of Sir Gerald and killed herself – leaving poor little Clio to the mercy of her father and her two horrible brothers.'

It sounded like a charming family. I could

almost feel the stirrings of pity for my sister's murderer. 'And what happened to bad Sir Gerald?'

'Hunting accident. Broke his neck.' He smiled. 'The earth is a far better place now that he's beneath it.'

'And where's the art student now?'

'Nobody really knows. After his second son was born, he disappeared without so much as a fare-thee-well.'

'So your poor cousin had to bring up her children on her own.'

'That's about the size of it, yes. Obviously the house then belonged to her in trust for the boys. She soldiered on a bit, and then Redmayne came along. Plenty of money there, so my cousin was free to do what she really wanted, which was retreat into her own study and work. Even had the room soundproofed, if you can believe it!'

'Why?'

'So the noise of domesticity wouldn't disturb her.'

'What did you think of Mr Redmayne?'

'Never met him, my dear. Always up in London. Not that Clio encouraged anyone to visit. I don't think I saw her more than a couple of times after she went down from Oxford. Neither did most of the rest of the family.'

We heard the sound of wheels on the gravel drive, and David looked at his watch again. His face lit up. 'That'll be Omar,' he said. 'He promised to be here in time for lunch.'

'Omar?'

'My partner.' David got to his feet. 'You will excuse me, won't you?'

100

Six

Tidying myself up for lunch, I checked my watch and decided I just had time to read another of Sabine's letters.

Dear Little Sister,

Big excitement yesterday! There was a rather elaborate dinner party here last night, loads of the rich and famous (or perhaps they only looked rich and famous) plus a few of the local gentry. Trevor Barnard, the tenant-farmer, who I met the other day. Some titled dude called Forshawe and his wife, a weird woman with hair like a fishing net. A couple of art dealer colleagues of Harry Redmayne's, plus wives. Plus Clio's publishers, who have a country cottage nearby, and some other people I can't remember. There were eighteen guests in all: so the outdoor staff (I'm getting into the upper-class swing of it now!) opened up the massive dining room and put leaves into the huge mahogany table, while we women brought out the best crystal and the monogrammed silver and the most gorgeous hand-painted Spode dinner service. Gosh, I thought I was above materialism, but I would kill to own that Spode.

Anyway, it was really grand. They had a caterer come in, and Jill and I helped out with drinks first. Harry said we had to wear black and put on these dinky little white aprons, which I kind of objected to, on democratic grounds, but of course I went along with it. The food was delicious. Jill and I gorged on leftovers. Especially the pheasant in a chestnut sauce, and funny little puffed-up potato slices, like flat-sided balloons, can't remember their name, and fabulous asparagus hollandaise and soft-poached eggs with smoked salmon.

The Hon Clio didn't look particularly thrilled about her guests, I must say, but she looked totally fabulous, given how pale she is. She was wearing this dark green velvet dress with medieval sleeves, all decorated with gold, straight out of any illustrated manuscript you care to mention. In fact, now I think of it, she looked rather like that girl in the Uccello painting of George and the Dragon – without the silly hat and veil, of course.

Anyway, I hope you guys are gearing up for the festive season over there in sunny California. I ought to miss you all, but I absolutely haven't had time to do anything other than prepare for Christmas and keep an eye on those boys. Have to say they keep me pretty much occupied.

Harry is almost never here at the moment. Finalizing some big art deal going down with a client in Japan, so he's staying in his flat in town. And Clio's working towards a deadline and rarely comes out of her study. So I'm very much in loco parentis. *Jill told me yesterday, in the strictest confidence, that the study was soundproofed a few years ago, so Clio can't hear the Hoover going or the boys shouting or anything. I suppose it's one way to deal with unwanted noise. And, strictly* entre nous, *as they say, a good way for her to avoid being Mom to her children. Because I'm starting to wonder if that's what's at the root of all this weird behaviour of hers. I've got friends (well, you know Lindsay, and also Charlene, the daughter of Mom's friend Megan) who say it can drive you mad, the relentless twenty-four hours a day, seven days a week thing with kids. 'It's the mindless repetition of it all,' Charlene says. And Lindsay's always saying things like, 'To think I gave up a high-powered job for this.'*

And I can tell you now that if (IF) Malc and I ever have kids, I shall love them to little bits and spend every day thinking how wonderful they are. And telling them, too. It's what Mom always does and I think it's a good thing. But I'll also be hoping their aunt Chantal will be popping over from California all the time, to take the pressure off. (I'm only almost joking!)

According to Jill, poor Clio is of a

nervous disposition – (well, even I, a total newcomer, can see that!) – and has actually spent time in the psychiatric wing of the local hospital. She's apparently always been sort of screwed up, ever since she was a child. She usually eats alone in her study, unless Harry is around, and the boys, when they're here, usually eat with me and Jill in the kitchen. It's not exactly ideal family life, is it?

Especially when these boys, George and Edward, are the most adorable lads you could ever hope to meet. Thick blond hair, deep blue eyes, a lovely open manner . . . very very charming and well-brought up, as you'd expect. A bit naughty, by all accounts (actually, very naughty, according to Jill!), but they're healthy boys, after all. And the third boy – Gavin – is cut from exactly the same cloth: I guess maybe there's something to be said for private education after all.

I managed to slip out for a walk late this afternoon. Went round the fields and through the woods. It gets dark here quite early, so lights come popping on in the houses around the valley. I came back along a little path which led to a marvellous little chapel sort of hidden behind yew trees and holly bushes. I peeked in and there was a stained glass window above the altar table and a couple of candles lit. It was really magical. Dusk falling and there were a few bursts of

*snowflakes, just in time for Christmas (did
someone organize this specially??!!), and
inside the chapel someone was playing
the little organ – I think it was Bach.
Totally lovely. You know the way we used
to nominate special moments that we'd
remember for the rest of our lives? Well,
that was definitely one for my list.*

*No idea who was playing but he or she
is very talented.*

*Bed calls. Looking after the boys is
quite tiring, actually. Plus there's all my
other duties. Plus I'm trying to keep up
with my reading for when I go back to
uni. NOT that I'm complaining 'cause I
really love it here.*

All love, your sister,
Sabine

I had come here in the hope of sharing in my
sister's final days. Instead I was learning far more
about her killer. I went downstairs and ran into
Maggie Fields on her way into the dining room
and asked if I might join her. We sat down
together at a table for two and ordered. Soup and
salad for me, duck paté for her, followed by
salmon.

'You might not think it,' she said, seeing my
glance, 'but archiving is hard work. I need to
stoke up.'

'It must be a fascinating job.'

'Oh, it is. It involves so much more than merely
making lists of objects in a room, or itemizing
the contents of a cupboard. Reading long-ago

diaries, going through old bills of sale, or dipping into letters describing long trips abroad and the purchases made along the way. Learning the life and times of people long dead, who still live on through their papers and possessions.'

'Did you train as an historian?

'Yes.' She beamed. 'God, I can still taste the delight when I got the letter saying that I'd won a scholarship, that I'd get to spend three whole years in Oxford. Almost no one from my inner-city school in Salford had even gone to university, let alone Oxford.'

'It must have been amazing.'

'It was the culmination of all my dreams, all the hard work I had to put in.' Her smile was huge, as though she'd just heard the news that very morning. 'Oxford, home of learning and all that, all those dreaming spires. I imagined everybody wandering round in mortar-boards and gowns, attending lectures in ancient build-ings bursting with academic achievement and intellectualism. Not to mention punting and college balls and summer picnics beside the Cherwell, all that Alice-in-Wonderland pastoral jazz which probably bore as little relation to reality then as it does now.' She spread paté on a piece of wholemeal toast and happily chewed it.

'And did Oxford live up to your expectations?' I asked.

'It fulfilled them all, and more.' Reminiscently, she shook her head. 'Yes, absolutely.'

I coughed. Sipped some water. 'Uh . . . I over-heard you talking last night to . . .' I discreetly pointed my chin to where Fingal sat, three or four tables away, eyeing Maggie in a manner which seemed to me to verge on the possessive. He caught my eye and scowled.

'Fingal Adair? Did you?'

'You were right beneath my window.'

'I was up at the same time as his . . . uh . . . girlfriend. She and I were studying the same subject and became good friends, which is how I came to meet him.'

'She?' I knew the answer but wanted to hear her tell me.

'Um . . .' For a moment Maggie seemed disconcerted. It was obvious that she had been enjoined by David Charteris not to mention Clio or anything else that had taken place here. 'Someone called – um – Clio Palliser. Who used to own this house, incidentally.'

I nodded.

'Fin was a little older than us two, a junior lecturer, but we hung out together. Until Clio left.' Frowning slightly, she pressed her table napkin to her mouth, as though to prevent further injudicious words from tumbling out.

And then she laughed suddenly, her pale eyes bright. 'Oh, why am I being so coy? Goodness, that Clio. She was a real live wire, zipping about Oxford on her bike or rushing into lectures, out of lectures, in and out of parties, up and down the stairs in college, wearing the most amazing brilliant colours, trailing scarves and shawls and ribbons. She was like a . . . like a dragonfly on speed.'

'She sounds like fun.' Talking in that familiar

107

way about my sister's killer felt as though I was chewing barbed wire.

'Oh, she was. "Calm down, girl," I used to say. "Relax. Take it easy." And she'd look so distressed . . . She'd say, "But I *can't*. Don't you see? I can't *afford* to stop. I haven't got *time*."'

'I wonder what she meant.'

Maggie spread her last piece of toast and crunched it down. 'Who knows? But I could tell even back then that something had to be very wrong. It was fairly obvious that all that whooshing energy was being powered by something kind of dark and corrosive. Maybe even dangerous.'

Energy that turned into the darkest of rages, I thought. Danger that had culminated in mutilation and murder. Maggie was making allowances, even excuses. But then she had been the woman's friend. I had not.

She pursed her mouth. Dabbed at her lips with her napkin. 'Oh, hell,' she said. 'I've already been so indiscreet . . .' She glanced towards the door of the room as though worried that David Charteris was standing there, lip-reading our conversation. 'I might as well come clean and tell you – in confidence – that my poor friend was . . . uh . . . involved in some fairly nasty goings on here, some years ago. For obvious reasons, David doesn't want people to be aware of what happened, but it's difficult to keep it all under wraps. It was such a *cause célèbre* at the time.'

'Too late for discretion,' I said. 'There are several people here who were involved in some way or another.'

108

'What?' She seemed alarmed. 'Does David know?'

'No idea.'

'Who, for instance?'

I gave her a quick run-down: Stonor, Fingal Adair, Malcolm MacDonald (if my suspicions about his identity were correct), Brian Stonor, Gavin Vaughn.

'Gavin Vaughn,' she repeated. 'As in Metcalfe-Vaughn?'

I nodded.

'My God. He's here? The third boy? The one that got away?'

'If you can ever be said to get away from something like that.'

'And the policeman who was involved in the original investigation. That's rather bizarre, isn't it?'

'It's because of Mr Charteris's advertisements for this special weekend. We all saw them, and that's the reason each of us came.'

'But why, after so long?'

'I don't know about the others.' I avoided her inquisitive grey eyes. 'But I came for my sister's sake.'

There was a small hiatus in the conversation as we glanced at each other and away. On the terrace, the plants in their pots were swaying, caught in a gust of the wind which was wiping out the fine day. Cobweb-grey clouds drifted across the sky, casting irregular shadows over the fields. A small pale bird landed on the flat stone balustrade and began to sing, its little body throbbing with the strength of its music.

Then she said carefully, 'Your sister?'

I fiddled with my water glass and took a deep breath. Eventually, I said, 'Look, I know all about Clio Palliser and what happened here.'

She drew in a sharp breath. 'You do?'

'Yes. It was my sister who Clio killed, along with her own sons.'

Slowly, she nodded. 'I see. At least . . .' She smiled fleetingly. 'I don't know exactly what I see. But something. And I'm so very very sorry. About your sister, I mean. That's not an easy thing to live with.'

'Tell me . . .' I could feel my throat thickening. 'Since you knew the . . . uh . . . assailant, tell me how she could possibly do such a thing.'

'I've asked myself that a hundred times. When it first hit the headlines, I just . . . I didn't know what . . .' Maggie shrugged her shoulders, lifted her hands. 'I mean, it was so unlike her. Her own children . . .'

'But just now you used the word corrosive about her. And dangerous.'

'I know. And when I knew her at Oxford, I can't pretend that she didn't sometimes fly into terrible rages, usually about something completely trivial, like her bike having a puncture, or an ink-blot on an essay – we didn't use computers back then.'

'Was she ever violent?'

'No. Not at all. Well, not really. Oh, she might have aimed a kick at her bike or thrown a book across the room, but nothing more than that. Broken a cup or a mirror or something. I can see that there was a lot of stored-up anger there. But

110

murder . . .' She shook her head. 'I couldn't get my head round it. Still can't. OK, she was always a little strange, a little different. But God! Her own kids. How *could* she?'

'Did you know Mr Adair would be here?'

'Fingal? Not in the least. What a pleasant surprise it was to see him again after all these years.' When she smiled, dimples showed in her cheeks. She pushed her plate away. 'Excuse me, won't you? I have to get back to work.'

'Just before you go . . . what was her second husband like? Harry Redmayne.'

'I never met him. I went to New York after I graduated, and Clio and I lost touch. It wasn't until I saw something about the murders in the *New York Times* that I even realized it was her.' She stood up. 'You could try talking to Fin, but I don't think you'll find him any more enlightening about it all than I've been.'

'One last question: what happened to all the stuff here after . . . after she was found guilty?'

'I believe most of the valuable pictures went into storage, along with some of the furniture. And a company specializing in maintenance of places like this came in every three or four weeks and gave the entire house a good clean, got rid of spiders and moths and rats and so on, made sure the soft furnishings weren't succumbing to the ravages of damp and mice and all the other nasties which try to invade a neglected house. Which is very nice for me, compared to some of the places I've had to work in.'

'So basically the house was left more or less as it had been that night?'

111

'As far as I know. At least, until David and Omar began doing the place up.'

'Thank you.' I watched her walk away across the room, stopping at Adair's table to speak with him briefly. Shoulders straight, figure melding into late middle age, good legs. A nice woman.

I debated getting up and joining Adair, but before I could do so, he got up himself, following Maggie out of the door.

Another time, then.

Meanwhile, there was Gavin Vaughn. I desperately wanted to speak to him. He might have seen Sabine just before she died. But I didn't want to open wounds that I suspected were nowhere near healed. Not his, not mine. I'd worked out why he'd been so upset when I quoted A.A. Milne at breakfast. It was a line Sabine and I often repeated, if Dad started making a fuss about something; she must have done the same here.

Despite the rising wind, coffee was being served outside on the terrace. I took my cup over to one of the slatted wooden tables and looked out across the parkland. About three minutes later, Gavin Vaughn joined me. 'May I?'

'Of course.'

He sat down, and we both sipped coffee in silence, until he said, 'I'm going into the town shortly. Anything I can get you?'

'No, thanks. But might I come with you?'

For a moment, he hesitated.

'It's supposed to be rather picturesque,' I said.

'All right.' It wasn't exactly the warmest of responses, but I wasn't about to quibble.

112

Seven

When we got there, the steep little High Street was strung with red, white and blue bunting, and the old-fashioned wrought-iron lamp-posts trailed tricoloured beards.

Gavin edged his car into a space I wouldn't even have contemplated and we got out. He stood on the pavement and stared up and down. 'It's hardly changed,' he said softly.

I followed him as the street opened out into a pretty square with a fountain in the middle. Stalls were set up all round, selling the usual things: cheap clothes, local honey, hand-thrown pottery, cheeses, flowering bulbs, second-hand books. There was a flower stall and a trestle table laden with earth-crammed leeks and weird-looking potatoes.

Gavin found a little café behind a pots-and-pans seller who stood guarding his wares with folded arms and a thin cigar in his mouth. We sat down, ordered a pot of tea and a cheese scone each. We were silent until the waitress appeared with a homely brown pot and a couple of bright yellow scones with tiny brown bits on top.

'OK,' he said, when cups had been filled and scones spread with butter. 'Who exactly are you? Are you the police?'

'The *police*?' What a bizarre idea to come up with.

He scrutinized my face, his brow puckered, not

quite a frown but very far from amiable. He blinked a couple of times, looked at me again, said, 'All right. I think I can guess. You're Sabine's sister, aren't you?'

I nodded agreement. Before I could say anything else, he went on: 'Ever since we met, I've had this feeling I knew you. She used to talk about you all the time, how pretty you were, how clever. She showed us photos of her family.' He pressed fingers against his forehead. 'You live in California, don't you? Your mother's French. Your father's a professor of something.'

'Did. Was. Was,' I said. 'A potted biography: my mother never got over losing Sabine and died a couple of years later. After that, my father gave up teaching and moved to Rome with me, where he took up antiquarian book-selling. I attended a small liberal arts college in California for my first degree and then went on to Edinburgh, just like my sister.'

'So why did you come for this weekend?'

'There were a number of reasons, most of them fairly vague, mostly to do with Sabine. Why did *you* come?'

He looked across the bustle of the crowded market square. 'Like you, I'm not entirely clear about my motivation. But I . . .' He stared down at the earthenware tiles beneath our feet. 'The thing is, I've been haunted for years by – by what happened. As you have too, I'm sure. It's not simply the blood and . . . the other things. I've just . . . ever since it happened, I've had this terrible feeling that I'm responsible for . . . well, for ruining someone's life.'

114

I could see his hands trembling on his knees, until he folded them together. 'Ruining *whose* life?'

He ignored my question. 'And what did I think I'd achieve by coming here? Did I think I could wipe the slate clean? God only knows.' He wiped his hand over his face. 'When I saw the advertisement in the in-flight magazine coming back from Singapore, it seemed like serendipity. You know, not only a relaxing way to recoup after eight years at the cutting edge of the financial markets, but also a possible means of coming to terms with it all.'

I smiled. 'My sentiments precisely.'

'I'd love to know what my therapist would say if she could see me here. Something like, "Smart move, Gavin. Face your demons. Way to go, boy!" That's the irritating way she talked. I'm sure I came across as a complete nutter, but really, I'm not.' With a sort of laugh, he added, 'But then I would say that, wouldn't I?'

'You seem perfectly sane to me.'

'It was my parents' idea that I should go to therapy. They thought it would make me feel more optimistic about life. In actual fact, the wretched woman never said anything even remotely positive in all the time I went to her.'

'Mine was the same. She had a way of shaking her head in a pitying manner which always made me feel I'd slipped up in some indefinable way.'

He laughed, his nice face relaxing for the first time since we'd met the day before. 'Mine used to say, "And how do you feel about that?" and hand me a box of tissues when I started blubbing

115

on her sofa. As if the answer wasn't always going to be, "Bloody terrible, since you ask, which is why I'm sitting here bawling my guts out and droning on about my worst nightmares, while you doodle on a pad of recycled paper and surreptitiously look at your watch."'

It was my turn to laugh. 'How long did you go to her?'

'Three years. And I didn't feel any better at the end of it. Didn't feel any worse, to be fair, but no better. I suppose I shouldn't blame her, really, with some thirty-something neurotic constantly banging on about his nightmares. She was probably dying to shout, "Get. Over. It!"'

'I'm sure she wasn't.'

'You're probably right, but that's what it felt like. I know she thought I should get out more. To tell you the truth, leaving Singapore and coming back to England made me feel better almost immediately. And that was only a couple of days ago.'

'I must say I nearly backed out at the last minute from this weekend,' I said.

'Oh God. Me too. It suddenly seemed absolutely insane to choose to return to the very place which was turning me into a nut case.'

'I was more or less the same. Actually, if I hadn't put down my deposit . . .'

'I thought I could always drive back to London if it turned out that I couldn't handle it.'

'Exactly!' We grinned at each other. A moment shared.

And something unexpected happened. For the first time since my sister's death, I felt the ropes which had tethered me for so long at last begin to loosen. I was no longer alone. Someone else's ghosts flanked my own ghost. Someone else was beside me, experiencing some of the same nightmares. After so many years, it was an extraordinary feeling. I set my cup back on its saucer, feeling stronger than I had for years. 'Come on,' I said. 'We have to talk about it.'

'I know.' He looked at me sombrely. 'And before you ask, coming back to Weston Lodge after all this time has already cleared some cobwebs from my head. What happened, happened, nothing can change that. Perhaps it's the same for you.'

I considered my reply. Eventually, I said, 'To a certain extent, yes.'

He leaned back and stuck his hands into his trouser pockets. 'I feel as if I've been carrying poor Edward Palliser round with me for most of my life. He was my best friend, and we used to spend hours planning our lives once we'd left school. Sheep-farming in Australia, panning for gold or herding cattle in the Wild West, diamond-mining in South Africa or exploring the Amazon . . . You name it, we were going to do it. Living gloriously, free spirits roaming the globe! And when I left university, I felt I owed it to him to do some of that. I even tried some of it, but it wasn't the same without him and eventually I gave up. Which of course made me feel I'd let him down even more than I already had.'

I was about to ask what he meant but he carried straight on. 'Silly of me, really. Life's paths always prove so different from how we think they'll be.'

'Gavin . . .'

'What?'

I hesitated. Was it fair of me to be posing such a question in the first place, and what might his reaction be? 'I . . . I hate to ask you, Gavin, and please *please* feel free to refuse, but . . . could you bear to go through that whole . . . well, tell me precisely what happened that evening? My family, we felt so helpless, living so far away, and though my father came over, we never really . . . we've always wanted to know about Sabine's last mo— How it all went down, and what you saw or heard.' I was getting fairly upset myself by now, and Gavin took my hand in his and squeezed it.

'It's all right,' he said. 'As a matter of fact, apart from the police at the time, you're the first person who's ever asked me that.'

'Not your parents?'

'Definitely not them. They were terrified that it would ruin my childhood if it was ever brought up, so it just lay inside me like a stone. If I ever mentioned it, my mother would say something really bland, like, "Oh, darling, you don't want to be talking about that, much better to forget it." So stupid. As if I could possibly forget it.'

'Have you even *wanted* to talk about it?'

'No. Not until now. But something's beginning to change . . . It's like an emotional tectonic shift.' He gave a wry smile.

I nodded. I knew exactly what he meant.

For a moment he pressed his lips against his

118

teeth. 'Yes, that evening . . . I'd been out to supper with one of the neighbouring families who knew my parents from when they were all young, and they dropped me back about half past seven. I could see Clio through the windows, working at her desk in her study, and I knew all the staff had gone off for a couple of days, and Mr Redmayne wasn't going to be back from London until later so I sat down at the piano and played for a while—'

'Was it you playing the organ in the chapel this morning?'

'Yes, did you hear me?'

'I listened for a bit but didn't want to disturb you.'

'Anyway, the boys came down and we sang a few carols and then Sabine appeared to get Georgie, and I played some dance tunes and they all pranced about and then we went upstairs.'

'And Mrs Palliser didn't join you?'

'I don't suppose she even knew we were there. Her study was soundproofed, you see, so she wouldn't have heard a thing.'

'People keep telling me about the sound-proofing.' I smiled at him. 'I'm so glad to hear about you all dancing about in the hall . . . that Sabine had fun that evening.'

'So Georgie got into the bath, while Edward and I went to our bedroom – we always shared when I was staying with the Pallisers, because he and I were in the same form at school. Sabine – gorgeous Sabine whom Edward and I, our hormones boiling away, were madly in love with – went back to her room along the passage, saying

119

she was keeping an ear out and we'd better behave.'

'More or less as normal?'

'Absolutely. Up until then, everything was just as usual. Edward and I were working on our Lego model of a monorail transport system and hugging ourselves with the thought that we might get a kit to make a castle or a pirate ship for Christmas. Even aged thirteen or so, we still loved those sets – we were much more naive than today's kids. And then, just a few minutes later—' He stopped abruptly.

'Then?'

'Suddenly, Georgie started screaming.' Gavin held his hands to his face. 'It was the most ghastly horrible sound I'd ever heard, before or since. He was yelling at his mother, begging her to stop . . . Edward and I stared at each other – and then we heard Sabine come out of her room again and demand to know what was going on, and then she started screaming too, you c-could t-tell she was in t-terrible terrible pain.' He dropped his hands and stared at me, his eyes wet. 'Oh, *God.*'

I put a hand on his arm. 'Look, if you don't want to, you don't have to tell me.'

'It's all right.' He swallowed. Tried unconvincingly to laugh. 'Better out than in, as they say. So Edward and I looked at each other and ran to the door of our room—' He broke off. 'I don't know if you've been in that part of the house, but there was our room, then Georgie's room, then the passage turns at a right angle where the bathroom and Sabine's room were. And we looked towards the bathroom, where Georgie had stopped shrieking his head off, and was moaning, and we could see one of Sabine's feet sticking out, hear her kind of gasping . . .' He looked at me nervously. 'You did ask . . .'

I nodded. 'Yes.'

'We didn't have a clue what was going on, but we could tell it was pretty nasty, so we turned and ran towards the back stairs. And at the bottom, E-Edward fell over and in-instead of stopping to help him, I ran even faster. I could hear him scrambling into the little broom cupboard under the stairs and then . . . and then . . .' He swallowed once, then again. 'Then I heard Edward screaming, shrieking, begging his mother not to hurt him, please not to hurt him, "*Stop! Mummy, please stop!*", he didn't mean to be naughty, he was sorry, sorry, until his voice died away and I should have turned round and tried to help him, but I didn't, I raced into the cold pantry and squeezed through the air vent at the back and out into the snow.' He looked at me with tear-filled eyes. 'I've blamed myself ever since.'

'What on earth for?'

'Maybe if I'd stopped and helped Edward, we could both have escaped. But I was too much of a coward. I wanted to save my own skin and the hell with anyone else's.'

'Come on, Gavin. What were you, twelve years old?'

'Thirteen. Easily old enough to . . . to behave more . . . *honourably*. It was that voice she put on. That's what really spooked me. A sort of nightmarish whisper.' He shuddered.

121

'What was she saying?'

He put on a voice like something out of a horror movie, which sent shivers crawling over my body. 'I remember it so clearly: *"All the doors are locked, boy. You can't get away, you can't get away, you can run but you can't hide . . ."*'

'But you could hide. You *did*.'

'True.' Gavin grimaced. 'But all these years later, she still comes after me. Over oceans, across continents, through space and time. My God, it was so *terrifying*. And then I was outside, no shoes, snow beginning to pile up. And I had to duck under the yew tree at the end of the lawn and all I could think of was that moron, Charlie Leeming, telling us in the dorm that yew was poisonous, one touch and you'd shrivel up, turn blue and die.'

I laughed.

So did Gavin. 'Of course I didn't believe it, not one hundred per cent, anyway, but I always gave yew trees a wide berth. Still do.'

'So then what?'

'I could see lights in Farmer Barnard's place, half a mile away, but I didn't dare go there, in case she followed me, pushed into their house after me, killed us all. And then I remembered a kind of little stone shed place in the woods, buried in undergrowth, covered in elder trees and brambles – we sometimes played there – and I made for it, pushed myself into the big catcher of the farmer's ride-on mower, pulled some horrible bits of sacking over myself. I can still remember the scratch of that filthy straw against my legs and a ghastly stink of old droppings and pee. And

122

rats, the brush of rat-fur on my skin. Ugh, horrible. I couldn't help hearing Leeming's voice again, saying that if a rat bites you, you go into convulsions and grow grey fur all over you. I wanted to be sick. I'd seen blood on the carpet of the passage. And . . .' He paused and stared at me.

'And what?'

'I shouldn't say. Not considering your poor sister.'

'I need to know as much as you need to tell.' I could feel my stomach begin to curdle in antici-pation of what he might say.

'Maybe it was Edward's . . . It was . . .' His voice seized up. He coughed and started again, avoiding my gaze. 'I saw a . . . a finger. And . . . and bits of flesh. Clio must have been completely insane by then. She'd thrown them down the passage, which is why I saw them . . .' He pressed his hands together. 'Oh *God* . . .'

I felt nauseous. Tried to remove the images from my brain before they could settle there. Gritted my teeth and pressed on. 'What was she like?'

'I always felt a bit sorry for Edward and Georgie. I couldn't say she was warm. Or maternal. Nothing like my own mother, always giving me a hug and saying she loved me.' He thought back. 'But I was – am – an only child, and my mother was just a homemaker, not a high-powered academic writer like Clio.'

'I don't see that being clever stops you from being a loving mum,' I said.

'Maybe she'd never learned to be loving. You

123

wouldn't believe some of the things I've heard about her family . . .'

Sabine's letters had mentioned murder and madness, sudden disappearances: the stuff of gothic novels writ large. 'Looking back afterwards, even allowing for her lack of motherly warmth, were you surprised that she could do such a thing?' Why was I so insistently asking these questions, as though I were a reporter, or a detective investigating a crime?

'Of course I was. I'd known her all my school life. Prep and public. I'd seen her fly into the most ghastly rages over the most trivial things. And get over them fairly quickly. Given that she never wanted children in the first place – or so my mother told me – she didn't do a bad job, considering. I mean, the boys *were* a bit mischievous sometimes, but that's partly because they were neglected, in my opinion. A sort of negative attention-seeking.'

There was a long silence, both of us digesting what he'd just told me. Eventually, I said, 'Thank you for telling me all that.'

'Will you pass it on to your father?'

'I very much doubt it. He wouldn't want to know about Sabine in such . . . such detail.'

He put a big hand over mine. 'You may not believe this, but I've never talked so much about that dreadful evening. Not even to my therapist. And at the trial, I was too traumatized to help much, and nobody wanted to press me too hard. Even Clio's defence lawyers. Besides, it seemed pretty much open-and-shut.'

Across the square a man came out of the

124

ironmongers and stood looking about him. Checked shirt, weather-beaten face, corduroys, sturdy shoes: unmistakably a man who lived and worked in the country, rather than the town.

'Isn't that one of the people who were there last night?' I said. 'Terence Barnard?'

'Trevor,' said Gavin. 'Farmer Barnard.'

Barnard looked in our direction, and I beckoned him over. For a moment he hesitated, then came slowly across the cobbles to our bench. 'I met you at Weston last night, didn't I?' he said to me, looking from one to another of us. 'You too . . .' he added, to Gavin.

'That's right,' said Gavin.

'Why don't you join us?' I said.

He checked his watch, pulled out a chair, sat down. When he was settled, I said, 'We were intrigued by David's potted history of the Lodge last night. He's certainly turned the place into a charming hotel.'

'I hope it'll succeed,' Gavin said.

'So do the locals,' said Barnard. 'It would certainly bring the village back to life. Make it more like the old days, when the house was full all the time. Comings and goings, visitors down from London, big orders placed with the butcher, the baker, the candlestick maker. Good for all of us, really. It was a bad day for this place when . . .' He paused. 'Well, when the household broke up.'

'What happened to the original heirs?' I asked innocently, though I already knew the answers.

'People died, mainly. So the house came down to the daughter, rather than the sons.'

Gavin picked up. 'They must have been young, to die.'

'One of them was killed in a skiing accident. The other was murdered during a burglary.'

'Goodness,' I said. 'Did he have a lot to steal?'

'He was something of a collector,' said Barnard. 'He wasn't a very pleasant character. But none of the males in the family were.' He lifted his teacup, and a signet ring flashed on his fourth finger.

'What did he collect?' Gavin asked.

'Paintings, mainly. And modern silver.'

'Did they ever find the burglar? Or murderer, I suppose he'd be.'

'Not as far as I know.'

'It would be interesting to know where those paintings are now,' I said.

Barnard frowned. 'Why are you asking all these questions?'

'I'm in the art trade myself,' I said. 'I was just wondering whether they'd ever been offered for sale. That way the police might have been able to find out who killed this guy.' Again I looked innocent. 'I don't suppose you remember the names of any of the stolen stuff, do you? If you did, I could go through back catalogues, see what's come up over the years.'

'At the moment I haven't a clue. Something might occur to me if I think about it hard enough.' He stood up. 'Someone called Lucian Freud, does that sound right?'

I nodded.

'And I do remember Cl—the victim's sister saying that he'd taken some stuff of hers, Swedish painters, or Danish, I can't remember. I have a feeling those were stolen from the brother's flat too. Anyway, I'm sure the police looked into it at the time – it was years ago now.'

He raised a hand and turned to go. 'Enjoy the rest of your time here.' He pushed aside a couple of chairs in order to get out, then came back. 'She didn't do it,' he said. 'I know she didn't do it.'

Gavin and I stared at each other after he'd gone. 'Do we know what he means?' I said.

'I think we can guess.'

Later I returned to my room to change for dinner. I ran my fingers through my cropped hair, watching the cows move slowly from one side of the field to another and thinking what completely boring lives they must lead.

Downstairs, in the bar, I stood with a glass of red wine in my hand and examined a small Dutch landscape of leafless willows along the banks of a frozen river, which hung near the door.

'It's beautiful, isn't it?' I turned to find Malcolm Macdonald at my shoulder.

'Exquisite.'

'Don't forget that I'm to show you the armillary spheres, will you?'

'Tomorrow morning after coffee.'

Later, after another excellent meal, coffee was served round the fire in the hall. Urged on by me, Gavin sat down at the grand piano and started to play, classical stuff at first, then songs from shows, and finally rock and roll numbers which had most people up on their feet. I tried very hard not to think of Sabine doing the same thing, in the same place, never knowing that she was no more than an hour away from death.

Someone replaced Gavin at the piano. Gavin came over to me and asked me to dance, and we stepped out on to the floor. I'm not a particularly good dancer, but in his arms, I felt relaxed and happy; I felt safe. He towered over me, but when I put back my head, he was looking down at me, a smile on his mouth. It was a small smile but it said a lot. I'd known that some day I'd meet another man I could love as I had loved Hamilton; I began to wonder if, by some extraordinary happenstance, Gavin was the one. As he twirled me around, placed his hand on my waist, drew me against his chest, I thought, *Dad, for once you're wrong*.

It was a good decision to come here. Maybe one of the best I ever made.

Eight

I said at the beginning that it was difficult to know where to start with a story such as this. It's even harder to continue. The characters have been laid out like chessmen, the settings are in place.

But what about the plot? In this case, the significant events unfolded nearly a quarter of a century earlier: surely there could be no further development. Yet the past has a way of redefining itself as it becomes further separated from the present. Matters which seemed transparent at the time are revealed in murkier colours, and conclusions once unhesitatingly come to can now seem flawed, even irresponsible.

I was fully aware that nothing would bring back my sister, nor restore to me the carefree childhood I had lost; I knew my enquiries were pointless. Yet at the same time, the reactions to them seemed to lead me further and further into a situation far removed from the one I had anticipated. What did I hope to achieve by asking questions to which I already knew the answers?

Nonetheless, the restless human spirit constantly seeks revelation. Not just answers, but answers which satisfy. And I could not rid my mind of Trevor Barnard's earnest expression, the hostility in his blue eyes as he told us *she didn't do it.*

'She' being – obviously – Clio Palliser. I should have gone after him, asked how he could be so sure.

His remark was the first slice of doubt slashed into the hard ball of my hatred.

My father rang me from Italy almost as soon as I had closed the door behind me on my return from Weston Lodge.

'How'd it go, hon?' he asked, his casual tone making perfectly clear his worry that I might have suffered some further trauma.

'It was good, Dad. Really good.'

'You sound . . . lighter, somehow.'

'I am. I met some interesting people, too.' I gave him a brief rundown of the weekend. For some reason, I left out Malcolm Macdonald. I'm not sure I was ready to face the fact that I was unaccountably drawn to the man who had once been my sister's lover.

But then I was equally drawn to big Gavin Vaughn, though in an entirely different, much more visceral way.

'So you're glad you went?'

'Very. No regrets at all.'

'And . . . and your sister? Any – uh – further-ance there?'

'Dad, I've barely drawn breath since I got back. I need to get my head round it all before I can answer the question I think you're asking.'

'Fair enough.'

'How's the *contessa*?' I asked, and we drifted off into a conversation about the villa on the coast south of Rome and a couple of prestigious antiquarian book sales the two of them had been involved in.

'Lovely weather down here,' he ended up. 'Come down and see us.'

'I'm planning to.'

I couldn't sleep. Night after night I found myself back in the hall at Weston Lodge, decorated as both Sabine and Stonor had described it, logs burning in the hearth, snow falling outside, the smell of mulled wine and mince pies in the air. The children upstairs, the murderess still in her soundproofed study, my sister writing her last letter home. The night before Christmas Eve, the excitement, the anticipation, the shimmer and twinkle of the big tree, the sparkle of the foil-wrapped presents underneath. And, everywhere, the blood.

It had never before occurred to me to wonder what the Honourable Clio had planned to give Sabine for Christmas. Nor what happened to all those gifts in the aftermath of the tragedy. Were they still mouldering in some forgotten police storage facility, along with the bloodied knife Clio had used, the bloodstained dress she'd been wearing? Brian Stonor would probably know.

Four days after I got back from the weekend, I rang him. 'You told me to telephone you at any time,' I said.

'And I meant it.'

'Could I buy you a drink some time over the weekend? Or lunch?'

'A drink will be fine. Name the day and the place, and I'll be there.'

131

'How about next Sunday?'

'That's good for me,' said Stonor.

So we arranged to meet on the terrace of the Festival Hall at one o'clock. Inside if the weather was lousy, outside if it was fine.

So now I leant on the balustrade, looking over the Thames, the Eye to my left (thinking, I'd never been on the Eye and likely never would, since I have no head for heights) and Scotland Yard across the river.

Stonor joined me, carrying two glasses by their stems, along with a bottle of wine, and we seated ourselves on a bench. 'So what's on your mind?' he asked, pouring for us both.

'Give you one guess,' I said.

'How can I help?'

I stared at a passing passenger launch, the amplified voice of a guide resonating across the water, the words blown away from us by the breeze. Eventually, I said, 'For the past quarter of a century, I've carried this . . . this ugly weight of loss and hatred with me. The loss of my sister, hatred for the woman who murdered her. But now I'm beginning to think there's more to it. Things I heard while we were at Weston Lodge, things you hinted at . . . I've thought about it a lot, and I'd guess you suspect that what happened was not as straightforward as was made out at the time.'

'Suspicions are all I have,' said Stonor.

'Like what?'

'I felt that my superiors at the time didn't dig deep enough into the events surrounding the case. As far as they were concerned, it was all cut and dried: they had their victims, their perpetrator, their motive . . . Why start casting about for anything more when it was all too clear what had happened? And the suspect herself wasn't talking.'

'So what are you saying?'

'I'm not saying anything.' He swallowed an over-large mouthful of his wine. 'Haven't, for all this time.'

'But something about it bothers you.'

A slight pause before Stonor nodded. 'I think that's a fair assessment.' Everything he said seemed to pass through a kind of central processing unit before he actually gave voice to it.

'What is it you're uncertain about?'

There was a longer silence, until I said slowly, 'You're not implying that maybe the Honourable Clio wasn't guilty after all, are you?'

His voice was policeman-cautious. 'I'm implying nothing.'

I ignored that. 'But if *she* didn't do it, who else could possibly have done?'

He shrugged without speaking.

'But you nonetheless believe there was something odd about the case. Something not quite right.'

After another long silence, he said, 'Yes, I believe that. But I don't know – I've never worked out exactly what it was.'

'Tell me about it.'

He looked at his watch. 'How long have you got?'

'As long as it takes.'

'All right, then.'

This is the story he told me:

He'd seen the ad for the bank holiday weekend at Weston Lodge while idly leafing through the Travel section of the Sunday newspaper, his attention immediately caught by the name of the hotel. *Weston Lodge, set in the Cotswolds*. He read it again. It just had to be the same place, and there was no way he wanted to miss the opportunity of checking it out, though he wasn't clear quite why. He had no intention of attempting to do a Sherlock Holmes on it; too much time had gone by for there to be any possibility of anything new turning up. On the other hand, perhaps things which had seemed obscure then might look a lot clearer now.

In addition, after too many years of ready-meals and convenience foods, he liked the sound of the gourmet dinners. And the on-site gym might encourage him to start exercising again, get back into shape. So why not? he'd asked himself. The last few years had been tough, what with Rachel's slow dying, and Hamish suddenly upping sticks and moving to Australia to start a new life.

Stonor had no faith in such concepts. In his experience, the new life usually turned out to be nothing more than an echo, or even a straight copy, of the old one. But the worst thing about his own life, old *or* new, was the sense which sometimes caught him of being utterly alone. With Hamish gone, if he were to fall down the stairs of the tall narrow house he and Rachel had shared for so long, who would know? If he were to have a sudden heart-attack or a stroke, who would alert the emergency services? Nobody would know until the smell of his decomposing body alerted the neighbours – like Clio Palliser's elder brother in his exclusive Hampstead apartment. (Never got anyone for that, incidentally.)

So why *not* give in to temptation, spoil himself? Change the dull routine of his days, get out of his rut. He might even meet someone there, someone new, someone to start again with. Part of him felt guilty at the mere thought of another woman, let alone a woman who might one day take Rachel's place. Another, perhaps saner, part felt that there had to be an end to mourning, that he needed to move on. Increasingly, his life seemed to be stuck down a dead end. Or was he, he asked himself in his more optimistic moments, perhaps simply dithering at a crossroads?

The idea of a weekend at the Weston Lodge Hotel triggered something he had not felt for so long that he barely recognized it: a flicker of excitement, an awareness of possibilities. He'd been there before, of course, but then only as an outsider looking in. Now, as a resident, albeit only a temporary one, he'd be able to poke around a bit more, maybe even ask questions he couldn't ask last time he was there. He had been in his early twenties then, and his memories of the place were edged with blood. While he couldn't pretend that he had been haunted by that gore-spattered bathroom, the body in the bathtub, the desperate little corpse tucked under the stairs, the case had always intrigued him, and in fact intrigued him still.

He went over to the neat-as-a-pin roll-top desk in the corner of his living room. It had belonged to Rachel's father and was a big old-fashioned

135

thing, full of little drawers and pigeonholes, with a nice leather top, though the gold tooling had long ago lost its gilt and the wood was stained here and there with spilt ink. He took out his address book, turned to the page for R and found the number for his old guv'nor, Roy Richards. Hadn't spoken to him for years, he might even be dead – though he'd probably have heard about it in that case. Either way, it was certainly worth a try.

Lilian Richards answered, sounding depressingly old and shaky. 'What do you want?'

'Lil!' he said, pitching his voice too loud, too heartily. 'It's Brian Stonor here. Long time no hear, eh?'

'Brian? Do I know a Brian?'

'You remember . . . I used to work with Roy, years ago.' Now was the point at which she would tell him if Roy was still around or had departed for the great cop-shop in the sky.

'Roy? Who's Roy?'

Brian's heart sank. The poor woman was obviously suffering from some form of dementia. He heard a voice in the background, some kind of struggle for the receiver, then someone else spoke. 'Roy Richards here.' The voice was exactly the same as it had always been: firm, brisk, capable.

'It's Brian Stonor.'

They spent a few minutes briefly catching up, before Richards said, 'So what's on your mind, Brian?'

'Remember that case years ago, out at Weston Lodge?'

'Remind me.'

'Christmas Eve. Kids. Snow.'

'Oh, yes. Your first homicide, wasn't it? What's your interest, after all this time?'

Brian explained that he'd be visiting the place and why, but before he'd finished, Roy interrupted. 'You're not seriously expecting to find out anything new, are you? It was an open-and-shut case. She didn't confess, but she did everything but. 'Sides, look at the evidence, who else could possibly have done the dirty deed?'

'I don't know. Somehow I've always wondered if justice was really done.'

'If she wasn't guilty as charged, why didn't she speak up?'

'She couldn't, Roy. According to the psychiatrists who examined her, the killings caused a psychological trauma. It's called elective mutism or something similar. She'd had episodes before.'

'Come on, Brian. She could have put pen to paper. Most people would, faced with the prospect of a lifetime in Broadmoor.'

'Suppose she didn't do it? That's all I'm saying.'

Roy heaved an exasperated breath. 'You're not going to bring in the passing tramp or the mysterious twin, are you?'

'Come on, sir. You know me better than that.'

'Of course I do. Which is why I'm going to wish you a very good weekend at the place and say goodbye. And if you're ever down this way, etcetera etcetera.'

'I'm sorry it's been so long.'

'So am I, Brian. So am I.' Roy put down the

phone, but not before Brian heard Lil's quavering voice wanting to know who Roy was, and what he was doing in her sitting room.

What must it be like to live with a dementia sufferer? Twenty-four hours a day watchfulness, constant vigilance, relentless anxiety, never knowing what lay ahead. And there he'd been thinking that losing Rachel had been bad . . .

All in all, although he was generally a cautious man, since there was nobody else to think about, he had a good pension, and the mortgage was long since paid off, he felt that for once there was no reason not to indulge himself.

Seeing the first signpost to Weston, his hands tightened on the steering wheel. Twenty-three years on, his wheels were somewhat smarter than the car he'd owned back then. A bit Inspector Morse, truth be told, though he himself went in for racing green rather than Morse's maroon. A vintage Jaguar Mk II, leather upholstery, polished walnut fascia. It was about the only similarity between him and Morse, more's the pity: he didn't really listen to classical music, and he couldn't abide the taste of beer. Nor were women constantly giving him the eye.

Now it was springtime, and on either side of the road, hedgerows were bursting into green, lambs were springing, catkins quivered from trees all along the line of the river. Very nice. Not a bit like the first time he'd been to Weston Lodge . . . He relaxed his grip and let the memories of twenty-three years ago flow into his mind.

The day before Christmas Eve, it was. Newly

promoted to DC, he'd been called away from the bosom of the family, as his dad liked to put it, though by then the bosom was only him and Dad. Their first Christmas without Mum. Truth to tell, he'd been relieved to leave the house, so that he didn't have to go on seeing poor old Dad doing his best to act as though he were managing perfectly well on his own, putting on a show for Brian which convinced neither of them.

It was snowing when he set off in his third-hand Cortina – took him a year to save up for it – to drive to Weston Lodge, three miles away. 'Make it quick, lad . . . I mean sir,' the duty sergeant had said. 'There's kids involved.'

'Kids?'

'Someone's been murdered, three people, not clear who, but it seems a bit of a nasty business, 'specially so close to Christmas.'

Quick wasn't an option. By the time he'd negotiated the first couple of miles of narrow lanes that was the quickest way to the Lodge, black ice was making driving conditions extremely hazardous, and it was just over an hour before he slithered into the drive and parked as close to the house as he could. Emergency vehicles were already standing around, and even as he mounted the stone stairs, a pair of ambulance men came through the open front door carrying a stretcher and began sidestepping down the icy steps. A nasty wind had lifted a corner of the covering, and he glimpsed the bloodied body of a young kid. Boy or girl? He couldn't tell which. He felt sick. Kids dead . . . He hoped he would be able to act professionally.

At the top of the steps, he'd halted briefly to stare through the wide open double doors at the festive scene within. A vast hall, a big tree sparkling with Christmas lights, presents wrapped in shiny striped paper and coloured ribbons, enormous logs burning in the grate. It was his first murder scene, and he'd paused longer than he should have done, reluctant to go in, so that Inspector Richards had impatiently motioned him forwards into the house, wanting to know what had kept him.

A man in a pinstripe suit was standing in front of the fire, his bloodied hands shuddering every now and then against the seam of his trousers, while a woman in a reddish dress sat slumped in a high-backed tapestry sort of chair beside him. Took Brian a moment or two to realize that the dress was actually greeny-blue. Bloodied woman, nervous man, glittering tree: the image had stayed with him for years. He'd been prepared to face the fact of death, but at that stage, the only death he knew anything about was his mother's, and that had been in hospital, clean and clinical, any pain obliterated by drugs. The cold reality of murder, of living sentient beings reduced to bleeding flesh, hunks of meat, like the slaughterhouse where he briefly worked one summer when he was fifteen, struck him with the chill of a knifing wind. Even now, he felt ill, thinking about what he had seen when Richards sent him upstairs: slashed limbs, ripped hands, a gaping throat almost severed from the head, the unbelievable redness of recent blood.

If the truth be told, he had needed little

persuasion to come on this Gala House Party Weekend or whatever it was called. Not just because of needing a break, but for professional reasons. OK, so the case had been wrapped up within five minutes of the police arriving, the trial had been open-and-shut, the murderer had been sent to Broadmoor indefinitely. But he'd always thought that there'd been something a little off about it. He'd never been able to pinpoint it – no sudden flashes of intuition for Brian Stonor, just dogged police work. But there'd been the prickle at the top of his spine every time he mentally reviewed the case: glittering tree, silent wife, uneasy husband. Over the years, he'd learned to trust that occasional prickle, had stood by it, when it made him dig a bit deeper, look a bit harder. It had lifted him up through the ranks, helped him do time with the Met, attain his Chief Superintendency, and then retire back to his roots. With . . . what was it? Maybe ninety-one per cent of his major cases solved. A pretty good record. But of the other nine per cent, perhaps half still niggled at him, including the Weston Lodge case.

Stepping in through the wide doors this time round, he had stopped. The spacious hall looked very different from the last time he had seen it. Instead of roaring fires and Christmas trees, there were containers full of daffodils and narcissi, huge vases of apple-blossom and lilac, bowls of grape hyacinths. Instead of the curtains of shabby red brocade which had previously hung from floor to ceiling, swags of fresh blue and white linen were arranged around the window embrasures in elaborate contemporary treatments, and on the floor lay a big Chinese carpet of blues and creams instead of that blood-soaked rug with the footprints of a man's shoes embedded in the stiffening pile. The air smelled of lavender and wood-fires. The seating was covered to match the drapes. A round rosewood table in the middle of the hall held tea things and a bowl of wrapped boiled sweets, as well as the receptionist and her paraphernalia.

The bedroom allotted to him was impressively large, with plenty of room for a big double bed, a sofa and two armchairs in front of the long window opening on to a balcony, a desk with a straight chair pulled up to it, built-in wardrobes, a television set and a chest-of-drawers. He checked out the en-suite bathroom: high-pressure shower as well as tub, luxury toiletries in a cotton-lined willow basket, thick blue towels. All very nice.

A folder lay on the desk and he opened it, absorbing the information it offered – time of meals, telephone numbers for the various facilities, a guest list. None of them were in any way familiar – until one name, which lunged out at him . . .

What the hell could have brought Gavin Metcalfe-Vaughn back to this house? How could he even bear to step foot over the threshold? Stonor had reached into the top of his suitcase and brought out the thick file on the Weston Lodge case that he'd brought with him, God knew why. He was well aware that, as a boy, Gavin had regularly spent his school holidays here, that Clio and Harry Redmayne were his legal

142

guardians since his father worked abroad, that Clio had been best friends with his mother, Paula, ever since the two women were children.

He knew, too, that in the aftermath of the tragedy, Gavin had been whisked overseas to live with his parents and that his architect father had resigned from his prestigious job in Nigeria and moved to Australia, taking a job at lower remuneration because it was less demanding in terms of constant relocations and absences from his family. Gavin had been in therapy for a while, in order to help him cope with the inevitable PTSD, but as far as Stonor could determine had otherwise led a normal boy's life until he went off to university, then on to work in the Asian money markets, before now returning to England and taking a flat somewhere in the Canary Wharf area.

So why would he come to Weston Lodge, where he was bound to be confronted with memories he must have much preferred to leave behind? Stonor poured himself a small whisky from the well-stocked fridge, brushed his hair and put on a tie, and determined that, one way or another, he would make it his business to find out.

Downstairs, at the ridiculously named Mingle, he had identified Metcalfe-Vaughn without difficulty. The boy had hardly changed in twenty-three years: same dark hair, wide eyes, slightly startled expression. Same gangly body and large hands. He was talking to a girl when Stonor arrived, a girl he instantly recognized. Until he caught himself short: that girl had died a long time ago.

The following day, buffed, honed, polished,

fifty lengths of the hotel swimming pool achieved, massaged muscles as relaxed as glycerine, Stonor made his way back up to his room feeling as though he had shed ten years. Half an hour until lunch, a walk round the estate, maybe a quick poke about, see what was what, maybe talk to the kitchen staff, see if anyone had been here twenty-three years ago, or knew someone who had.

He opened the door of his room, took in the made bed, the replenished toiletries, the fire newly laid in the grate, window slightly open to let in the soft breeze. This was the life, he thought. Delightful, absolutely delightful. Worth every penny. He glanced at his watch, wondering whether to snatch a half-hour nap after the morning's labours – after all, he wasn't a spring chicken any more (if he ever had been) – or to go downstairs to the bar and see if he could find a congenial companion or two to enjoy a pre-prandial drink with. He was about to opt for the latter when he took note of his folder lying on the writing desk beneath the window, neatly aligned with the blotter which lay in the middle of the polished surface.

Buff-coloured, scruffy, with some kind of frayed white octagonal label outlined in blue. The edges of the flap had felted, the back fold was torn. Despite knowing the contents by heart, he approached it with the caution he might have shown towards a man-eating spider which had just dropped from the ceiling. Inside were cuttings from newspapers, the one on top being a 'think' piece about the Honourable Clio, the violent murderess who'd been put away for life. *A Family Steeped in Blood and Death*, the American journalist had called the Pallisers, writing:

> *. . . her family and ancestors, the early suicide of her mother, the murder of one brother and the skiing fatality of the other witnessed by her at the tender age of seventeen, the hunting accident which killed her father, must have caused her trauma enough. Add to that the way the women in her family had been used for generations merely to produce an heir before being forced to watch the ruthless philandering of their husbands and the gradual squandering of their own money at the card-table, on horses or other women: were these some of the factors which led inevitably to that bloody evening just before Christmas?*
>
> *There is the added mystery concerning Clio's first husband, who disappeared after the birth of his younger son, George, and has never been seen since. Given the number of deaths within the Palliser family, it is tempting to wonder whether he lies undiscovered among the peaceful fields and fruiting orchards of the lush countryside surrounding Weston Lodge. But that is mere conjecture, and there has never been any real suggestions of foul play. Perhaps as a young man wishing to make his way as a creative artist, he found the demands of a family*

145

and a centuries-old mansion in constant
need of repair to be too much and decided
to leave.

Instead of going downstairs, Stonor had fetched himself a beer from the mini-fridge and focused on the question of why he had kept this file of cuttings for so long, why he had never whole-heartedly accepted the verdict brought against Clio Palliser. He didn't know, though every now and then – he told me as we watched the river heave and churn in the wake of the constant movement of the shipping going by – an idea buzzed briefly in his mind like a lethargic wasp and then was gone. Not even an idea, more of a faint connection which he couldn't quite grasp. The dinner gong had left him still puzzling over it.

Over the years, Stonor had used his seniority to keep tabs on the Honourable Clio, and had thus been aware of the report received by the Home Secretary, the subsequent acceptance of the Resident Medical Officer's opinion that there was no longer any danger to the public, the recommendation of her release on a conditional discharge. He had even stood among the people outside the gates as they opened to let out those who'd served their time.

Eventually, a woman had emerged between the big wooden doors. He could only presume it was her although there was not the slightest resem-blance to the Clio Palliser whose palely elegant face and slim figure had once featured in news-papers and magazines around the world. All he could see now was a bloated, hollow-eyed, unrecognizable woman who was met by a car and driven away.

'And since then,' Stonor said to me now, 'I've found neither hide nor hair of her, despite searching everywhere I can think of, using all kinds of access to Scotland Yard's files and so on. It's as if the world had opened and swallowed her up.'

'She's probably changed her name,' I said. 'Gone to live in quiet obscurity.'

'Possibly. At one point, I actually thought about hiring a private detective to look for her, until I started wondering what the point would be. Even if I discovered her whereabouts, I'd be no further forward. And the niggle would still be there.'

'What's your own view on where she might have gone?'

'I wondered if she might have gone back to Redmayne, but it's pretty unlikely,' Stonor said. 'After what happened, I wouldn't have thought so, would you? Besides, back then, the word on the street was that he was a bit of a womanizer. Leopards and spots department: he's not likely to have changed much, ergo he's not going to go for a fat old ex-con murderess, when he could still pull nubile young flesh.'

'Even if she's his wife?'

'*Was*. He divorced her as soon as sentence was passed.'

'And then what?'

Stonor shrugged. 'No idea. Like the first husband, he disappeared. Not literally, of course. But from the day sentence was passed, he took

147

off, and so far, I've not been able to trace him, either.'

I frowned. 'Do you think *he* could have done it?'

'Believe me, from what I've heard about him, he would certainly have been capable of it. By all reports, both he and his wife were given to explosions of rage. And the boys weren't his, they were hers, so if it was him, he might not have had the same qualms about killing them.'

'What on earth could trigger that kind of murderous fury?'

Again Stonor shrugged. 'If you're that way inclined, could be anything that set you off.'

'Did the police actually look at him for it?'

'Of course they did. At first he seemed a more likely candidate than she did. After all, they'd scrawled or scratched an obscenity on one of his paintings. If you're a collector or dealer, I can imagine you would be incandescent with rage if you encountered that kind of vandalism. I don't know anything about art restoration, but I imagine the canvas would never be the same, and its value considerably reduced. But whether that would lead you, however fanatical you were about art, to murder your stepsons in cold blood is a bit of a moot point.'

'And in any case, he had an alibi?'

'Try as we might, we couldn't see how he could have driven to Weston Lodge, done the deed and driven away, then reappeared, all innocence, at the station as usual. Besides, the station master thought he recognized him, arriving on his usual train.'

'Only thought?'

'Two of the platform lamps had been vandalized for months: the lighting was very dim. Also, it was snowing, and freezing fog was swirling round.'

'And where was his car? He's coming home for the Christmas holiday: he'd need his car, wouldn't he?'

'It was in the station car-park, as usual.'

'How do you know?'

For a moment Stonor looked disconcerted. 'Because that's what he told us.'

'Just a minute here.' I held up my hand. 'The guy didn't come home with murder on his mind, I imagine. He wouldn't have been expecting the damage to the picture. So if it *was* him, he would have been on the train as normal.'

'That's the conclusion we came to ourselves. And believe me, we went into it very thoroughly. And later, I checked it all out on my own. The only theory I came up with was the possibility that he came home earlier than expected, saw the damage the boys had done, did the deed, then went to the station before his own and got on the next train when it arrived, getting off at his usual station as per normal. But in that case, how did he get there? And wasn't he taking a huge risk of being seen the first time?'

'Anyone else who could have been responsible for the killings? The locals, for instance?'

'All investigated, all with unbreakable alibis.'

'Who were they?'

'The farmer, Trevor Barnard. Lord Forshawe and his wife, in the nearest house. She'd been out walking the dogs that evening; he'd been staring into the bottom of a whisky bottle, it being Christmas and all. He told us he didn't often get to fill a glass, so when she went out, as she did every night so the dogs could do their business, he always snuck a nip or two out of his private bottle.'

'Poor chap. I got the impression she very much wore the trousers.'

'As well as them, there were a couple of houses on the Forshawe estate. The police even interviewed my poor old dad, as a local. Not as a suspect, of course, but to see if he could shed any further light on anything. Which he couldn't.'

'The domestic staff? There was a live-in housekeeper, wasn't there?'

'Jill Jones. She'd left that morning. We could trace her up to Manchester, to her sister's house, where she was spending Christmas. The domestic staff had gone home the night before and weren't expected back until the day after Boxing Day.'

'Is it feasible that one or other of them might have some deep-seated grudge against the family?'

'Not a big enough Christmas bonus, you mean?'

I laughed. 'You're hardly going to commit three murders just out of pique, are you?'

Stonor didn't laugh. 'Stranger things have happened. Anyway, naturally we interviewed them but, as I said, they were vouched for by numerous family members. We also talked extensively to the villagers, the people at the pub, the couple who'd rented one of the holiday cottages for a couple of weeks over Christmas and the New Year. Nothing.'

150

'So all in all,' I couldn't resist saying, 'the police did a pretty lousy job of finding out anything helpful.'

'They didn't need to do much, Chantal. To everyone, including me, it seemed obvious what had happened. And even when I started to wonder, I had absolutely no evidence to base my doubts on.'

I shook my head. For some reason, I was beginning to develop a grudging sympathy for Clio Palliser, whose life seemed to have been a sad and sorry one, especially given the hints that Lord Forshawe had let drop. Just suppose she was innocent of the crimes, just suppose she had spent more than twenty years mourning for her butchered sons – let alone my sister. And if she *was* innocent, did she know who had done it? Surely, it would have been simple enough for her to deny that she had anything whatsoever to do with the murders. Instead, she had withdrawn into self-imposed silence. Following my own train of thought, I said, 'If she felt she couldn't speak, wouldn't she at least have been able to write down her version of events?'

'Of course she could. But she didn't. She refused to cooperate or communicate with the medical authorities at Broadmoor. Refused to discuss the case in any way.'

'So what *did* she do while she was there?'

'She read a lot, that I do know.'

'What sort of books?'

'Just about everything, from thrillers to mathematical treatises to biography and history. Lots of academic stuff, things she was working on before the murders. She was very bright.'

'Wasn't that supposed to have been the trigger, the fact that the boys had burned – or tried to – her manuscript?'

'That's right.'

'But what about the third boy, the one who escaped, didn't he explain?'

'Gavin Vaughn, you mean. Explain what? He hadn't even been there during the early evening; he was having supper with some neighbours, friends of his parents – which we verified, of course – then they brought him back to the house when it was nearly bedtime.'

'Did she have any visitors while she was in Broadmoor? Her brothers and father were dead, her husband had run off, her sons were gone.'

'According to my source inside, she didn't have a single visit during her time there.'

'That's rather sad.'

'I think most people who might have gone to see her were repulsed by what she did.'

'*If* she did it.'

I astonished myself. Why had I said that? Or even thought it? All these years I had known how I felt about losing my sister, but now my certainties were being gradually eroded. Did I still believe Clio Palliser had murdered my sister? Yes, I did. But not quite as emphatically as before, though I had no theories to put in the place of the ones I'd always held on to. 'Farmer Barnard – Trevor – was quite definite about it when I saw him the second day we were there,' I added. 'He said categorically that she didn't do it.'

'That means nothing at all,' said Stonor. 'First of all, what did he know about it? Secondly, interviewing him I got a definite feeling that he was more than a little in love with her, had been ever since they were young. So he would say that, wouldn't he?'

I frowned. 'Ever since I've started thinking about this again, it does strike me as odd that she never denied that she did it.'

'My own personal theory? Whether she did it or not, she wasn't bothered. Partly because, by all accounts, she wasn't a particularly good mother. Not materially neglectful, but certainly a bit lacking in the warmth and love department. So my feeling is that she felt so guilty that she had no choice but to take her punishment like a man, so to speak.'

'That's a fairly bleak scenario.'

'I know. But it fits either way, don't you think?'

'You said earlier that you had a niggle about it. When you first saw them, you felt that something wasn't quite right.'

'And as I also said, I've never been able to put my finger on exactly what it was. If I could only . . .' He looked back into the past. 'He was standing in front of the fire. She was sitting in a chair. Both of them were covered in blood. Neither had much expression on their faces, though he did appear to be faintly upset.'

'That must have been slightly odd.'

'Yes. You'd have thought one or other of them, or both, would have been registering some emotion, wouldn't you?'

'Perhaps they'd done all that before you got

there. How long after she'd killed them did he come home?'

'About three hours, if I remember rightly.'

'And what do you think she was doing between the . . . the killings and the time he got back?'

'Who the hell knows.' He shook himself. 'Probably getting rid of the weapon, among other things. Because we never found it. And even if I were now to work it out, it's far too late for most of the players.'

'One question, Mr Stonor. Do you in your heart of hearts think she did it?'

There was a pause, long enough for Big Ben to strike four. Then he said, very slowly, 'I don't know.'

'Crunch question then: if not the Honourable Clio, then who?'

'Again, I don't know.'

Nine

That year, as spring gave way to summer, the weather deteriorated. Unseasonable rain lashed the country, rivers burst their banks, floods devastated areas from Scotland to Devon, people and animals drowned, cars and houses were washed away. London itself was dreary and miserable. In the small back garden behind my house, grey rain slanted down on to sodden earth, despairing plants lay collapsed on the beds, roses were weighed down by the sodden mass of their blooms. It was too wet for me to enjoy my usual weekend activities of strolling in the parks, or walking through the city. Instead, I made a point of visiting all the art exhibitions on show, catching up on missed films or eating out with friends.

I had evaluated the days I had spent at Weston Lodge nearly two months before and found that although my visit there had only partially achieved its intended purpose, at least the horror and rawness of Sabine's death, which in all these years had never left me, was now so muted that I knew I was finally putting it behind me. For good, I hoped.

A few weeks weeks later, while I was drinking a cup of coffee before heading for Chauncey's, my mobile bleeped.

Gavin Vaughn. 'Hope I'm not calling at an antisocial hour,' he said.

'Eight fifteen? I don't think so.'

'I've just got off a flight from Singapore. And all the way across all those mountains and oceans, all I could think of was calling you to see whether we can meet up.'

'I would think so.' I felt my heart lift.

'Tonight would be bad,' he said. 'I'd just fall asleep over the soup. But tomorrow?'

'You're on.'

We met the next day in front of the National Gallery. I'd spent the years since Ham's death taking responsibility for everything in my life, and I felt a huge relief as Gavin gave me a friendly hug. For this evening, at least, I would have to make no decisions.

He took my arm and folded it into his as he led me towards a small Greek restaurant tucked away behind the London Coliseum theatre. I remembered my certainty, the first time we met, that this was a man who would always have a spare can of gas in the boot of his car. Steady, reliable – but also full of enthusiasm and vitality. And very sexy.

'I wanted to get in touch much much earlier than this,' he said over a Greek salad and kebabs – I don't mind gastronomic clichés: at least they have the ring of *faux*-authenticity about them – 'but my firm sent me off to Valparaíso almost as soon as I got back from that weekend, and I've been on the run since then. But that didn't stop me thinking about you.'

I couldn't help smiling. 'Good,' I said.

'And before we go any further, shall we agree not to discuss . . .' He made a comic face,

widening his eyes and raising his eyebrows. '. . .
you-know-what?'

'Oh God, yes,' I said. 'Anyway, what else is
there to say about it?'

So we talked about everything under the sun,
as they say. He told me about his days in
Singapore, that clean, crime-free city; I told him
about Rome.

'Never been there,' he said. 'Maybe I should
go some time.'

'My father lives there,' I said. 'I'm sure he'd
love to see you.'

'Or *us*. I couldn't just show up on his doorstep.
Remember that guy who wrote a book about
doing up an old house in Provence? He made it
sound so idyllic that he had every third cousin
twice removed of anyone he'd ever spoken to in
his life showing up for a free holiday.'

'OK.' I laughed. 'We'll go together.'

'When, when? The Eternal City . . . there's so
much to see and do.'

'Soon. I'll call my father and let you know.'

'You're on!'

We looked at each other. Broke into sponta-
neous laughter. Tipped our glasses at each other.
And that was it. The beginning . . . or perhaps
the continuation . . . of exactly the kind of relationship I had been longing for.

As someone once said, though, men are like
buses. Either none at all, or six in a row. A couple
of weeks later, Malcolm Macdonald called me
up. 'I'm in London for the weekend,' he said.
'Could I take you out for dinner?'

'That would be great,' I said, really meaning

157

it. He was a nice man, and I had enjoyed his company at Weston Lodge.

'This evening? Tomorrow?' he asked.

Having fixed time and place, I wondered what Dad would say if I told him. All too easily I could hear his voice: *'Isn't this a step too far, honey? First the same courses as your sister, then her university, then the kind of job she wanted. And now dating her boyfriend? Come on, Chantal. Get a grip. Time to get a life of your own.'*

And he'd be perfectly right. Except for the dating bit. Since Malcolm's main connection to me was my sister, that would really be bordering on the crazy. And, in any case, it wasn't the fact of Malcolm's former relationship with Sabine that I had liked. It was his Scottishness, the voice that was so like Ham's, the person behind the kind eyes.

That first time we met up, I told myself that I wouldn't mention Sabine at all. We'd talk generally, learn a bit about each other, have a nice evening, maybe at the end of it make a date for the next time he came down to London.

And as all women do, and despite Gavin, I asked myself whether, if the opportunity arose, I could go to bed with him. Could I sleep with a man who had slept with my sister? If we got that close, would Sabine have any bearing on what might occur? I really didn't want to go there.

Malcolm was wearing a business suit when we met at the restaurant he'd suggested in Soho. He looked elegant and in charge. I liked that.

'Right,' he said, after orders had been placed,

wine ordered, small talk exchanged about how nice it was to see each other again after . . . what was it? . . . goodness me, over three months, 'I wanted to talk about your sister.'

'Is there anything more to say?'

'I thought you might like to know some of the things she wrote to me about before her death. They would be very different from the kind of information she was sending home to you in California.' He reached into the breast pocket of his jacket and pulled out a few envelopes with my sister's distinctive hand on them. 'Obviously, I don't mean the personal stuff. But things about the family, the house, the . . . uh . . . lads, her employers.'

'She wrote pretty comprehensively to me,' I said. 'Actually, Malcolm, if you don't mind, I'd rather not talk about Sabine at all. Not tonight, at least.' How was that for not taking decisions?

He seemed surprised, even taken aback. 'Oh. All right. If that's what you—'

'Are you married, Malcolm?' I asked.

'I have been.'

'What happened?'

'Oh.' He shrugged. 'The usual. She found someone she liked better than me.' He refilled our glasses. 'What about you?'

'Would you and my sister have got it together?' I asked, avoiding the question.

'Who knows?' He smiled. 'It was lovely while it lasted.'

'How often do you get down here?'

'At least twice a month. Maybe next time, we could—'

'I'd like that,' I said. The second interruption in three minutes. 'We could take in a play. Or a concert, maybe.'

And suddenly we were away from what had originally brought us together. We began to discuss our likes and dislikes in music. From there we moved to books, theatre, the worst programmes on TV, the best, our favourite movies – all the trivia that two newly met people talk about. Of course there had been men in my life since I lost Ham, but until Gavin, none of them had been very important. Nor did I perceive Malcolm as being of any importance, either, but I liked him more than others I'd met.

When the evening came to a natural end, he pulled out his diary and told me when he would next be down in London. He said that he would telephone in advance. He didn't try to extend the evening. Was I disappointed? Maybe, just a little.

This is not a story about a love affair. But that summer constituted some of the happiest weeks of my adult life. Gavin and I seemed destined for each other. He knew a tremendous amount about the kind of world I moved in, and I knew almost nothing about his. But we had a shared enthusiasm for rugby, and frequently found ourselves at Twickenham, or in Wales at Cardiff Arms Park, as it was still called then, cheering on one side or another. 'My father's from Abergavenny, as it happens,' he told me. 'So I get to root for two sides.'

'What happens when Wales plays England?' I asked.

'Then I can cheer them *both* on.'

All our conversations seemed to lead to hilarity. It was simple, harmless, frivolous stuff, and I loved it. I began to see that over the years I had smiled little and laughed less. Now everything, seen through the prism of Gavin's far-from-solemn gaze, amused me.

The question of whether we should eventually move in together was one which hovered over the two of us, though we never discussed it. I think we both felt that although there was no hurry, it was inevitable. And we did indeed go over to Rome to visit Dad and his *contessa*. The first night we were there, Gavin gave my father a present wrapped in soft tissue paper. 'It's not valuable,' he said, sounding almost shy, 'and you've probably got a copy already, but it's such a pretty edition that I couldn't resist buying it for you.'

'Oh, my goodness.' Dad gazed down at the beautifully bound volume of Thomas Hardy's poems which lay between his careful hands. Seventy-five years old, it was bound in scarlet leather with gorgeous marbled endpapers, and the covers were decorated with gilt titles and double rules around the panels. The paper was tissue-paper thin, with a hardly faded scarlet silk-ribbon bookmark. Having lived with my father for so long, I knew the jargon. 'This is incredibly kind of you, my boy.'

'I'm really glad if you like it, sir.'

'Iss beautiful,' said the *contessa*. 'Where did you find it?'

'There's a little second-hand bookshop round

the corner from my flat. Chantal told me you were both into books, and when I saw it, I thought it would be just right.'

'It *is* just right,' said Dad.

My heart was touched by Gavin's thoughtfulness. He couldn't have chosen a more apposite gift. 'Oh, darling,' I said tenderly, my heart melting. I rested my hand on his shoulder.

He smiled and reached up to cover my fingers.

Rome was wrapped in the amber light of autumn, and we walked hand in hand through narrow streets to visit galleries and churches and the usual tourist destinations, or simply to sit at pavement cafés and watch the world go by. I was happy in an unshadowed, uncomplicated way, and I believe Gavin was too. We were at the start of the rest of our lives: we both knew it.

Gavin had to get back for work on the following Monday, but I had a few days of leave owing me, and I travelled with Dad and Ingrid to her villa on the coast.

After a lunch of freshly caught fish and salad, Dad and I were sitting on the patio of the seaside house. We could see for miles, to where the horizon misted into nothingness in the heat. Far below us, the peacock-blue sea rolled slowly in to a small white beach.

'This is almost too much,' my father said. 'Sometimes I feel that something dreadful needs to happen, to make up for such beauty. There needs to be a grain of sand in the oyster. A serpent in the Eden.'

'Why not just enjoy it?' I said from where I

162

sat on the swing-seat. Tomorrow I would be returning to England, and the weather reports had not been encouraging.

'It's the Protestant work ethic,' said Dad. 'I was brought up to believe that we were not put on this earth to enjoy ourselves. We're supposed to work hard and live frugally, not lounge about in sybaritic idleness.'

I wasn't really listening as I lazily turned the pages of the *Corriere della Sera*, which was delivered every morning by the store down in the little white town.

'Yes,' Dad continued, sniffing the thyme-laden air, shading his eyes to look out at the sea. 'Plain living and high thinking, as the poet has it: that's what we were supposed to be aiming for.'

I looked at him with love. He wore nicely cut shorts and a striped shirt: he was tanned and fit, with a head of thick greying hair. He looked good. He looked happy.

'Do you miss Mom?' I asked suddenly.

'Of course I do. But life is not about regrets, it's about moving onwards as well, bursting joy's grape and all that. Don't you miss Hamilton?'

'All the time.' But, I realized, with a sharp pang of disloyalty, I had dwelt on the loss of Sabine to a much greater extent than that of Ham.

A bird trilled suddenly from one of the fruit-laden lemon trees which stood in blue ceramic pots around the garden. The sky was criss-crossed with vapour trails from planes taking off or landing at the nearby airport. There was no sound except the distant murmur of the sea.

'So what did you think?' I asked.

163

'About what?'

'About Gavin, of course.'

'I thought he was extremely nice. So did Ingrid.'

'Nice? *Nice*? What kind of a word is that?'

'It's the first time we've met him,' he said mildly. 'Give us a chance to get to know him.'

'You sound as though you have reservations.'

'Absolutely not. It's just . . . the two of us would like to know more. But that's our age, I guess. Certainly, on first meeting, your Gavin seems intelligent, thoughtful, energetic – and he's resolved to win you, like some medieval knight. Bringing that beautiful edition of Hardy was a master-stroke.'

'You make him sound so calculating.'

'Not in the least, darling. But he's obviously a determined young man—'

I couldn't help thinking of Sabine, those mutilated little boys: lucky, lucky Gavin, to get away physically intact from that madwoman, even if not completely emotionally, and lucky me that he had.

The *contessa*'s manservant appeared across the marble tiles of the patio on well-trained silent feet and asked if there was anything he could get us. Dad looked at his watch. 'Thank you, Sergio,' he said, 'I'd like a glass of rosé. How about you, Chantal?'

I looked at my watch. Four o'clock in the afternoon. 'Whatever happened to plain living?' I said.

'The hell with it,' said Dad.

I smiled. He and my mother had been happy together for many years, but the new Dad had settled easily into a different kind of happiness.

More hedonistic, less earnest. And why not? The premature deaths of two of his family must have contributed largely to his current *laissez-faire* attitude.

'I'll join my father,' I said, trying hard to sound as if my arm were being twisted.

Below us, light flashed like electric signals on the kingfisher-blue of the water. Two white-sailed yachts drifted from one side of the bay to the other; a group of seagulls bobbed in the waves. Sergio reappeared with a tray holding a silver bucket and an opened bottle of wine. He poured us each a glass, handed us each a small dish of black olives and returned to the house.

'Here's to heaven,' my father said, tipping his glass at me.

Over the roof of the house, we heard the swirl of gravel from the courtyard in front of the building. The slam of a door. Brisk footsteps. The *contessa* had arrived.

She swept out on to the patio, all exclamations and kisses, a poppy-splattered white sundress showing off her tan and long Scandinavian legs. 'Sandro! Chantal! *Buongiorno, buongiorno! Come stai?* Ah, you are drinking. I too shall have a glass of *vino*. No, no, do not call for Sergio, I shall share your glass, *caro mio*.' She sank down beside my father and took the glass from his hand.

'And how are you, *cara*?' he said. 'Did you get your business done?'

'Perfectly, thank you, perfectly. And now see what I have brought you, Alessandro.' She handed Dad a small package.

He opened it and gazed at the contents trans-
fixed. 'My God, Ingrid, where did you get this?'

'I have been looking for some time, *caro*. And
then it came up for sale. I knew you wanted it, so
I bought it for you.' The *contessa* stroked my
father's thick white hair, then playfully pinched his
cheek, while I looked elsewhere. I was so glad that
Dad had found new happiness, but that couldn't
stop me wishing that *maman* was there instead.

'Look at this, Chantal.' He held up a small
book.

'What is it?'

'It's an extremely rare first edition. Take a look.'
He handed it to me.

I opened it at the title page and read: *The Life
and Strange Surprizing Adventures of Robinson
Crusoe, of York, Mariner.* There was a frontis-
piece illustration of Crusoe in his goatskin coat
and hat, and behind him the posts of the stockade
he built. A large starfish lay beside his bare feet,
while his ship – supposedly wrecked – tossed on
the stormy waves out to sea. 'Lovely,' I said.
'Lucky you.' The little volume felt smooth and
gentle in my hands.

Later, after a dinner of grilled lamb and *risotto
ai funghi*, eaten under the grape arbour at the
side of the house, accompanied by a carafe of
the coarse local wine, and served by Sergio in a
starched white jacket, I borrowed a torch and
made my way down the steep little steps which
had been cut out of the rock and led down to the
beach. There was nobody about so I stripped off
my clothes and ran into the milk-warm sea.
Phosphorescence trailed behind me, sparkling in

the dark water like the tail of a comet. Floating on my back, I gazed up at the stars, languidly lifting an arm now and then to watch the incandescent light pour down my arm. No other lights were visible from Ingrid's private little bay: I felt as though I had the entire world to myself. And my life at last seemed to be on an even keel.

When I got back, my father and the *contessa* had retired to the small private sitting room attached to their bedroom. I poured myself a last glass of Ingrid's excellent Chianti and tiptoed along the marble corridors to my bedroom, where I dialled my closest friend and colleague in London.

'Hi, Lorna,' I said. 'How's it all going?'

'Dreadful, darling. We need you. Desperately! We're going to rack and ruin without you. Come back!' Lorna was always theatrical.

'I'm only away for a week, you know. Home tomorrow, back at work the day after.'

'Seems longer, that's all.'

'Anything new to report? Any exciting developments?'

'Not on the artistic front. But if you're talking personal . . .' She paused meaningfully.

'What?'

'Mr Right,' she said, sighing blissfully. 'I want you to meet Nat A-SAP. Give me your opinion. Because, honestly, darling, I think this is The One. The Real Thing!'

'That's wonderful. Lorna, I'm so pleased for you,' I said. 'Though I can't imagine why you'd want me to endorse someone you've obviously already made your mind up about.'

'I was thinking we could make up a foursome,

167

give me a chance to meet this Gavin of yours. Knock back a glass or two, have a laugh.'

'Sounds like my sort of thing, though Gavin's not hugely into the social whirl,' I said. 'But I'm sure he can be persuaded.'

'Still at the honeymoon stage, are you? Spending the weekend in bed, calling in pizzas, watching DVDs with all limbs entwined?'

She was so accurate that I blushed. 'More or less.'

'Been there, done that. But if you could persuade him to get out from under the duvet, honey-babe, why don't we make it this Thursday, at that nice fish restaurant?'

'I don't know any fish restaurants.'

'Yes, you do. We went there the other day. The Golden Carp.'

'Harp, Lorna. The Golden Harp. And it's not a fish restaurant.'

'Never mind. Eight o'clock all right?'

'We'll be there.'

I liked Nat as soon as I met him. Warm, smiley, losing his hair and not bothered. A calming influence on Lorna; that much was obvious from the start. We ordered champagne and drank a toast to each other. Gave our orders to the waiter and asked for another bottle of wine to be brought to the table. Chattered about this and that: affairs of the day, the dick-heads currently running the country, why no major government was bothering to intervene in the Middle East, the disgraced disc-jockeys being exposed by their victims. Nat and Gavin discovered that they had both spent time in some of the major financial cities of the world and began chalking up mutual acquaintances, while Lorna and I eyed them fondly.

'Aren't they sweet?' she said.

And I had to agree that they were.

'So, what does your mother think of Nat?' I asked.

'She hasn't met him yet. I thought I'd try him out on you first. But she *loves* the sound of him. The right age, the right job, the right religion . . . What's not to like?' Lorna laughed raucously and drank down the remains of her glass of red. 'In fact, it wouldn't matter if he was brain-damaged, as long as he can produce those grandchildren she's after.' She laughed some more. 'I keep telling her, "Mum, I am not a childbearing vessel. I have a brain and I use it. I don't want to sink into that sour-milk-smelling, unbrushed-hair, not-enough-sleep syndrome that's trapped my sisters." But Mum just laughs. "You just wait!" she says.'

'So are we thinking of making this a permanent thing?'

'*I* am. Hope he is too.'

'Has he proposed?'

'Not yet.'

'Well, just tell me in good time, so I can start saving up for my frilly pink bridesmaid's dress.'

'Frilly? Pink? Are you kidding me?' Lorna shrieked. 'I'm thinking a gorgeous saffron brocade for the bridesmaids, to offset my white dress, with matching hooded coats, since it'll be a winter wedding.'

'You already have the date?' I asked, surprised.

'January eighteenth next year.'

'Does he know?'

Lorna giggled; a dribble of red wine ran slowly down her chin. 'He'll be there, I expect. If not, I'll just have to go through it without him. I mean, I've been planning this wedding since God was a boy, and I'm not going to let the lack of a groom ruin my arrangements. Fill-ups, guys?' She seized the second bottle of red wine and started slopping it into our glasses, a lot of it landing on the tablecloth in the process.

Gavin frowned. Leaning forward, he tried to take the bottle from her.

'I can do it,' she said.

'I can do it better,' he said firmly. He was sitting well back from the table, worrying, I could tell, about his pale-coloured chinos, worn for the first time that night. 'Give it to me.'

Reluctantly, she did so, while Nat and I watched the exchange with some amusement.

Later, we walked down the Soho pavements, two couples hand in hand, laughing up at the orange-shaded sky. Thirty-somethings, in love with life, our horizons were bright. Lorna was on a high, leaning on Nat's arm, happiness crackling in her hair. Every now and then she tottered on her heels, or sloped sideways against a lamp-post.

'Ooof,' she said. 'I don't think I shall ever be as happy as this again.'

'You will,' Nat said seriously. 'I promise you that you will.'

In the cab back to my place, I snuggled up to Gavin. 'That was fun, wasn't it?'

'On the whole, yes, it was. Apart from your drunken friend. Nat's a nice fellow.'

'She wasn't that drunk.'

'Drunk enough. Falling about all over the place. I really dislike women who make a public spectacle of themselves.'

'Gavin! That's a bit harsh.'

He pulled me closer. 'I don't think you should spend too much time with her, if you want to know the truth.'

'But she's my best friend.'

'Maybe. She's also a bad influence on you.'

'What do you mean?'

'I've never seen you being so loud and noisy before. Don't you read the government health warnings? You drank far more than is good for you.'

'I did not, thank you.' I moved away from him. 'And where do you get off, telling me who I should be friends with?'

'I was only saying—'

'Yeah, well, don't,' I snapped. We were on the edge of our first row.

After a short pause, he said, 'I honestly thought she was going to pour wine all over my new trousers.'

'So did I!' I sank against him once more. Row averted; thank God for that.

And, of course, he was right. I'd drunk far too much. Certainly too much to take part in the vigorous love-making he initiated as soon as we got into the flat. So for once, I just lay there and let it happen as he touched and kissed me in all the places he had come to know, loving it, loving him.

* * *

171

The following Sunday, Gavin and I drove out to a waterside pub near Oxford for lunch. It was a gorgeous autumn day, the rivers soft and still, gulls following busy tractors as they ploughed up fields that had been abundant a month ago.

Gavin had been away all week, and I had been extra-busy with a new sale coming up, so this was intended as a bit of concentrated us-time before he dashed off again – to Toronto this time – and I got back to my own job.

It was a pretty place, with a terrace stretching down to the river and an ancient three-arched bridge leading from one side of the water to the other. Narrowboats plied slowly up and down, full of people sitting out in the cockpit with glasses in their hands, smiling and waving as they passed. Earnest young men sculled rapidly along, obviously training for some very important river-based event. We sat in the golden sunlight of autumn, studying the menu and looking appreciatively round at old stone and copper-coloured chrysanthemums, the gleam of brass from inside, the iridescent green necks of the mallards which waited patiently for something edible to be thrown in their direction.

By the time we were called inside to eat, the restaurant had filled up. We sat down at our reserved table in the conservatory annexe and contemplated pleasant though unexciting food.

We smiled at one another. He took my hand and turned it in the sunlight, which filled the conservatory. 'Darling,' he said fondly, 'I really—'

'Christ, it's Vicious Vaughn, as I live and breathe!' a voice said.

172

We both looked up at the florid man who stood beside our table. He wore a dark suit and a black tie, highly polished black shoes, a gleaming white shirt with the kind of creases which advertised the fact it had only been removed from its wrapping that morning.

For a moment Gavin said nothing. Then he grinned. 'Good God, Brutish Barnesy,' he said. 'Darling, can I introduce Leo Barnes, former rugby player, brilliant sawbones, and all-round bastard. Leo, this is my . . . uh . . . fiancée, Chantal Frazer.' *What*? I tried to assume the kind of demure expression a fiancée might adopt while Gavin got up, and the two of them went into one of those half-embarrassed male embraces.

'Good to meet you, Chantal.' Barnes gave me an up-and-down look. 'And congratulations on getting engaged to this bugger. Just as long as you know what you're getting yourself into.'

'I love you too,' said Gavin.

'No, seriously,' Barnes said to me. 'I hope you can control the lad. He can be really nasty when roused, as many a one-testicled prop-forward can confirm!'

'Bollocks,' said Gavin.

'Precisely,' said Barnes, sniggering like an adolescent boy with a copy of *Playboy*. 'Or not, as the case may be.'

'What are you doing down here, anyway?' said Gavin. 'I thought your sphere of influence was in Hong Kong.'

'It is, but . . .' Barnes waved across the room where a table of four men, all with black ties,

173

were guffawing over some joke or other. 'We're here for Charlie Leeming's funeral.'

'Charlie's Leeming's . . . Charlie's *dead*?'

'Heart attack. He was at some bankers' do, stuffing meat and two veg into his face, keeled over, died on the spot. I assumed that's where you two were off to.'

'Barnesy, please. Do we look as if we're dressed for a funeral? Anyway, I wouldn't cross the road to rescue Leemers from a rabid tiger, as you well know.'

'We weren't any fonder of him than you were, old man. We're just going along to show support for poor old Sally—'

'Sally?'

'Sally Preston as was. Clive's sister. She married Charlie all those years ago, and now, at last, her luck has turned and she's shot of him.'

'A charming sentiment,' said Gavin. 'Is Clive here too?' He twisted round to look at the guys over at the table, who had stopped laughing and were staring over at us. Their expressions were not particularly friendly.

'Clive. Woodsy. Bradley. Edwards. You remember them. They certainly remember you!' Barnes looked at me. 'Rugby's a violent game, Chantal, but Gavin here turned violence into an art form, didn't you, old boy?'

Gavin shrugged. 'No more than anyone else.'

Barnes raised his eyebrows, but didn't comment.

The waiter appeared with our food, and Gavin sat down again. 'Give them all my best, and condolences to Presty, on his sister's behalf.'

'Will do.' Barnes moved back to his own table.

174

Gavin had his back to them, but I could see them hunched forward as they cast sideways glances in our direction, clearly discussing us in lowered voices. It wasn't a particularly pleasant encounter, as I could tell from Gavin's expression. 'What was that all about?' I said.

'Bunch of boys from Singapore,' he said briefly. 'We used to play rugby on Saturday afternoons. It was good fun.'

'You don't sound as if you liked them much.'

'I didn't. Any of them.' He put a forkful of food in his mouth and chewed slowly. 'No, that's not true. They weren't a bad lot. You met Charlie Leeming at that weekend, didn't you?'

'That's right.'

'Did you like him?'

'Heavens, no.'

'That lot over there were all supposedly friends of his. Says it all.'

'But he was young to die, wasn't he?'

'You saw him, sweetheart. Face like a tomato about to burst. That's always a sign of high blood-pressure.'

'Poor chap. You wouldn't really wish such an early death on anyone.'

'Of course you wouldn't.' He laid his big hand over mine, and we were both silent, both remembering those much earlier deaths.

After a long while, I spoke hesitantly. 'Gavin, I know you wish I'd just leave it to lie, but is it possible that Lady Forshawe was responsible?'

'Who?' He was astonished. 'Jennifer Forshawe? Clio Palliser's best friend? I don't think so.'

'Why not?'

175

His reaction was mixed: irritation that I kept on and on about it all, and a strange sort of excitement. 'Why on earth would a respectable woman like Jenny Forshawe want to kill two kids? It's just unbelievable.'

'But you agree that it's at least possible.'

'It would never in a million years have occurred to me, but yes, I suppose it's at least possible.'

'Which could mean that poor old Clio spent twenty years in Broadmoor for something she didn't do.'

'Yes.'

'And if we can prove it, then finally my sister is avenged.'

'That too.' He squeezed my fingers, which he was still holding. 'Does it still mean so much to you?'

I smiled at him. 'You wouldn't believe how different I am from when we first met. All the angst and horror and fury . . . it's almost gone, though of course I'll never get over the regret. But nonetheless, I would still like to have it settled.'

'Look, I hope you didn't mind me saying you were my fiancée. I thought they'd show a bit more respect that way.'

We drove home in friendly silence and spent the rest of the day in bed, enjoying the touch, the feel, the smell, the taste of each other.

Ten

Gavin rang. 'My mother is coming over from Australia. I want you to meet her, if that's all right. Or her to meet you, whichever's more apposite. Can the three of us get together for dinner one night while she's here?'

'Of course. If . . .' I hesitated slightly. 'If you think it's appropriate.'

'What's that supposed to mean?'

I was embarrassed. 'Nothing, really.'

'You mean because introducing my girl to my mother is a significant gesture?'

'Precisely.'

'It damn well is appropriate. She'll love you. Not as much as I do, of course, but . . .'

I laughed aloud. 'Excellent. Wonderful.' He'd never said it before. Not when we made love slowly and quietly on a rainy Sunday afternoon, nor when we woke in the night and turned to each other, or were tearing our clothes off before we'd even got through the front door, collapsing on to the floor in a frantic urgent coupling, nor when we sat over dinner gazing into each other's eyes.

'Would you like me to cook at home?' I said. 'Use all the best china and silver and so on? Show her how suitable I am?'

'Not this time. She likes eating out.' He hesitated. 'Besides . . .'

'Besides what?'

'It's all yours, is it?'

'What do you mean?'

'The silver and so forth. Damask tablecloths, crystal glasses, all that fancy stuff.'

'I didn't shoplift it from Harrods, if that's what you're asking.'

'No, I meant, did it come from your family?'

'Gavin, I bought some of it with Hamilton, I inherited some of it from my French grandmother, I bought some of it with my very own money, and some of it was wedding presents. Satisfied?'

'There's no need to get snippy. It's just that I'd prefer to use stuff that's ours, rather than things to do with your first husband.'

'You are being so extremely stupid that I'm going to put the phone down now, quite carefully,' I said, annoyed, 'before I slam it down.' And I replaced the phone on its stand. Gavin had done this before: shown an over-the-top jealousy which was entirely misplaced. I'd explained about Ham's death. I'd said that, yes, I missed him sometimes but that I had moved on long ago. I'd pointed out that we were a couple now, that we were beginning to build up our own stuff. And I'd also added that I had no intention of getting rid of my possessions because of some stupid prejudice on his part. Probably not the best way to demonstrate my commitment to us as a partnership, but it was how I felt and he'd have to get used to it.

I met them at Gavin's favourite Greek restaurant. Paula, his mother, was tall and somewhat remote,

178

with anxious eyes that rested frequently on her son, searching his face for something she couldn't always find. I guessed it to be the natural reaction of a protective mother when a child has been through the kind of ordeal that Gavin had suffered, especially since she had been a single parent since her husband's death. I hoped that seeing him with me would provide the reassurance she must have sought over the years. Apparently, she ran an import–export business and did very well at it.

'Gavin's father and I set it up together years ago,' she told me. 'After he died, it seemed silly to sell up; I couldn't think of anything else I wanted to do, and I certainly wasn't ready to take up golf or sit around gossiping at the country club.'

But now, she said, she was thinking of moving back to England. 'I don't want to be idle, though,' she said. 'I like a garden to dig, hills to climb, rugby to watch and so forth. Gavin's father was a great rugby fan.' She glanced with affection at her son. 'I'm planning to buy a season ticket or whatever it is over here so I can watch all the big internationals.'

Gavin took my hand. 'Chantal loves rugby too, don't you, darling?' He smiled at us both. 'Maybe you can go to matches together.'

Oh, great, I thought.

Paula didn't seem all that thrilled, either. 'Is that how you met?' she asked distantly.

Gavin and I each waited for the other to answer his mother's question. In the end, I said, 'We met when we were both staying in the same hotel.'

'Liked the look of him, did you?' Paula said to me.

'Something like that, Mum,' he said frostily. 'In actual fact, Chantal had run out of petrol and was stranded in the middle of nowhere, and fortunately I came to the rescue.'

'Knight in white armour,' Paula said.

It took me a moment to realize what was wrong with the phrase. 'I was very lucky he came along,' I said.

'I was lucky I came along too,' said Gavin. 'Very.'

I grinned hugely. 'Otherwise I might have sat there for the rest of the week.'

'Oh, surely not,' Paula said. 'Someone would have eventually come.'

Another tick on the debit side for Gavin's Mum: no sense of humour.

'Still got your Morgan roadster?' Paula asked.

'You bet. I'm not getting rid of that at any price.'

'Not very practical for children.'

'Mother dear,' Gavin said lightly, 'you may not have noticed, but I haven't *got* any children.'

'They'll come soon enough, love.' Paula glanced at me in such a meaningful way that I would have blushed if I'd known how to. Children? As with Ham, if they came along, I would be delighted, but not devastated if they didn't.

'Where does your family live?' Paula asked me.

'There's only my father: he lives in Rome.'

'Is that right?' She gazed at me thoughtfully. I

180

wondered if she knew about Sabine; I wasn't
going to launch into any of that and hoped Gavin
hadn't mentioned it. But given that her own son
had been right in the middle of what had happened,
it seemed unlikely that Gavin hadn't told her of
my own connection.

'How long are you in England for this time?'
I asked.

'I haven't quite decided. As I said, I'm keen
to come back here, but it's a question of where
I move to. And, I suppose, what I can afford.'

'Will you be looking at any area in particular?'

Again she stared at her son rather than at me.
'That would depend on . . .'

I could see she was dying to know if Gavin
and I had any plans of a permanent nature, and
if so, what they were. But beyond the next week
or two, we had none. Not yet, anyway.

Call me undutiful or cold-hearted, but I was
already quite sure that whatever the future might
hold for Gavin and me, I was not going to want
his mother coming along for the ride. I could
envisage it quite clearly: the endless Sunday
lunches, the offers to pop round for tea, the kindly
suggestions of days out together, phones ringing
when we were making love on weekend morn-
ings, the hurt if she weren't included in some
outing we wanted to undertake, the constant
poking-in of noses. No, thank you. It's not that
I'm antisocial: I just like to choose my company
rather than have it thrust at me.

I glanced across at Gavin and could see he was
thinking very much along the same lines. Where
the hell could we escape to? Outer Mongolia?

North Korea? Feet would have to be very firmly put down, I thought. But how to do it without hurting someone? Not someone: *Paula*. Oh dear.

Gavin was spending a few days with his mother, visiting family in the Lake District, and although I always had plenty of stuff to do, I was quite glad of a diversion.

'That guy down there's been hanging round across the road for at least half an hour,' Lorna said late one afternoon, one ample hip perched on the edge of my desk as she slurped coffee from a stained mug and stared down at Bond Street.

'And I'm interested because . . .?' I clicked a button on my computer and brought up images of aboriginal art. Something I find intrinsically boring, mainly because I know perfectly well that the images have not sprung out of any artistic impulse but have been created to order. Usually by unscrupulous whitefella dealers.

'Because a) he's looking up at these windows. And b) he's holding up a sign saying, "I love you, Chantal, will you marry me?"'

'*What*?' I jumped up to stare down at the street below. There was no man with a sign saying anything. But there *was* Brian Stonor. I waved and made signs indicating that I'd be down shortly. 'You are a barefaced liar,' I told Lorna, and she laughed.

'Looks like my last depilation treatment worked, then.'

'Oh, *très* droll,' I said, cross with her for making my heart lurch when, for a moment, I had really thought Gavin was down there, proposing.

'Would you have accepted if it'd been Gavin?'

'I would have – until I met the mother.' I threw a few things into my shoulder bag and headed towards the door. 'I might have to rethink my strategy.'

'I'll have him any day,' Lorna said. 'Talk about dishy.'

'You'll have to make do with Nat.'

'Hope you didn't mind,' Stonor said as we settled at a table in the Royal Academy restaurant.

'Not in the least.' I poured tea from the pot we'd ordered. 'So what did you want to tell me? Or ask me?'

'Discuss with you, actually.' He reached into the briefcase he'd set on the floor beside his chair and pulled out a file. 'The Palliser case: I've spent the last few days boiling down the evidence in the police files to a manageable size. Your final question, when we last met, is the one I've been concentrating on. That's to say: if not Clio Palliser then who?'

'And what's your conclusion?'

'I haven't got one. Not yet. But first I asked myself who had the means and the opportunity; that was relatively easy. It was the motive I found difficult.'

'So who did you put on the list?'

'I went back, first of all, to Harry Redmayne. To be honest, I always liked him for it.'

'I thought you'd established conclusively that he couldn't have done it.'

'I've looked again. But I'll come back to that. Next, the locals and the neighbours. We investigated them thoroughly at the time, but looking again, I can see gaps where anyone could have done it, if they lied about it. Farmer Barnard, for instance. He was in and out of Weston Lodge all the time, knew his way in, knew the layout of the house. I think he could have done it. He certainly had the opportunity. But why? That's what I can't work out. Neither with him nor with most of them.'

'Let's get the list sorted first, and then see if we can come up with a motive.'

'There's also Sam Windrow,' said Stonor. 'Son of Linda Windrow, one of the Weston Lodge cleaning staff. Sixteen years old at the time. We didn't investigate him all that thoroughly, though perhaps we should have done. Supposedly watching TV in his bedroom, but easily capable of getting over to the Lodge, carrying out the murders and slipping back home again, no one the wiser.'

'He'd have been chancing his arm a bit, wouldn't he?'

'Maybe he'd got the hots for your – excuse me – your sister.'

'I don't think she ever mentioned him, but I'll have to check up on that. But at sixteen, to kill her?'

'Maybe she rejects him. Laughs at him. So he strikes out at her. Turns away and sees one or other of the boys witnessing all this, so does them too.'

A thought struck me. 'Do we know who was killed first? I never thought to ask.'

'According to the evidence offered by Gavin

Vaughn, it seems that poor little George got it first. Then your sister. Then Edward. Then it would have been Gavin, if he hadn't found an escape route through the pantry.' He looked thoughtful. 'But maybe it was the other way round. Like I said, Sam the Son comes into the house, up to Sabine's room, she rejects him, he kills her in a fury, sees one of the boys watching and goes after him, has to do the other, can't catch the third boy and races on home to finish watching *Dallas* or whatever.'

'That's possible, I suppose.' A party of Japanese tourists clutching guide books settled like a flock of starlings at the tables round us.

Stonor looked down at his file. 'Now, Lord Forshawe. Desmond. I looked at him more closely, and he could certainly have done it. Had the means and the opportunity. Wife was out walking the dogs, Mrs Stanton, the housekeeper at the time, had gone home. What was to stop him driving round to the Lodge and committing murder? He was a career soldier once, you know. Saw active service all over the world. Perfectly capable of killing someone if he wanted or needed to. But as we've said, even if you believe a guy like him could have killed children in cold blood, what the hell was the motive?'

'I wouldn't believe it, anyway. Not Desmond.'

Fort a moment he stared at me thoughtfully. 'You don't think your sister could be at the root of all this, do you?'

'You mean Desmond Forshawe had got the hots for Sabine and decided at eight o'clock in the evening to go round and proposition her, when

Redmayne might have returned from London, Clio could be having a glass of wine in front of the fire, the boys were still swarming about? I absolutely do not think so.'

'It does sound a bit far-fetched, doesn't it?' He put a hand on his papers as though to prevent them from flying away. 'Now here's an interesting one. With a motive, too.'

'Yes?'

'You know that picture which the boys had scrawled "Fuck You" on?'

'Harry Redmayne's newest acquisition, you mean?'

'That's the one. Well, it turns out it wasn't his, after all. It was lent to him: guess who by?'

'Cut to the chase, Brian. I can do Sudoku but not guessing games.'

'Lady Forshawe, if you can believe it.'

'I knew she was quite a connoisseur. Why would she lend Redmayne a painting when he had so many of his own?'

'I would guess it was loaned to Clio, rather than Harry. They were good friends. The thing is, she was out walking her dogs at the crucial time. Suppose she took it into her head to borrow it back for Christmas. So she walks over to Weston Lodge, goes inside – all the staff were gone, don't forget, Clio's beavering away in that soundproofed study of hers, the boys and your sister were upstairs. She thinks she'll unhook the thing from the wall, sees it's been scrawled with rude words, picks up a paper knife or whatever is to hand and flies up the stairs, knowing it must have been the children who damaged it, not Clio

186

or her husband, starts laying about her with the knife, kills your sister just because she happens to be there.'

'As a theory, it's certainly got legs. And who told you about the loan?'

'The extremely helpful Mrs Linda Windrow, mother of the aforementioned Sam. Turns out we used to go to school together. Funny, isn't it?'

'Hilarious.'

'I just happened on that snippet of information this time round. I should have looked at it more closely at the time. It certainly provides a motive, something we're a bit short on.'

'But isn't it a longish way to walk the Forshawe dogs, on a snowy winter night?' I remembered Desmond Forshawe's rueful laugh as he said that his wife had loved her dogs only second to her paintings. 'On the other hand, I suppose they were big dogs, needed exercise.'

'And nobody would suspect her for a moment, would they?'

'What about footprints left in the snow?'

'By the time we got there, it was snowing quite heavily. They'd have been covered up well before then.'

'Clothes covered in blood?'

'Gets back to her house, strips off down in the mud room or whatever they call it, throws them into the furnace that powers the central heating. Creeps up the back stairs and into her bedroom, gets dressed in a fresh outfit and down she goes to make supper for herself and her husband. Easy as standing on your head.'

'I, for one, have never found that particularly

187

easy.' I was mulling over what he'd said. It certainly hung together. But knifing two children to death because of a swear word or two seemed pretty extreme. 'If by any chance you're right, you'll never get her for it.'

'I know. She's dead.' He grimaced. 'More tea?'

'Thank you. And of course you've already explained why the Honourable Clio might have gone along with having the blame laid at her door: remorse over her lack of warmth and so on towards her two dead children.' I raised my cup and peered at him over the rim. 'So what do we do now?'

'Attempt to establish someone else as the guilty party.'

'Or, of course, Clio's innocence. Either way would do.'

'If she *is* innocent. At this distance in time, almost impossible to prove, wouldn't you say?'

'Pretty much.' I thought of my father's mantra, *It's not going to bring her back.* I knew that. What I wanted now was some kind of justice. I wanted, if not exoneration of Clio Palliser, then at least some understanding. And if she *were* to prove blameless in the matter of the foul slaying of her own children, then I wanted that established too, if only for Sabine's sake. 'But it's worth a try.'

'So what's the first move?'

'If you seriously think Farmer Barnard or Lady Forshawe could have done it, I suggest we go down to Weston Lodge again, stay a night or two, visit Desmond Forshawe, meet up with some of the locals. I'll pay for you, if you like.' I

188

thought of the money my darling Ham had left me: investments, stocks and shares, cash in different places, the leasehold of my house. I was never going to be short of money.

'I'm not short of a bob or two,' Stonor said, echoing my thoughts. 'Thought the place was well worth the money. No, prices will have increased by now . . . Let's pay for ourselves. I agree with you that bearding the lion in his den is as good a place to start as any. And as soon as possible, eh?'

'Absolutely. Let's go for it!'

Across the table, we shook hands.

'Motive, though. We have to establish a motive.'

Easier said than done.

Eleven

We drove down to Weston Lodge early on Saturday morning, intending to take pot luck. If there weren't rooms available at the hotel, we'd find a B&B somewhere.

David Charteris remembered us from the last time we were there. 'How nice to see you back again,' he said.

'Good to be here.' Stonor nodded. 'We're travelling together, but quite independently, in case you're wondering.'

'No, no. I wasn't,' Charteris said hastily. 'None of my business, anyway. So two bedrooms, and will you be here for dinner tonight?'

'Certainly,' I said. 'The food was brilliant when we were here over your promotional weekend.'

'Good, good.'

'Same for me,' said Stonor.

'Is it going well?' I asked. 'The new hotel, I mean.'

'Very much so. In fact it's only because we had two cancellations just this morning – two American couples travelling together – that we even have any spare rooms.' He handed over two sets of keys. 'We're even thinking of expanding: converting some of the existing outbuildings to add more accommodation.'

Once settled in my room – not the same one I'd had last time – I used the house phone to tell

Stonor I was going to stroll through the woods to see Desmond Forshawe and maybe set up another meeting with him.

'Better tread carefully, Chantal,' he said. 'Nobody wants a relative stranger appearing on the doorstep and implying that his wife could have killed three people twenty-three years ago.'

'I'd already worked that one out,' I said. 'I'm planning to use all my feminine wiles on him. Hens, roses, Balthus, it'll be a cinch.'

'I just hope you know what you're doing.'

'What will you do while I'm gone?'

'I've thought about Trevor Barnard, and it might be better if you were there for pursuing that line of enquiry. So I'm going to visit friends and relations round about the area who were here at the time and knew some of the people involved. Then, if that peters out, we're back to looking very hard indeed at Redmayne, yet again.'

'Is there possibly an X factor here? Somebody we haven't yet considered. Or don't even know about.'

'We can explore that one when we've seen how this comes out. But I need to say that I still think in the main that Clio did it. I'm going to have to be very very convinced to believe otherwise.'

'Right. I'll see you in the bar before dinner.'

'I'll be the one holding a half-pint of beer.'

I felt like a completely different person from the one I'd been last time I walked through these woods. Looking back, I could see the sort of limited person I had become over the years, emotionally bent low and seeing only the ground

191

beneath my feet. Now I walked tall, head held high. Taking on the world. It was partly to do with Gavin, I knew that. But more because I had at last properly faced my demons.

The landscape had changed, moved into russets and golds, after the rich green of summer. The fields off to the right were amber, tawny, more than ready to be harvested. In among the trees, there were already bare branches and a thickening carpet of fallen leaves. Somewhere above my head, pigeons cooed forlornly and intermittently, a woodpecker rat-tat-tatted for insects. When I arrived at the edge of the woods, I could see Desmond Forshawe pottering about on the stone-flagged terrace, holding a pair of secateurs in a useless kind of way.

'Good morning!' I called, when I got nearer. 'How are the roses doing?'

'Chantal Frazer!' he said. 'What a welcome sight you are, my dear.' He looked at his watch. 'A glass of sherry would be appropriate, wouldn't you say?'

'Definitely.' I mounted the mossy steps and gave him a buss on the cheek. 'So how are you? How are the hens? And the dogs?'

'All the better for seeing you.' He led the way into the drawing room and poured us each a generous sherry. 'Let's sit outside, while the sun's still shining. It'll be winter all too soon.'

We sat on weathered teak outdoor chairs and contemplated the view. A couple of dogs sidled up, gave me a desultory sniff, and lay down beside their master.

'So,' I said. I couldn't think of much to say

after that. As Stonor had pointed out, the subject of Lady Forshawe's possible murderous activities was a difficult one to broach. 'Thank you for contacting the chairman of Chauncey's on my behalf.'

'Think nothing of it.'

I sipped the excellent manzanilla he'd offered. 'Your intervention has done wonders for my profile at Chauncey's. I'm going to be in charge of a sale of miniatures early next year.'

'Excellent, excellent.' He tipped his glass at me. 'You seemed fairly sound on the subject when we last spoke.'

'Mmm.' I willed him to make the connection with the miniatures we'd discussed on my last visit. And, bless him, he did.

'It'll be interesting to see if any of those missing Palliser miniatures comes up,' he said.

'It will indeed. I shall be keeping an eye out. Not that I've seen them, only read descriptions of a few.'

He stirred in his chair. 'I'm fairly sure m'wife had a file on them, now I come to think of it. I'll see if I can look it out for you. She was a good friend of the Honourable Clio Palliser, as I may have mentioned before.'

Just the opening I had been hoping for. 'I imagine the two of them spent a lot of time together.'

'Yes, they did. Back and forth between the two houses all the time, actually.'

'Through the woods, I suppose.'

'That's right. M'wife often walked the dogs that way – big dogs, need a good stretch of the

193

legs – and stopped in for a coffee with Clio. Though, mind you, once Clio had shut herself up in that study of hers, it was pretty hard to winkle her out of it. If she hadn't married that art student fellow and popped the two boys out so quickly, I reckon she would have been very happy indeed to stay put in Oxford, join the academic community there. Much more suitable for her, too. Frankly, I don't think the poor girl was cut out for motherhood.'

'As I understood, she left university unexpectedly early, before the summer term was over, and married the artist almost immediately.'

Forshawe looked shrewdly at me and tapped the side of his nose. 'Want my honest opinion? She was already up the spout when the wedding took place.'

'Interesting,' I said, though I wasn't sure what bearing it might have on anything. 'Where did the art student come from in the first place?'

'I don't really know the answer to that. One minute he wasn't here, the next he was carving Green Men all over the shop, stained glass windows and that sort of thing.'

'Apparently it's not a Green Man,' I said. 'It's Cronus.'

Desmond clapped his hands together delightedly. 'Oh, wonderful! That's exactly what Jenny – m'wife – said. "It's a portrait of Gerald, only he's too thick to see it. Devouring his children, just like Cronus." All a bit above my head, I'm afraid.'

I was fairly sure it was not. 'But how did he get here? Where did he come from?'

Forshawe screwed his face up in a questioning

way. 'Was he a friend of Piers . . .? That's Clio's eldest brother. Or did Gerald recruit him from the local College of Art? I can't really remember. If I ever knew. M'wife was always chattering away about something or other, and I'm afraid I didn't always pay close attention.'

'Was Sir Gerald pleased when Clio got it together with the student?'

'Remarkably sanguine. I remember thinking so at the time. I'd have expected him to fly into one of his famous rages about it. I'm sure he aimed higher for his daughter than an impoverished art student. We went to the wedding, and although you felt there were certain tensions simmering beneath the surface, everybody conducted themselves in a perfectly civil way.'

'And then one day he just upped and left.'

'That's right. By then Sir Gerald had gone upwards or, more likely, downwards, and the younger son had died several years earlier in that ski accident, not to mention Piers getting himself murdered. So it did rather leave Clio in the lurch. Not exactly gentlemanly behaviour, I felt at the time.'

'I wonder where he is now.'

'Who knows? I seem to remember someone mentioning that he'd gone to Australia, but I may be mixing him up with one of m'great-nephews.'

There was another piece of information I needed to try to establish. 'And did your wife take the dogs out that evening? The evening when everything –' I tried to adopt the same ironically dispassionate tone as Forshawe's – 'went pear-shaped?'

195

'Yes, indeed. She always did, come rain, come shine. Come snow, even.'

'Even in the dark?'

'Definitely.'

'And she wasn't scared?'

'Scared? It's not a word that was in Jenny's vocabulary.' He laughed, throwing back his head to display his long yellowish teeth. 'By God, I'd like to see the man who tried to take on Jenny: she'd have him on the floor howling for mercy within seconds.' He stared at me thoughtfully. 'Why do you ask?'

'I'm sure the police interviewed her at the time, but I just wondered if she'd seen anything. Some stranger hanging round. A car she didn't recognize. That sort of thing.'

'But I understood that Clio – poor girl – was responsible for what happened to your sister and her boys. I thought that had been established years ago.'

'Yes, but . . . I'm interested in puzzles,' I said, improvising. 'And I've been asking myself what if . . . what if, after all, somebody else did it?'

'An intriguing thought, I must admit.'

'So, as I say, she might have seen something.'

'I suppose Jenny could have done it.' He glanced sharply at me then gazed out across the garden. 'Yes, I can see exactly how she might have done it. Walks the dogs to the Lodge, goes in, sees or hears something that causes her to fly off the handle – you'd need to establish what – does the deed, then comes home, stuffs her blood-stained clothes into the washing machine, goes upstairs and showers, puts clean clothes on and

196

comes down all ready for a glass of G and T with her dear husband, who's been snoozing by the fire all the time she was gone and wouldn't have noticed a thing.'

This was so uncannily close to my own speculations that I could feel myself flushing with embarrassment. 'I really didn't mean to imply—'

'Don't worry, my dear. I can understand your feelings. But I assure you she loved Clio like the daughter we never had. No way she'd have been round there sticking knives into Clio's children, let alone allowing their mother to take the blame.' Belatedly, he added: 'Or your poor sister, of course.'

'Just as a mental exercise, what might have caused your wife to fly so far off the handle that she could have murdered three people?'

'Well, you see, that's where you venture so deeply into the realms of fantasy that you lose me. I absolutely cannot imagine what could enrage Jenny to such a pitch, short of someone dismembering one of the dogs in front of her. Or slashing one of her paintings.'

Not slashing, but possibly defacing . . . I waited but he didn't vouchsafe any further information. I longed to ask about the picture his wife had lent Clio, and whether that was the painting disfigured by the boys, but I didn't have the gall. Nonetheless, as I walked back to Weston Lodge, I wondered how he could be so certain of his wife's innocence. He'd even produced a logical, and possible, scenario. And what other motive could Jenny Forshawe possibly have for killing anyone?

As I stood on the edge of the woods and watched the sun falling away behind the distant hills, it struck me how many people in this dismal story had tempers so terrible and so easily aroused that they might easily be capable of murder.

'But in the end, it's not the *how* or the *who*,' I said to Stonor later, as we sat in the bar of the hotel with a pre-dinner drink, 'it's the *why*. Get the motive and you've got the killer.'

'This is always supposing that, after all, the Honourable Clio wasn't responsible?'

'If she was, she's taken her punishment, although nothing could atone for the crime she committed,' I said. 'And if she wasn't, then it's worth seeing if we can work out who was. So how did you get on this afternoon? I imagine it was easier for you to make enquiries than it was for me, you being a policeman and all.'

Stonor drank heartily from his beer glass. 'Even after all this time, everyone seemed to remember what happened quite clearly and was also perfectly willing to talk about it. I suppose it's because the Pallisers were one of the big families round here. Plus Linda was working here then. And there was the timing, of course, the horror of two children being killed so close to Christmas, the third boy getting away only by the skin of his teeth.'

'Did you learn anything new?'

'As a matter of fact, I did.' He leaned towards me, looking back over his shoulder to make sure we weren't being overheard. An old policeman's trick? It seemed a little out-of-place among the mainly American clientele currently crowding out the room. 'You're not going to believe this, but it turns out that there's a strong possibility Clio Palliser may have been pregnant when she got married!'

He spoke as though this were mind-boggling news, but since I'd already heard much the same possibility suggested earlier in the day, I was less impressed than I might have been.

'Desmond Forshawe hinted at the same thing,' I said.

'Oh.' Stonor's face dropped. 'Thought you'd find that interesting.'

'I do.' I found myself remembering the conversation I'd overheard on the terrace below my bedroom window, the first night of my last visit here. 'I wonder if that's why she left Oxford without taking her degree,' I said slowly. 'Which would mean that the art student came into her life earlier than we thought.'

'So she met him at Oxford?' Stonor ordered us refills by waving at the bartender then pointing at my glass and his own.

'Or in the Easter vacation. No, we can be reasonably sure that the art student was the father of both boys,' I said. 'And you got the last round so these are on my tab,' I added as the glasses appeared on our table.

'Thanks. Cheers.'

'It seems to me we absolutely need to track down this artist. Unless . . .' I widened my eyes. 'Oh my God. It can't have been Fingal Adair, can it?'

'Do I know him?'

'He's that dour sort of guy who was at the special weekend. You must remember. Fin, who seemed to take a bit of a shine to Maggie Fields, the woman who was doing the inventory on the house. Still is, for all I know. He was madly in love with Clio when she was at university, and she with him.'

'He wasn't an art student, was he?'

'Of course not. He was her history tutor.'

'And he got her up the duff?'

'Nicely put, Stonor.'

'Knocked her up. Got her in the family way. Gave her a bun in the oven, take your choice,' said Stonor, laughing like a man who was well into his third pint of the evening.

'Well, they were certainly sleeping together.' I frowned. 'But if it was him who made her pregnant, why wouldn't she have married *him*, instead of this mysterious art student?'

'Search me. Anyway, the artist was long gone by the night in question, so I can't see that he's got any relevance to anything.'

I nodded. 'This is true.'

I'd started on a quest that was only semi-serious, almost as an intellectual exercise, to see if there were any alternatives which pointed to Clio *not* being the murderer of my sister. But as Stonor said, what possible relevance did the vanished artist husband have? Or, for that matter, Fingal Adair? If we went to Oxford and questioned him, he would undoubtedly turn out to have an unbreakable alibi and an entire family to vouch for his presence at the significant time.

Maggie Fields came into the bar. Her too, I

thought. I waved at her. She came over with a drink in her hand. 'Couldn't keep away, I see,' she said.

'And looks like you couldn't *get* away.' I introduced her to Stonor. 'How's the job going?'

'Exhausting. There's so much stuff here. Not that I'd have it any other way.'

'Cupboards, drawers, storerooms, attics . . .?' I trailed them in front of her like a matador's scarlet cloak.

'That's right. You name it, they've got them stashed to overflowing with artefacts,' she said. 'Most of them historically interesting, many of them valuable, some of them priceless.'

'Do you start at the top or the bottom?'

'Bottom, usually. Funnily enough, the attics are often where you find the least valuable things. Families tend to stow their unwanted possessions up there, not their more precious belongings. So I generally leave those until last.'

'The broken-backed rocking chair,' I said.

'Granny's chipped teapot,' added Stonor.

'That sort of thing. Though, as everyone knows, it's also where you can stumble across some forgotten treasure.'

Which meant that I could, if I dared, and the opportunity arose, return to the attic I had climbed up to last time I visited Weston Lodge and find out what – if anything – had been hidden there. Better still, I could go right to the top and ask for permission. One of the more surprising things I've discovered about myself over the years is a distinct talent for lying through my teeth. But don't we all do that? Doesn't everyone occasionally pretend to be happier or richer or healthier than they really are?

I excused myself to Stonor, saying I'd be back shortly. I knocked at the door of David Charteris's office. 'Oh, David,' I said diffidently, when I was standing in front of his desk. 'You remember about my sister Sabine . . .'

'Yes, indeed. Terrible, terrible.'

'The thing is, after it all happened –' I twisted my hands nervously – 'someone sent her possessions back to us in California, where we were living at the time. But there were one or two items missing. And it just occurred to me this morning that possibly they'd been overlooked, stowed away in . . .' I took a deep breath. 'In an attic or somewhere.'

He nodded encouragingly.

'So I wondered if you would allow me to look here and there, maybe start upstairs, just in case they might still be here?'

'I can't see why not,' he said. 'You'd better liaise with Ms Fields.'

I produced a shy smile. 'My father and I have managed without them for all these years, so it's not that critical, but since I'm here . . .'

'I understand completely.' He got up and came round his desk to take both my hands in his. 'It's the very least I can do, considering the fact that she . . . well, that it was in this house that she . . .'

'Thank you,' I said. Humbly.

Sometimes I think I'm not a very nice person.

I found Maggie and explained that I'd been given permission to poke around in the attic in the hope of locating some of my late sister's (non-existent) possessions. 'I promise not disturb anything. Nor to take anything away without reference to you.'

'Fine.' She smiled kindly. 'I do hope you find them.'

I felt even guiltier.

Twelve

When dinner – pheasant stuffed with walnuts and figs, pumpkin soup, a delicate chestnut sorbet, all locally sourced and seasonal – was over, I told Stonor that I had stuff to do upstairs. I didn't specify what.

'Fine,' he said, jovially. 'With her agreement, I intend to buy myself and Ms Fields a brandy at the bar. Then we're going to sit in front of the telly and watch some programme about wildlife in the Amazon Basin.'

'The Gobi desert, actually.' Maggie winked at me.

'Same difference.' Stonor grinned, a man enjoying himself for all he was worth. From what he told me some weeks back, in recent years he'd led a pent-up kind of existence, so I was glad to see him having such a good time. And even gladder to know that Maggie would not be upstairs in the attic with me, monitoring my movements.

When I got upstairs, the attic appeared not to have been touched since I was last there, except for the strangely clean, dust-free atmosphere. What exactly was I looking for? What fictional object should I come up with, were anyone to question me? But this time I wouldn't have to skulk behind the racks of dresses: I could breathe freely, since I had permission to be there, even if fraudulently obtained.

I looked carefully around. Where should I start? I opened the trunk which had contained the photograph albums and removed a couple. There were two or three yellow Kodak wallets sitting haphazardly on top, and I started with those.

I got a shock. The first one contained snaps of my sister, bundled up in winter clothes, flanked by various combinations of the three boys. They were wearing winter coats and scarves in the first few photographs, and Sabine wore a woolly hat which I recognized with a wrench as one I'd given her when she first went off to Edinburgh. The wintry landscapes behind them were recognizably those visible from the front windows of the Weston Lodge Hotel. There were some interior shots: the three boys posed in front of the Christmas tree in the hall; the two sons of the house with their parents; Sabine with the children leaning into her, laughing, with Redmayne and the Hon Clio standing behind them, hands on their shoulders. I'd seen many shots of Clio in the past, though usually they used a stock photograph, as they always did for the Moors Murderers. The one in my hand was the only one where she looked remotely relaxed, even cheerful. I felt a sudden pang for the woman. I'd heard more than once of her complete lack of parenting skills, but here she seemed like any normal mother posed with her family around her, all of them anticipating Christmas.

The place was thick with candles and holly, wreaths of ivy, bunches of mistletoe. Branches of pine lay all along the mantelpiece and on the window sills. Sabine had done all that. In one of

205

the snaps, the big Christmas tree stood against the carved banisters, lights twinkling, presents piled beneath it. And here was the family again, this time with my sister snuggled among them, presumably taken by Gavin since he wasn't in the shot.

Which led me to believe that this must have been only a day or two before the murders took place, after Jill the housekeeper had gone home to Manchester, otherwise they would surely have called her in to join in. Or so I deduced. The poignancy of it made my eyes wet. All having such fun, and none of them with the slightest inkling that all of them, in their various ways, were on a countdown to doom.

I put the photo wallets at the top of the stairs, ready to take them down to my bedroom for a closer examination. The under-eave storage with the small brass handles was the place I really wanted to investigate, but first I turned round the canvases stacked again the pine panelling. There must have been an unusually large number of Scandinavian paintings in the house, if what I'd been told was correct. Clio had accused her brother Piers of stealing a lot of her paintings; the burglarizing murderer who'd killed him had made off with a load of Danish paintings which must have been the ones her brother had taken. And now here were half a dozen more. Including a painting by the Danish Janus La Cour, which I'd never seen anywhere, had never even seen reproduced. *The painter of silence*, they called him, because of the tranquillity which pervades his works.

Strange . . . Were they the same paintings Clio claimed had been taken? And if so, how had they found their way back here? But it was years ago, and I hadn't been around: it was perfectly possible that they'd been recovered and returned to the family home of the man murdered in the execution of the robbery.

I stood with puckered brow in the middle of the huge attic, thinking that there was a piece of this complicated jigsaw that it would be more than useful to locate, and that was Clio's first husband, father of her two sons. The man who had not only produced – or designed – the stained glass window in the little Palliser chapel, but had also sculpted that formidable image above the lintel. Cronus, the Green Man, Sir Gerald Palliser . . . whichever, it was a powerful piece of work.

And somewhere in the depths of my befuddled brain, I had a faint memory of seeing work very like it, and not all that long ago. I must try and dredge the information up, I thought. But meanwhile, I wanted to tackle the under-eave storage. I shifted some of the canvases leaning against the low wall and tugged at the nearest brass handle. The door opened easily, and I gazed in dismay at the jumble of objects which had been thrust inside. There was very little floor space; by the time I'd gradually removed everything from the triangular space and piled it up on the floorboards, I'd need to learn to levitate in order get about the room. Carefully, terrified of knocking some priceless *objet* to the floor or irreparably damaging a *bibelot*, I started on the job.

I was looking for something, but until I found it, I had no idea what it might be, even if it existed. Or, if it did, whether it was in this attic. I carefully examined each object I hoicked out of the storage space and found I was mostly looking at more of the same stuff that already stood packed around the room, though on a smaller scale.

No furniture, no dresses, no more canvases, no rocking horses. But plenty more boxes of glasses. Venetian ones, for instance, with elaborate stems and delicate gold tracery on the bowls. More gorgeous antique porcelain. A carton of leather boots. A box of skates. Fur stoles and what I believe were called tippets. More boxes of papers. And more. A treasure trove for Maggie, maybe, but not for me. Folded linen, thick and heavy and going yellow along the creases. All the detritus of generations of family life.

Stop, I told myself. Stop dithering around and be logical. What is it you really hope to find? The answer, when I'd sat down on one of the brocade-covered armchairs and closed my eyes, was some hint as to the whereabouts or identity of the art student. In my heart of hearts, I knew that my searching was a waste of time, that the whole matter was done and dusted, had been for years. Clio had killed her sons and my sister, and that's all there was to it.

And yet, and yet . . .

I flicked through the photo albums again, hoping to find pictures of a younger Clio. A wedding album. Family fun with the two baby boys, before the husband ran off. I didn't find that; instead I was looking at Oxford days, spires against the sky, undergraduates in overloaded punts, bridges across willowed rivers, more students capped and gowned, an unmistakable Clio cuddled up to a man I easily recognized as a young Fingal Adair, more snapshots showing Maggie and Clio and Fin, the three of them dressed for a ball in long gowns and white tie, groups of students waving wine bottles at the camera, groups of them making silly faces.

This was a family which kept records, and surely the logical progression from university life would be the sober stuff of marriage and children. But there was nothing. I thought there might have been christening photographs, children's birthday parties, first day at school: all the fond and silly events that parents like to record. I was willing to bet that the significant milestones in Gavin's life had been recorded, as had mine. But there was nothing here.

Perhaps there were other albums elsewhere. Or – if they even existed – perhaps Redmayne had got rid of them, horrible reminders of what had once been. Carefully, I stowed them back in the trunk. The single wallet with pictures of Sabine I would keep. I was owed those snaps.

Back in my room, I brought out my precious cache of Sabine's final letters. I hadn't looked at them on my return to London. They were too poignant, almost too uncomfortable to read; it was like having second sight, knowing as I did that three lives were about to be snuffed out. The one I picked at random was dated about ten days before she was murdered.

Hi, Babes:

I've got half an hour, so I thought I'd write to you. Once those boys are home, I doubt if I'll have much time for setting pen to paper . . .

Today Clio summoned me to her study. I knocked at the door, and when she let me in, I could hardly believe my eyes! You can't imagine more of a contrast with the rest of the house. Her room is at the back, very large, with big arched windows, all painted pure white, except for one wall which is shocking pink and has a pink velvet sofa pushed up against it. There's a stunning abstract painting hanging above it, all patches of gorgeous colour, by <u>Howard Hodgkin</u>, if you've heard of him. And even if you haven't, I have to say I could hardly believe my eyes. The floor was polished wood, absolutely bare except for a gorgeous rug which she said had been specially woven for her in Skye, beautiful swirls of rose and violet and blue and magenta, with just a touch here and there of a kind of acid green, which reflected the painting. There's another sofa, big enough to sleep on, and lots of white-painted bookshelves with two or three pieces of ceramic art-ware. And a couple more paintings, one of them a Hockney, no less! David Hockney!!!! Unbelievable! The other was also rather gorgeous, by someone called Laura Knight, a woman standing at a window,

210

looking down at the sea. Dame Laura Knight, to you.

Outside are these fabulous views of the open countryside spreading for miles into the distance: hills and lines of willows along streams and rivers, and the odd church spire peeping out of the greenery, some roofs, furrowed fields – you know the sort of thing.

It's an absolutely stunning room, especially given the traditional look of the rest of the place. I suppose it reflects the real Clio, since she must have chosen it all herself, rather than the inherited persona she's been carrying around all her life, along with the burden of being in charge of part of England's heritage, when all she really wanted was to be an academic and lead an uninterrupted life in the ivory towers of some prestigious university or other. At least, that's how I read her.

She's a strange woman, slightly hysterical, very nervous when interacting with other people, finds it hard to meet your eye. Anyway, she says she's absolutely up to her ears in work, and she can't believe Christmas is only a week away and it's going to drastically upset her schedule, and she's getting absolutely frantic but it's not fair to the children, let alone her husband, not to make it wonderful for them, mistletoe and holly, all that jazz, and the upshot is, if I would take over all

211

*responsibilities for it – pretend it's my
home and my children, sort of thing – she
would give me free rein to decorate etc
etc (she showed me an album with photographs of the way the Lodge has been
decorated in the past, and notes made by
housekeepers in the glory days, and gave
me lists of local suppliers of turkeys and
vegetables and handmade Christmas puds
etc etc) and – get this! – she'd double my
salary into the bargain! Well, you can't
say fairer than that, can you? It was an
offer I had no intention of refusing.*

*The boys come home tomorrow for the
Christmas hols. I'm really looking forward
to meeting them.*

What fun it will be.

*Your Big Excited Sister . . . no, make
that Your Excited Big Sister.*

I was snuggled under the covers when the telephone rang beside my bed. It was Gavin.

'How's it going, sweets?' he said.

'Not well.'

'In what way?'

'I can't seem to find a focus.'

'Just focus on me.'

I smiled. 'Always.'

'You know I love you, don't you? And that I
think you're mad.'

'Why?'

'What do you think you're going to find down
there, especially after all this time? Evidence that
Clio Palliser didn't commit those murders?'

212

'I guess.'

'There's absolutely no indication that anyone else at all could have done it, Chantal.'

'Yes, but just suppose someone *did*?'

'I still don't understand why you think that the verdict of the court was wrong.'

'It's not that,' I said. 'That's not the *point*.'

'So what *is* the point?'

'I don't exactly know.'

'Darling Chantal, when are you going to drop it and let the two of us get on with our lives? Because until we can put it behind us, we're not going to be able to do that.'

'I know, I know. It's just . . .'

'It's just *what*?'

Again I said, 'I don't know.'

There was sigh from the other end of the line. 'Ever since I met you, and we talked about it all and I finally got it off my chest, I've honestly felt like someone who's been let out of prison. Or released from a cage. I so much don't want to go back to those dark places again.' There was a pleading note in his voice. 'Please, Chantal. Can't you drop it?'

He was right, of course. Or was he? 'Gavin,' I said, 'I'm convinced that there's more to all this than we realize.'

He sighed again. Louder this time. Irritably.

'Thing is, I was like you,' I said. 'I thought I knew exactly what had happened.'

'But I was there,' he said. 'I *know* what happened.'

'You didn't actually see Clio committing the murders, did you?'

He drew in a hissing exasperated breath.

I rushed on before he could say anything. 'And it's quite possible that if I did find the missing piece of the jigsaw—'

'If there is one.'

'—it won't alter anything. Everything will still point straight at the Honourable Clio as the culprit. But until I can be sure – and I know, I know . . . until that weekend back in the spring, I was absolutely sure – I feel this stupid urge to investigate further. Especially since Brian Stonor feels much the same way. Do you understand?'

'No,' he said sulkily. 'And anyway, what's it got to do with Stonor?'

'Well, you know he always said he had what he called a niggle.'

'A niggle? Not another stupid word like that Mingle thing we had to attend before, I hope.'

We both laughed. 'No,' I said. 'It was sort of a feeling he had at the time that there was something wrong. That he and his colleagues might have overlooked something, or hadn't probed deeply enough.'

'I never heard about that.'

'It's what he told me. And the more I look into it all, the sadder poor Clio's life turns out to be.'

'Oh come on, Chantal. Lots of people have had sad lives. It doesn't give them the licence to go round knifing people.'

I felt an urge to justify myself. 'Remember Jennifer Forshawe?'

'Who?'

'Lady Forshawe. From Byfield Hall. More or less next door.'

'Good heavens, yes. A terrifying old biddy, she was. Not that she could have been old enough back then when I was spending the hols with the Pallisers. You'd have to be a certain age to be classed as an "old biddy", I should think.'

'Like what? Anything over twenty would have seemed ancient to boys of your age.'

'Whatever age she was, she'd have been fearsome. Very imposing, very commanding. Attila the Hun would have run screaming in the opposite direction if she'd come anywhere near him.'

'That's more or less what her husband told me.'

'He'd know, wouldn't he? She used to march into the Lodge and start bossing everyone about, telling them what they should be doing – which was never what they *were* doing – and ordering everyone around. She'd get horribly angry, too, if we didn't do what she said. Edward told her once that it wasn't her house, it was his, and she clouted him round the head so hard that he fell down and almost knocked himself out. Told him not to be so impudent.'

'Well, the point is that there's a faint possibility that she was responsible for it all.'

'*What*?'

'Sounds bizarre, doesn't it? Especially after all this time. But I went over to see Lord Forshawe and he came up with this scenario. Off his own bat, I may say, though he implied he was just doing it for the intellectual exercise. Jenny takes the dogs for a walk, as she so often did, decides she'll drop in at Weston to get back some picture she'd lent to Clio—'

'It was a rather rude picture, as I remember. A

little girl showing her underwear and some horrible old voyeur spying on her in the corner.'

'Anyway, she comes in, intending to take the picture back with her to Byfield Hall, sees that someone's scrawled a swear word all over it, knows it must be the boys, loses her cool, grabs a weapon – a paperknife or something – and races upstairs to start laying about her.'

Gavin was silent for a moment. 'I suppose that's a perfectly possible version of events. Only thing is, I'm certain the boys wouldn't have done anything like that. I mean, I know they could be a bit wicked, but they'd been taught a healthy respect for art. I remember Georgie once getting hold of a Magic Marker and drawing pubic hair on one of the marble statues that stood about everywhere. Edward made him clean it off pretty smartish, I can tell you.'

'Well, all I'm saying is that it was Forshawe himself who suggested this theoretical possibility. And *someone* scrawled rude words on the Balthus.'

'Strange. Almost as if he thought maybe she *did* do it.'

'That's exactly why I came down here. To see if there actually *is* an alternative to it being Clio. After all, she never admitted it.'

'Nor did she deny it. Anyway, I think that's more than enough about Clio and everything. I want to hear how *you* are, my darling Chantal. Whether you're having fun – though how you could without me around, I don't know – and all stuff like that.' And our conversation moved into a more romantic mode.

216

When we'd finished talking, I lay back on my pillows with my hands behind my head, listening to the noise of an autumn evening. Poplar trees shivered and an owl hooted, so close to my open windows that I could hear the whirr of its wings.

Funny that Desmond Forshawe hadn't mentioned that it was the Balthus the boys were supposed to have defaced. Or was it? I knew that his mind wasn't anything like as woolly as he'd have me believe, but it was more than possible that after such a long time he genuinely didn't remember. And of course he might say that it was none of my business or, alternatively, whichever picture it was had no bearing on the case.

Did I really think anyone other than the Honourable Clio Palliser had killed my sister? If I was perfectly honest, no, I did not.

Thirteen

The next morning I woke early. Waiting for the kettle to boil, I looked out at frost sparkling in the hollows of the lawns below me, and the fields beyond them. Leaves whirled madly in what I knew would be a bitter wind. Winter coming on apace, then. After a childhood in California and Italy, I was not very keen on the cold. It had been the worst thing about Edinburgh, and London wasn't much better.

There were only three more of Sabine's letters left. One of them I'd never even looked at. I wasn't sure I ever would. The one I took out now seemed to follow the one I'd read last night, although it was missing the first page:

LATER:
It seems like there's a serpent in this Eden. And I think it might be called Harry. Or possibly Clio. He's never been anything but charming and kind to me, but I was up in my room, writing to you, and heard him screaming at the boys for some misde-meanour or other. I wasn't sure whether I should get involved or not but in the end went down and found them in the morning room, the boys looking defiant but tear-streaked, shouting that they didn't, they didn't, while Harry was the colour of an

aubergine, fists bunched, eyes mad with rage. He turned on me like a rabid dog, demanded to know what the hell I thought I was doing, bursting into his private room like that, meddling in family matters which were no concern of mine, called me an interfering bitch, if you please. He picked a bronze statuette off the table and actually lunged towards me as though he was going to hit me! I couldn't believe it! He seemed completely out of it.

And then Clio appeared and asked what on earth was going on and shooed the boys out of the room. I followed them as fast as I could, but not before I heard her shrieking at him, using horrible language, sounding as though she too was having hysterics.

Upstairs I asked George what had been going on, and he said that Harry had been having a fit because he'd found them drooling over some nude painting or other. All strategically placed vine leaves and arms hiding nipples: you know the kind of thing. I'd have thought better a bit of appreciative drooling than complete indifference, wouldn't you?

'Apparently it's ever so valuable,' Edward said, 'but we didn't touch it or anything.'

'Yeah,' said his brother. 'Like we care about his beastly pictures.'

'But we'd never touch them,' Edward said. 'Not any more.'

'We know better than to do that, in case he flies into a tantrum.'

219

'Which he does all the time,' Gavin added.

'Scareee!' they said together, as though it was funny. But I'm not sure it was.

LATER STILL: Clio came up to my room when the boys had gone to bed, and apologized on Harry's behalf. Said he was a bit stressed at the moment as he's working terribly hard on some important project or other. I wonder how often she has to make excuses for him. She brought a bottle of Cointreau with her, would you believe, and between us we drank about half of it. Got very girly and confessional: I had the distinct impression she's pretty fed up with Harry, wants rid of him – and frankly, if he pulls a stunt like tonight's very often, I can't blame her. Though this morning, he was terribly apologetic, said the boys had just been in the wrong place at the wrong time, and had caught the full brunt of his anger. Hmm, as Mom likes to say.

Jill says he's hardly ever like that: he's usually very calm and controlled, it's Clio that seems to lose it.

Oh dear, I'm beginning to wonder what exactly I've let myself in for.

Meanwhile, the boys and I have decorated the entire lower floor with all sorts of wonderful decorations. There were boxes and boxes of them up in the attics, some dating back to Clio's own childhood, according to Edward. I don't know *who's more excited about Christmas: them or me. Only two more days until Christmas Eve. Harry comes home early tomorrow for the hols, and the staff all go back to their own homes tonight, so I'll be the only one on duty. Also I'm supposed to be doing the cooking (hollow laugh . . . you know what I'm like in the kitchen. Mom's fault: she's such a brilliant cook) for four whole days. Not that there's much to do for Christmas Day, just some vegetables, really, because Jill's prepared everything and stuck it in the icebox or the freezer. She's made something called Cumberland rum butter, a kind of hard sauce to serve with the Christmas pudding, which has already been cooked, just needs to go into the oven with rum poured over it, to heat up, and the chestnut stuffing's just waiting to be pushed up the turkey's backside. Jill's made mincemeat tarts, too. The boys and Clio have been detailed to do the vegetables under* my *supervision – because she's so vague, she's just as likely to sprinkle sugar on the salad and salt on the rum butter, so really all I have to do is shove the turkey in the oven and supervise the laying of the table – will they use that Spode service . . .? Oh please, God, yes – while Harry deals with drinks etc.*

So for the next two days they're going to have to make do with my signature dish, i.e. pasta in a cheese sauce. No, I can do better than that, obviously, and the freezer's full of goodies. I don't think any of us is going to starve.

I've bought everybody presents and wrapped them. There's this ginormous Christmas tree in the hall, which the boys and I have decorated, and I've stowed my prezzies under it. There's already quite a pile – and some of them actually have my name on them!

But of course she never got to open them.

The attic was chilly. On my hands and knees, I peered into the storage area beneath the eaves, now empty after my exertions the evening before. There was a short discoloured cord just inside to the left, which I pulled, praying not only that it would not break, but also that some kind of light would come on. Which it did. A dim yellow forty-watt light, admittedly, but it gave a weak illumination to the wood-lined space.

I wished I had brought a torch, and debated crawling back out and going to my bedroom for the one I'd packed in my bag before leaving London. Ham had taught me always to carry a torch, because you never knew when you were going to need it. But once my eyes had adjusted to the gloom, I could see quite well. I edged deeper in, the slanted ceiling only a foot or so above my head, peering into the interstices of the roof beams as I passed them. I found nothing.

Miraculously, I was able to turn round at the far end and start crawling back. I had an irrational feeling that I should hurry, that any moment someone would come up the stairs after me and slam the door shut, incarcerating me in there until I died and gradually desiccated, flesh vanishing from my bones, no one around to hear my weakening cries as I slowly died of thirst and hunger. It always amazes me how rapidly the human brain can paint these scenarios of doom and disaster. And as I made my undignified way along the unpainted wooden floor, feeling splinters embed themselves in my knees and the balls of my thumbs, I saw the faintest of gleams wedged between two intersecting roof beams. And another one. And another. Awkwardly I balanced on one hand and reached up. A frame of some kind. Oval, barely visible, and then only to someone going towards the door, rather than away from it. I tugged and pulled and finally managed to extricate what I could immediately see was a valuable miniature, portraying a curly-haired suitor with ruffles down the front of his shirt, plucking half-heartedly at a stringed instrument of some kind. Hadn't Sabine mentioned this very one . . . a Hilliard? Excited now, I looked harder into the interstices, and saw another of the crammed-in frames, which proved to be a portrait of a young boy, ten or twelve years old, perhaps, with a floppy blue cravat tied round a loose white chemise. Looking closely, I could see that the edges of the frame had been lightly coated in some kind of dark covering: ink, soot, paint? *Blood?* I shuddered at the thought. Presumably this was to hide the tell-tale glimmer of gold.

In all, I discovered eight more miniatures and

had no doubt that there were more of them secreted somewhere among the beams and crevices of the attic. Having tidied the place up, and loosely returned most of the stuff which had been stashed under the eaves, I took the entire eight downstairs with me. Obviously I had no intention whatsoever of keeping them – *stealing* them – I merely wanted to examine them at my leisure, and compare them with the ones Sabine had mentioned. At first glance, it seemed pretty certain to me that, despite her limited descriptions, these were the very same ones which had been displayed in Harry Redmayne's study when she was living here. So how had they found their way up to the attic and been so very carefully hidden? Who could have been responsible for that? And why?

I thought back, trying to reconstruct what might have happened. The police were called, the bodies identified and removed, statements were taken, an arrest was made. After that, was the whole place sealed off as a crime scene? Brian Stonor was the one to ask.

'Yes,' he said, when we met in the bar before lunch. 'Once Clio Palliser had been carted away to the nick, I – as the least experienced of the detectives present – was detailed off to go upstairs with Mr Redmayne and keep an eye on him while he packed up some clothes and necessities. He was anxious about the valuable stuff around the place, and I told him that an inventory would be made as soon as the SOCOs had done their work, after which the place would have to be sealed up for the foreseeable future.'

224

'And he went along with it?'

'Didn't have much option. He tried to trouser a few bits and pieces, some silver things, and those little portraits you're talking about, miniatures, insisted they were his property, he had every right, etcetera, etcetera, but we wouldn't allow him to since at that point, for all we knew, almost anything in the house might have some bearing on the case, or be needed to provide evidence at the trial. Bear in mind that nobody actually saw Clio Palliser perpetrate the crime, and she herself wasn't saying yea or nay. So the whole house became a crime scene: yards of yellow tape, nobody allowed in or out except the police, a copper on guard at the front door. That went on for weeks: it was a slow old process back then – and it's even slower now, believe it or not.'

'Perhaps because they're more thorough now. Anyway, what happened after that?'

'Eventually, Redmayne was allowed back into the house in order to pack stuff up under police supervision and have it taken somewhere for safe storage. But of course a lot of it wasn't his, it belonged to the Pallisers, so he had no claim to it. And once that was done, he vanished into thin air, as far as I can make out.' He chortled. 'Though of course he can't have done, when you think about it. But I've tried to discover his whereabouts and come up with a complete blank.'

'Do you think he's dead?'

'Not him . . . Too much of a slippery customer, in my opinion. Not that I've ever heard anything against him. Bound to be alive somewhere.'

225

'So where do you think he went?'

'Changed his name, I should think. Set up shop in New York, or San Francisco. Or even somewhere in South America.'

I could see it so clearly: Redmayne managing by some means or other to stuff the miniatures in his pockets – and anything else portable – and then hiding them upstairs in the attics while the removal men went about their business. I was willing to bet that if you could find someone who'd remember, they'd tell you that he was wearing a gamekeeper's jacket or something similar. He wouldn't have dared walk out of the front door with the loot, in case some suspicious or overzealous policeman demanded to search him or his briefcase, but getting up to the attic would have been easy enough; he must have been very confident that he'd be able to get back into the house at some point and retrieve the stolen goods.

And somehow, he had been unable to do so. I wondered what had stopped him.

'The solicitors handling the estate insisted on putting in a sophisticated alarm system right away,' said Stonor, answering my unvoiced question. 'Actually, it was the insurance company rather than the solicitors. Connected to the local cop-shop, so a would-be thief would have to be quick about it. But it did mean that the house was kept relatively safe.'

'Until David Charteris chanced along.'

'Precisely.' Stonor swallowed some beer and looked down into his glass as though wondering where the contents had gone.

'Very interesting.'

I remembered Desmond Forshawe's odd expression, the first time I had visited him, when I mentioned the miniatures. 'Was anyone else allowed into the house?'

'The boy. Gavin. They let him in to pack up his kit, take his presents from under the tree, say goodbye to the staff. And the dogs. This was before his mother had arrived to collect him. She had to fly over from Nigeria, where the father was working, so he went to stay with some family friends until she got there. The same ones where he'd been to supper the day it all happened.'

'He must have been in a frightful state.'

'He was. Mental and physical. In fact, I'm not sure he didn't develop pneumonia; not surprising after spending the night out in the woods in just his underclothes.'

'Poor kid.' No wonder he had seemed so uneasy, being back here. It made it all the more strange that he should have come, but no more strange, I guess, than my own attendance.

'After that weekend,' Stonor said, following an entirely different train of thought, 'I looked Charteris up on the Internet. He'd made a killing on the stock market – I think it said he was a multimillionaire by the time he was thirty – and that's how come he had the wherewithal to buy the place and turn it into a hotel.'

'Nice work if you can get it. And from what Maggie Fields told me, he hasn't a clue what's in the house.'

'Or isn't, as the case may be.'

I was assessing all this information as best I

227

could, wondering what, if any, bearing it had on any of the matters I was concerned with. Probably none. 'And you never found any trace of either Harry Redmayne, or Clio Palliser, after she was let out of Broadmoor?'

'Not a sausage. Strange, really. You'd think by now that some enterprising investigative journalist might have tracked down one or other of them. It was a notorious case at the time. Remember that Mary Bell, who killed a couple of kids when she was about ten? They found her, didn't they? And that was many years later. Clio, at least, must still be alive, to have sold the house to David.'

'So both of them, either separately or together, have managed to hide their identities.' I shook my head. 'God, I'd love to know where they are.'

'Would you really, Chantal?'

'Yes. Of course.'

'What would you do with the information if you had it?' He finished his glass, leaving beer-foam hanging like lace around the inside of it. Then he said, as though he was Dad's echo, 'Why bother? It won't bring your sister back. Nor those poor kids.'

'*You're* still on the hunt for them.'

'That's because I want to be sure that justice was properly done.' He put his head on one side. 'That's not your motivation at all, is it?'

I considered the question. 'Originally, I just wanted to get as close as I possibly could to my sister for the last time.'

'I can understand that.'

'And then you came along. And all these red

herrings were swimming around – if indeed they *are* red herrings. And then the waters were muddied even further . . .'

'This is the same water the herrings were swimming in?'

We smiled at each other.

He patted my hand. 'Come on, girl. Maybe it's time to let go. To move on. Have another drink and relax.'

'Brian,' I said, grabbing his fingers, 'I'm really glad you came here with me.'

'So am I. And you know something? I'm going to take my own advice and move on. Nothing's going to change what happened in the past: it's the future which matters.'

'What happened to the notion of justice being properly done?'

He wrinkled his nose. 'I know. But Clio Palliser's out now, whether she did it or not. Perhaps the truth doesn't matter so much any more.'

'I know you don't believe that.'

He nodded at me. Winked. Said, 'Too true.'

'So what are we going to do tomorrow?'

'Go down to the pub around lunchtime, make some general enquiries, see if we can pick up anything new. The locals usually know a thing or two. Especially with several of them working up at the Big House.'

'Didn't you do that at the time?'

'Different culture back then. People kept themselves to themselves, to their own community, didn't talk to the police if they could help it.'

'OK, that's the plan.'

* * *

229

Before I went to bed, I walked down to the chapel in the grounds. Again, dusk was falling and the sky glowed gold and purple behind the little bell-tower. This time, the door was firmly shut; when I tried the wrought-iron handle, it didn't budge. I gazed up at the magisterial carving over the lintel, Cronus devouring his children, and again felt the stir of recognition. Surely I had seen work in this same style very recently. I had likened it to Eric Gill's carvings, last time I looked at it, but I knew I had not caught sight of Gill's work for many months.

A flare of excitement caught light inside my head. If I had seen work like this not long ago, and I knew that the shadowy art student had executed the one here at Weston, then I must be able to track him down.

We left the hotel at around twelve. Although the temperature was cool, the sky was blue, and the walk through late autumnal lanes, bounded by bare hedges to which the occasional scarlet and crimson leaf still clung, was pleasant. We followed the roads for a while, then turned on to a track which led to the back door of the Palliser Arms. Not surprisingly, nobody was sitting outside, but the beer-scented taprooms inside were crowded.

At the sight of Brian Stonor, at least a dozen voices called greetings. We stood pressed together while drinks were bought and smiles exchanged. He went into jovial mode, and I remembered that he had been brought up in these parts, probably even went to school with half of these people.

I was wondering how we were going to get on

to the subject of Clio Palliser and the killings, when a woman pushed her way through the crowd towards me.

'I know you from somewhere, don't I?' she said.

'I don't think so.'

'I'm Linda Windrow. I'm sure we've met—' Her eyes widened. 'Hang about. I know who you must be. That poor girl's sister. Sabine Somebody. You're the spit and image of her.'

In my judgement, she'd already had at least two large sherries before the one she was currently in the middle of. But I wasn't counting. Besides, alcohol was a known tongue-loosener, which could be all to the good.

'That's right,' I said. 'My sister mentioned you in her letters home.'

'That was a nasty business,' Linda said. 'Really nasty. And your sister was such a nice little thing. Should never have happened, to my way of thinking.'

Three men got up from a table nearby, and I sat down on one of the vacated chairs. 'Why don't we sit down,' I said. 'And can I get you another of those?'

'That's good of you, love.' She turned and gestured at the man behind the bar, who was watching me with unconcealed curiosity.

'Why do you say that . . .? What shouldn't have happened?' I said.

'Oh, everyone knew Clio Palliser was a bomb waiting to explode. Nutty as a fruitcake, in my opinion.' She finished her sherry and picked up the new one which had arrived. 'And she hated

231

Christmas and all that malarkey. Couldn't be doing with it. Can't say I'm all that thrilled about it myself, too commercial these days, but you have to think of the kids, don't you?'

I nodded. 'So you weren't surprised when . . .' I lifted my shoulders.

She knew what I meant. 'Surprised, yes. I mean it was bloody terrible, pardon the pun, those boys killed like that. And your sister. But Clio was like a pressure cooker, and Christmas just wasn't her scene. I think that's why she hired your sister, to relieve the stress, not that it seems to have worked. But we all knew something dreadful would happen sooner or later. Not *that* dreadful, but . . .' She paused thoughtfully. 'Should have been in the loony-bin, if you ask me.'

'And I suppose you're absolutely sure it was her who did it?'

Linda stared at me, astonished. 'Not *her*? 'Course it was her. 'Course it was.' Another pause. 'Besides, who else could it have been?'

'I don't know.'

She patted my knee. 'How could you know? You weren't even there, were you?'

'I seem to remember someone mentioning one of the neighbours,' I said, deliberately naive. 'Some woman who lived up the road, a bit hot-tempered? Lady Something?'

'That'd be old Jenny Forshawe. Blimey, never mind hot-tempered, that one had a tongue on her that made sandpaper look soft. Used to walk in and out of the house as if she owned it, and anyone doing something she didn't approve of, or not doing it the way she thought it should be done, *wham*!'

I pretended shock and surprise. 'You mean, she'd barge into someone's else house and *hit* people?'

'Not quite. The boys, she didn't mind giving them what for, but us staff . . . she drew the line there, knew what the reaction would be if she didn't. But that didn't stop her tearing a strip off us, and no mistake.'

'Didn't Mr Redmayne object? Or Mrs Palliser?'

'Most of the time, he was up in London, so he didn't know how she acted. And Mrs P couldn't have given a damn, long as nobody disturbed her.'

'Goodness.'

'I remember Jill – that was the housekeeper – standing up to her, saying she had no right to come in and hit defenceless children, and Mrs Forshawe really having a go at her, saying Clio Palliser needed to be looked after because she wasn't the same as other people, and in any case, it wasn't Jill's place to be telling *her*, Lady Know-it-all Forshawe, what to do.'

'What happened then?'

'Jill said in any case it was wrong of her to be disciplining someone else's children, and that they might be a bit mischievous, but they were good boys on the whole, and didn't deserve to be knocked around.' She shuddered dramatically. 'She was a horrible woman. My husband used to say she was evil, really evil.'

'So do you think she could have been the murderer, and not Mrs Palliser at all?'

'Here. What is this? Are you some kind of journalist? Or one of them whatyoumacallits, cold-case detectives, like in that series on telly?'

233

'Neither of those things. Just someone wanting to know what happened to her sister, and whether the right person got blamed for it.'

Linda sighed deeply and stared into the bottom of her empty glass. Above her head, I signalled for another. 'You said they were good boys,' I said.

'Oh, they were. Could be a bit naughty, especially that Georgie. But I put it down to their mum. Distant kind of woman. Nothing warm about her. I mean, I've two boys myself, never stop giving them hugs and kisses, even now they're grown-up. My two sometimes played with the lads up at the Lodge, and even when they was kids they thought it was kind of funny that Mrs Palliser never seemed to have anything to do with her children.' She paused. Shook her head. 'Had that room of hers soundproofed, can you believe it? So she couldn't hear any noise! I never heard of that in my life, a mum who – what's the word? – barricaded herself away from her own kids.'

'Your sons got on well with the Pallisers, did they?'

'Very. They was kind kids . . . See, my Danny has a health problem, can't walk or run very well. But they never let it make any difference, always included him in their games, where they could. And Sammy, he was a bit sickly as a child – right as rain now – but they never teased him nor nothing. Not like at school.' Again she paused. 'No, they were nice kids – all three of them. There was this third boy, used to spend the holidays at the Lodge, parents worked abroad, so he didn't get to see them very often, but he was just like part of the family.'

I could see Stonor among his cronies, where a lot of loud guffawing and backslapping was going on.

'It's all so interesting.'

'You know,' she said, 'in all these years, it's never occurred to me that it could have been anyone but Clio who was responsible. Mind you, Leslie – that's Leslie Harris, used to work up at the Lodge with me – always used to say there was something a bit funny about it. Can't remember what it was exactly at the moment, it was years ago.'

I felt a rush of excitement. 'How can I get hold of Leslie?'

'You'd have to sprout a pair of wings and fly up to heaven!' Linda's guffaw matched any of those at the bar. 'She passed on five years ago now, breast cancer, very sad it was.'

Damn, I thought, sparing no more than a passing thought for poor Leslie. 'That's a—'

Pursuing her own train of thought, Linda didn't hear me. 'But now you ask me, I'm seriously beginning to wonder whether there's been a whatyoumacallit, a miscourage of jastuss. Misc . . . you know what I mean.'

'You think it's possible, then? That it wasn't Clio Palliser at all?'

'But if it *wasn't* her, why didn't she speak up? Why go to prison for something she never done in the first place? I certainly wouldn't.'

'The difficulty about it *not* being her is who in the world would kill two children?'

'There is that . . .'

'Nobody else could have done it. I mean, why would they?' I floated this like a fly landing lightly on the sea of sherry she had consumed.

'If you watch them telly programmes, there's always someone in the background who's got it in for someone else, isn't there? Maybe someone was after your sister and them poor kids just got in the way. Or someone wanted to get at Mrs Palliser.'

Amazingly, it had never occurred to me that the boys might have been murdered to injure Clio. I'd assumed that the defaced painting – the Balthus, as I now knew – was at the heart of the matter. And maybe it still was. It was perfectly possible that the rude message scrawled across the canvas was a nose-thumb at Lady Forshawe. To imagine some kind of revenge was at work seemed drastic in the extreme, I know, but you only have to read the tabloids to see how twisted the human mind can be.

'I guess so,' I said doubtfully. Would the fish bite? 'Someone you'd never think of,' I agreed. 'But of course I wouldn't know, I wasn't there . . .'

'I was.' She looked back down the years. 'There was always arguments going on in that house, mind you. Mr Redmayne, Mrs Palliser – I suppose she was really Mrs Redmayne, but everyone always called her Palliser – Jill the housekeeper. Bit of a temper she had. Didn't stand any nonsense from anyone.'

'What did they argue about?'

'Anything. Everything.' Linda suppressed a hiccup.

I knew that Jill had been up in Manchester with her family at the time of the murders, and it seemed too far out to be tenable to imagine her travelling back in order to get even with Clio Palliser over some quarrel, when she would have had plenty of opportunity when she returned from her Christmas vacation. 'Anyone else?'

'There was Trev Barnard, of course. We always used to think he was a bit sweet on Mrs P. But it couldn't have been him.' She finished the last of her sherry. 'There was my Neil, too. Gardener, he was, up at the Lodge. Clio was always putting him down, finding fault . . . but he didn't take it too seriously. That's just the way she was. Gawd . . .' Her somewhat unfocused gaze caught on to mine. 'You don't think? . . . Nah . . . The police took statements from everyone and nearly all of us were, whatdyamacallit, *vouched* for by everyone else.'

'Including Trevor Barnard?'

'Dunno about him. Funny: I'm still trying to get my head round her going along with it, if it wasn't her at all.'

'Maybe she didn't see much point trying to defend herself.'

'Well, I never. I'll have to talk to my Neil about this.'

Stonor was raising his eyebrows at me, ready to extricate himself from the crowd of his acquaintances. 'I have to go now,' I said, rising to my feet. 'I'm staying at the Lodge tonight, so if you come up with something, do please let me know. Or if you remember anything Leslie said about it.'

'I will indeed. Well, who'd have thought . . .'

I could see her brain whirring, rethinking all her previous assumptions, or at least giving them an alternative perspective. 'Thank you so much for talking to me, Mrs Windrow. You can't imagine how hard it was for my family, so far away in California and never really knowing anything about what happened. My dad came over, of course, but my mom couldn't face it. In fact, it more or less killed her.' I could feel myself going red, angry all over again at the killer who had taken my mother's life as well as my sister's.

'You poor thing.' Briefly, she touched my hand. 'I promise if we come up with anything, Neil and me, we'll send a message up to the Lodge.'

But Stonor was pulling at my arm, looking at his watch, saying we needed to get a move on if we were going to get back in time for lunch.

I still had time for another of Sabine's letters:

Hello, Babe:

Just a quickie . . .

The boys are getting more and more excited about Christmas, behaving like jumping beans or performing fleas . . . Take your pick, they do both! We drove down to the town this morning and I had a pot of tea and a scone in the café while they zoomed about from shop to shop, looking for presents. Just like you and I used to do.

They were still manic after lunch, so I

238

*took them out for a walk late this after-
noon. We went down to the edge of the
property; there's a pond – the boys called
it a lake, told me in the summer holidays
they have mock battles on the water,
pretending to be Nelson or Sir Francis
Drake, getting soaking wet. It's surrounded
by reeds and bulrushes, all rather dead-
looking now, but I can imagine it's very
romantic on a moonlit night. And they
showed me a secret place where they're
not supposed to go because it's dangerous.
A well, which they said goes down for
hundreds of feet, and there's all sorts of
things down there, including a couple of
their ancestors, if you can imagine! Sir
Humphrey, they said, who was their about
twenty-Greats Grandfather and was a
terrible drunk: he apparently fell in and
nobody heard him yelling for help, and
because they couldn't find him, he died
of cold, not drowning, because the water
is only about four feet deep. Actually, it
is a bit dangerous since once you move
the heavy wooden cover there's only a
very low wall around the edge, and
although they were having fun throwing
stones down to hear the splash, I hurried
them away. Wouldn't want them joining
their ancestor down there on my watch!
But I took photos of us all (enclosed) so
you can see them and a bit of the house
etc.*

Fourteen

'Strange thing is, none of them seemed a bit surprised that we were even asking whether there was any alternative to it being Clio,' Stonor said. At least, I think that's what he said. He was shovelling roast beef and Yorkshire pud into his mouth as he spoke, and speaking through it, severely hampering audibility.

'Linda Windrow said that everyone knew sooner or later there'd be some kind of a huge blow-up at the Lodge, but she didn't elaborate on why. Just said there was always some quarrel or other going on. And Clio was like a pressure cooker.'

'But the lads in the bar said they never really believed it was her. Mad as a March Hare was the general verdict, but not a murderess. And some of them had known her since she was a child.'

'Linda Windrow certainly seemed to like Jennifer Forshawe for it.' I considered my words and then amended them. 'The possibility of it being her, I mean.'

'My mates in the pub's money was on Redmayne himself,' said Stonor. 'And if not him, then Trevor Barnard. And if not him, then some guy who appeared to be hanging round the house. Lurking, according to Neil Windrow. Definitely lurking.'

'It makes absolutely no sense,' I said.

'Maybe he was after your sister. Ever thought of that?'

'The only person interested my sister was that Scotsman who was at the weekend we came to before. Malcolm Macdonald, the one in the kilt.'

'Maybe some pervo saw her and decided to try his chances.'

'Come on, Brian. Get real. He sees Sabine, somehow gets into the house, climbs up the stairs, murders a boy and then my sister and then another boy and then goes on his merry way? I don't think so.'

'Doesn't sound likely, put like that.' Stonor speared another roast potato from the dish in front of him and cut it in half.

An idea came to me. 'This lurking guy: it couldn't have been the missing first husband, could it?'

'Could easily have been. Casing the joint, so to speak, before making himself known.'

'Why would he suddenly come back after all these years away?'

Stonor shrugged. 'Who knows? Maybe because it's Christmas time, shops full of it, newspapers, magazines, and he gets all nostalgic, thinking about the little lads he abandoned before they were even old enough to know him.'

'So he goes up the drive, bangs at the knocker. Then what?'

'The Honourable Clio opens up and in he goes, shouting, "Guess who! Surprise, surprise!" and she tells him to fuck off, excuse my French, kicks him out of the house and slams the door in his face.'

'And that makes him so mad that he decides to break in and kill his own sons? Doesn't sound hugely likely to me. Why on earth would he do that?'

'Why does anybody kill anybody?' Brian asked tiredly. 'God, I've seen so many of these point-less murders in my time. Innocent people simply trying to live their lives as best they can, and some bastard with an inflated ego or high on something or drunk or angry with the way his own life has ended up decides to take them out. Don't ask me why, or what good it does. Simply means that they'll be spending the best part of the next twenty years behind bars.'

'We've come up with several different possible culprits,' I said. 'By the way, I think we can rule out the Windrow boys since they had physical problems of various kinds at the time, quite apart from the fact that they were kids themselves, and friends with the two boys. Plus the third one. Gavin. Is there anyone we've left out?'

'I'm starting to think about the lord, actually.'

'Getting that old time religion, Stonor?'

His smile was dutiful. 'Desmond Forshawe. If his wife could have done it, so equally could he.'

'Except she was known for her foul temper. And there was the painting the boys had damaged. And he seems as mild as milk. What would his excuse be?'

As the waiters cleared away our plates, Stonor propped his elbows on the table and rested his head in his hands.

'A question,' I said quickly, before he could

flat out refuse to answer any more. 'Why didn't the police come up with some of these scenarios at the time?'

'Partly because when we checked the alibis, they all seemed to hang together. But mostly because my superior officer refused to look beyond what was in front of his eyes.'

'OK. A final question: the murder weapon. I've never heard anything about it.'

'That's because we never found it. We decided that she'd had about two hours between the murders and the husband coming home in which to dispose of it. Which presumably is what she did. But short of digging up the entire estate, we didn't even know where to start looking. No suspicious piles of newly turned earth. Nothing in the ashes of the boiler or the fire in the hearth. Nothing hidden anywhere in the house – at least, not as far as we could see. We dragged that little lake, of course, but didn't find anything except a long-dead dog.'

I thought about the well Sabine had mentioned. 'Did you go down the well?'

'Didn't even know there was a well.'

'Doesn't sound like the police were all that conscientious.'

'You're right. Look, I'm beginning to get awfully tired of talking about all this.'

'You were the one who brought it up right at the beginning.'

He seemed weary. 'I don't think my brain is firing on all cylinders today.'

'Too much beer last night with Maggie Fields?'

He stared at me, gooseberry-eyed. 'Actually, I

remember the well. But it had this heavy wooden lid over it, and my guv'nor decided she couldn't possibly have shifted it.'

'Tell me about Trevor Barnard's house . . . Anything there?'

'Nothing that I could see. Some nice old country furniture, nice pictures on the walls, nice bachelor quarters, but it reminded me of my own place . . . Needs a woman's touch, if you know what I mean.'

'I hate to say that I do.' As if a man couldn't find a duster or pick some flowers. 'Anyway, let's not even think about it for the rest of the afternoon,' I said. 'I'm fed up with it myself. Too much speculation and no facts whatsoever.'

'Plus the strong possibility that there never was anyone else except Clio Palliser, as they said all along.'

'You're absolutely right, Brian.' I stood up. I bent towards him and stared straight into his somewhat bleary eyes. 'Just don't forget the niggle.'

After lunch, I went for a walk. I still had the miniatures in my room and wasn't sure what the best thing was to do with them. I could give them to David Charteris, who had after all given me permission to root around in the attic, though he might well have wondered how far the term rooting extended if I explained that I found them under the eaves.

The same was true of Maggie, though it would be easier to fudge it with her, make it appear that I'd been permitted to dig deep and wide in my search for these non-existent possessions of my sister's.

Or I could simply put them back where I found them. By the time I had returned to the hotel, I had decided that this was the simplest tactic. Accordingly, I gathered the pretty objects together and took a last look at them. How I wanted to abandon all my moral instincts and give way to a deeper more basic instinct: to steal one of them and keep it for my own. The thought of putting them back into their hiding place amongst the dusty interstices of the beams was physically painful. If I were to keep one, which one would it be? The child in a bonnet? The languid guitar player surrounded by eglantines? Or the dark-haired gentleman pressing a slender, calf-bound book against his heart with one delicate hand, his fine lace collar brushed by a goatee beard, his eyes soft but challenging?

I'm not ashamed to admit that my hand hovered over him for a moment. Unfortunately, when they were rediscovered, there were several people who might realize that one was gone, probably even which one. Eventually, I took them back up the attic stairs and carefully placed them among the silk petticoats in one of the trunks.

It was as I straightened up that I saw a small gilt-rimmed dish which had been obscured by a box of serving platters. I was very familiar with the plate: it had belonged to my French grand-mother and been handed on to Sabine by my mother. Hand-painted flowers decorated the rim; in the centre was an oval of gold leaves surrounding an ornamental letter S. My grandmother's name was Simone, my mother was called Sylvie. This I could take without the slightest twinge of conscience. I picked it up and went downstairs to the main hall to find David.

'I found this,' I told him. 'It was my sister's.'

'Then of course you must have it,' he said. 'It was obviously packed away in error.'

'I can't believe it's survived all this time. It means such a lot to me.' I held it to my chest. 'You can't imagine how delighted I am to have this back.'

He smiled benevolently. 'And I'm delighted for you.'

Fifteen

A couple of days later, I came up out of the Tube at Bond Street to see a poster advertising a mixed-media exhibition of contemporary Commonwealth artists at the Hayward Gallery. A pair of complimentary tickets for the same exhibition was sitting on my desk when I reached Chauncey's, and I could see Lorna raising expectant eyebrows at me as I picked them up.

'Wanna go?' she called.

'Sounds interesting.'

'Actually, darling, I'm not sure it does, but anything to get out of this dump.'

So in the lunch hour we took a taxi to the Festival Hall site. There was a stream of people going in, and the galleries were full of a jostling crowd.

'I'd no idea there was so much general interest,' said Lorna. 'Look, if we get separated, meet up at the front in a couple of hours.'

'Long lunch hour,' I remarked.

'Don't know about you, darling, but I look on this as work.'

'There is that.'

Of course we got separated, Lorna being a much more impatient soul than I am. And then meeting up with a group of three people she knew, pausing to chat while I moved on, taking my time. I passed from a gallery of paintings to another containing sculptures and carvings, bronzes set on plinths in the middle of the room, a large irregular piece of granite incised with an intricate frieze, carved stone plaques on the wall.

Even from across the room, one piece in particular caught my attention. The exhibition catalogue told me the piece was called 'Goddess', but I could think of a name which would have been far more apt. The face was unmistakably that of Clio Palliser; the artist was Paul Ferris, who lived outside Brisbane, Australia and, according to the catalogue, had several other pieces on show at the exhibition.

I was suddenly hugely excited. Paul Ferris: the man who must have carved the Cronus face, the man who must almost certainly have been the missing art student formerly known as Jarvis. The one with a name that had reminded me of a fairground. Had I finally stumbled on one of the last missing pieces of the Weston Lodge jigsaw puzzle? I made my way to the reception desk, showed them my Chauncey's business card and asked how I could contact Paul Ferris.

'Well,' the receptionist, an upbeat woman with a strong Australian accent, said brightly, 'he's here in London at the moment, staying with rellies.' She looked down at my card again. 'Look, there's a reception for the artists here this afternoon at three o'clock? Why don't I issue you with an invitation, then you could catch up with him there?'

She rootled around in her desk and brought out a deckle-edged invitation. 'I'm sure we sent at least three to Chauncey's . . .'

'Probably snapped up by the big boys,' I said.

'Isn't that always the way?' She wrote my name and workplace on the invitation-card and handed it over. 'See you at three. Meanwhile, enjoy the rest of the exhibition.'

'Thanks very much.'

I went back to the main entrance but there was no sign of Lorna, so I spent the intervening time looking at the stuff on display. In particular, the three other pieces by Paul Ferris. He seemed a little fixated on Greek mythology: there was a Gaia, a Poseidon and a Narcissus, all executed in the same solid style. They reminded me very much of the *moai* on Easter Island, but given that the two pieces of his work I already knew about were far more contemporary, I was fairly sure that the faces of these gods would prove to be disguised portraits of people in Ferris's life.

At fifteen minutes past three, I returned to the entrance but Lorna was still nowhere to be seen. By now, I felt I'd discharged any obligation to her and made my way to the room where already there was the sound of animated conversation. My invitation was accepted without question, and I took a glass of Australian Chardonnay from a tray as I moved further into the room. Almost immediately I heard a familiar guffaw and saw Sir Julian throwing back his head in laughter as he chatted with another of Chauncey's senior members. And beside them was Lord Forshawe.

Looking round the room, I could see the advantage of the kind of network to which they clearly belonged, ensuring that on the whole you met like-minded or familiar people and didn't have to go through the convolutions of meeting new people and having to be pleasant to them before you had a chance to assess whether they were worth being pleasant to. On the other hand, the network to which the rugby-playing friends of Charlie Leeming were attached was exactly the same sort of thing, which made ordinary people like me shudder with revulsion.

Desmond Forshawe saw me. He smiled delightedly and beckoned me over, at the same time coming to take my arm and lead me towards Sir Julian. I wasn't entirely sure that this was a good move, but now it was too late.

'A surprise indeed, Mrs Frazer,' Sir Julian said, lofty as a flagpole, and I know I didn't imagine the faint touch of frost edging his tone, as though I'd somehow infringed the rules by being here.

'Lucky, really.' I gave him my most winning smile. 'I happen to know someone who knows someone . . .' I let the sentence trail off, hoping he wouldn't enquire further.

He opened his mouth to do precisely that but Forshawe got in first. 'Your trouble, Julian,' he boomed, 'is you hog all the best invitations for yourself. You ought to be letting people like Chantal here attend these occasions as well.'

Sir Julian's eyebrows lifted at the use of my first name. 'Ought I?' he said.

Uh-oh . . . I felt a faint chill of apprehension. How much of a future with Chauncey's would I have left by the following week?

'Absolutely.' Forshawe winked at me. 'Give them a chance to meet the movers and shakers of the art world. After all, they'll be running it,

250

twenty years down the line, when you and I are drooling in our wheelchairs.'

'Speak for yourself, Des,' said the third man. 'Personally, I have no plans at all for a wheelchair. Not even a Zimmer frame.'

'Good for you, Francis,' Sir Julian said. 'Hoping to achieve immortality by not dying, rather than by the legacy of your work, eh?'

'Precisely.'

'I think I should circulate a bit,' I said. 'After all, if I'm going to be running the art world twenty years from now, I need to put myself about.'

They all laughed rather disconcertedly as I wandered off, and I could feel them watching my back. I went over to the man who had taken my ticket at the door and asked if he could point Paul Ferris out to me. He indicated a sixtyish man, not much taller than myself, with a dark grey-tinged beard and a plentiful supply of wild greyish hair.

I walked over to where he was standing in front of a garish painting of somewhere tropical or South American – it might even have been Easter Island, as there was what looked like a mask on a stick set to the right of the canvas.

'Do you enjoy these dos?' I asked. 'Most artists don't.'

He brightened at once, a man encountering a kindred spirit. 'Are you one yourself?'

'Unfortunately not,' I said. 'How I wish I were.'

'Have you ever tried? Painting, drawing, sculpting?'

I shook my head.

'Collage? Ceramics? Textiles? Stained glass.'

He was smiling now, thinking I was a harmless ignoramus. Which to a large extent I was.

'Stained glass?' I said, a terrier on to a rat. 'Yes. I saw a most interesting window the other day. It represented a Green Man, I think. Or was it Cronus?'

A defeated look crossed his face. 'And who are you, if I may ask?'

'Before I answer, may I ask you something?'

'What do you want to know?'

'In a previous existence, were you called Jarvis?'

He hesitated, and I wondered what he thought he might gain by denying it, when the hesitation itself made it self-evident that he must be the art student with whom Clio Palliser had fallen in love, and who had been the father of her two sons.

'My interest is entirely personal,' I said. 'I'm not the police, if that's what you're afraid of.'

'What's there to be afraid of?' He scowled at me. 'Yes, I was called Leo Jarvis, a long time ago.'

'And you married Clio Palliser, didn't you?'

'In a manner of speaking.' He smiled at someone behind me and crooked a finger in greeting.

'How does that work?'

'To marry someone implies a certain degree of willingness,' he said. 'In my case, I was bullied first, then bribed, then threatened. Poor Clio was already pregnant by then so I did what I thought was the decent thing and put a ring on her finger. Supplied by her bastard of a father, since I didn't have a brass razoo to my name.'

'I believe she had a relationship with someone at Oxford.'

He nodded thoughtfully. 'She might well have done. I wouldn't know. I was just the stooge in there to make things look respectable.'

A couple of people came up to us and excused themselves for interrupting, but could they ask Paul about one of his pieces and was it for sale because they were very interested.

'His work is really compelling, isn't it?' I said. 'Look, Paul, can we meet after this, say in the cafeteria across the way?'

It was hard for him to be rude in front of two prospective customers. He compromised. 'I'll do my best,' he said.

Before I left the room, I made sure there was no rear exit. Then I parked myself with the exhibition catalogue right outside the door. I sensed that Paul Ferris wouldn't willingly walk across to the Festival Hall to discuss highly personal matters with a complete stranger. I wasn't going to give him the chance to escape.

'All right . . .' I said an hour later as we sat with milky coffees in front of us, while two student musicians played violins nearby. 'I'm not apportioning any blame here, by the way.' God: I sounded so headmistressy. 'So you and Clio got married, to save her reputation. Then she got pregnant again. And then basically you buggered off. Have I got that right?'

'Absolutely right.' He gave the kind of smile which could only be called rueful. 'And also absolutely wrong.'

253

'Oh?'

'Right, we got married. Right, she got pregnant a second time. Right, I left for foreign parts. But the second child was no more mine than the first one. And when I left it was mostly because I couldn't stand that poor woman's pain and distress. I simply could not go on living with someone hurting so badly, when there was nothing I could do to help her.'

'She told one of her friends that she didn't know what happiness meant.'

'That I can well believe. And before you ask, I wasn't responsible for that.' Another grimace. 'Perhaps it was a bit of a cop-out to leave her, but to a certain extent, I felt that I was a victim too.'

'You're still hung up on her, aren't you? Your Gaia carving in the exhibition . . . that's her, isn't it?'

'It is indeed. She had – has? – marvellously strong features, no spare flesh on them, you could see the fine bone structure underneath and the way her eyes were set into her face. I've used her in several of my pieces.'

'You said you were bullied into marriage.'

'By the father. That evil bastard! I won't say he had my arm up behind my back as we went to the registry office, but the whole arrangement was entirely up to him, and Clio and I just went along with it, God knows why. He even opened champagne when we got back home, the filthy dipstick. He was a truly revolting person, in every possible way.'

'So these sons of yours . . .'

'They were *not* mine, poor little blighters.'

'Oh?' So Fingal Adair was responsible after all.

'Oh, nothing,' Ferris said. 'If you really must know, the first one was fathered, if that's the right word, by her loathsome brother Piers. And the second was the result of her own father raping her – yet again. God . . .' Ferris's face was red with remembered, and indeed unforgettable, rage. 'I only discovered this when I told her I couldn't stay in this sham marriage any longer, and that it wasn't fair to her or to her children.'

'Why didn't she ever say anything?'

'I imagine she was threatened by one or other of them. Or both, for that matter. Like father, like bloody son, if you ask me.'

'What a vile story.' I began to put together the events I already knew about. Sometime during the Easter vacation, she must have found herself pregnant by her own brother, and rather than let Fingal Adair take the blame, had cut off all relations with him. 'But why didn't she have an abortion?'

'God knows. The Pallisers were Catholic, in theory, at least. Maybe it was down to some notion of not wishing to make the sin even worse than it was already?'

'But by that time, she was twenty, twenty-one. Surely she was old enough to tell them to bug off, wasn't she?'

'In theory, yes. But she said her father threatened her, told her he would do terrible things if she didn't give in to him. She refused to tell me what they were – probably something to do with

255

the first child – but he was a fearsome man, and I can imagine she was just too frightened to refuse him. And there was probably embarrassment and guilt mixed in there, too. Anyway, by the time I knew anything about it, as I said, there was almost nothing I could do. And even if I'd known right at the beginning, I don't think I could have persuaded her into an abortion.'

I shook my head in disbelief at the sheer malevolence that the human mind is capable of.

'Poor, poor girl,' Ferris continued. 'I'll never forget how she cried when she was telling me all this. She kept saying, "They've taken everything." At the time I thought she meant – oh, it's a longish story, but basically she'd accused Piers of removing some paintings which belonged to her and refusing to hand them back . . . It was only some years later that I realized she meant much more than that.'

'How pitiful it all sounds.'

'Pitiful?' He turned his rather fine head away from me and stared into the past. 'It was bloody appalling. And on top of that, half the people in the area knew or guessed what was going on and not one of them lifted a bloody finger to help her, apart from that bloke who was the tenant farmer or whatever they called it.'

'I think the people at Byfield Hall tried, didn't they?'

'That was the bossy bitch called . . . um . . . Annie Something? Penny? No . . . Jenny. Yes, I think she tried to get Clio to do something about it, but she wouldn't. And, believe me, I'm not at all proud of the part I played in it all. The real kicker is that I sometimes wonder whether if I'd handled it differently, those boys might still be alive. But God, I was barely twenty myself. Came from the back-end of Bristol, didn't have a clue about anything. For all I knew, this was the way the nobs went about things.' Ferris looked down at the coffee in front of him. 'Look, I need something stronger than this muck. What say we get a bottle of wine?'

'Or a whisky,' I said. 'I'm buying, since I'm the one who's forced you to go back over all this.'

'Make mine a double. I feel as though I need to disinfect my mouth.' Ferris shuddered. 'That bloody awful man . . .'

'And you heard about the . . . the murders, did you?'

'Not at the time. Not until quite a bit later. I went travelling round India and it wasn't until I got back to Australia that I heard about it from my rellies here in England. What a bloody tragedy it all was.' He took a long sip of his whisky and looked at me with a sombre expression. 'Anyway, what's your interest in all this?'

I explained about Sabine's death and Stonor's feeling that the truth hadn't come out. 'Do you think Clio did it?' I asked bluntly.

'It all seemed so cut and dried that I can't say I ever questioned it. Especially since . . . This probably sounds as though I'm being wise after the event, but I . . .' He hesitated. 'Sounds bad, I know, but I have occasionally wondered if it was . . . well, *Clio* who killed her brothers.' He sat back and watched my astonished reaction.

'Are you serious?'

'Never more so. She hated them both. And who would blame her? The pair of them had been raping her ever since she was a little girl. Not that I ever met Miles, he was gone long before I came on the scene. He died on a skiing holiday, and I've often thought she could easily have suggested they go off-*piste* and then pushed him over the edge of a cliff. Perfectly possible: she was a really good skier. "*Oh, Miles, look at that strange cloud . . .*" or "*the light on that mountain . . .*" or even "*that weird bird . . .*" then when his attention is focused elsewhere, she could have poked him in the back with her ski stick and watch him slide over the edge. I'm not a skier myself but it could easily be done, I should think.'

I stared at him in amazement.

'As for that that bloody Piers,' he continued, 'the sick bastard was killed in his own flat and the body wasn't discovered for a week.'

'Why would that be down to Clio?'

'Why not?' He laughed. 'You're looking at me as though I'm off my rocker, but I can assure you that if you'd known any of the Pallisers, you wouldn't find it at all far-fetched. I'm not saying she *did* do them, either of them, I'm just saying it wouldn't surprise me if she *had*. Because when I checked it out, I discovered that Clio had been up in London the same day they reckoned he died, to do some research at the British Library. So she had motive *and* opportunity. Which doesn't make her a murderer, I realize that. And the police didn't seem to think it was significant. But . . . and this is the interesting thing . . . I'm

258

certain I saw some of the very paintings she said Piers had stolen from her. Hanging right there in her study, bold as brass. No attempt at concealment. Real beauts. Scandinavian ones, which her mother had given her.'

'I've seen some of them too. Were you sure they were the same ones she said her brother had taken?'

'Too right. She had a list of them.'

'Wouldn't someone else have noticed them too? The police or someone?'

'Maybe she kept them hidden until the fuss had died down. Look, how did they get back to Weston Lodge, if she didn't steal them back again?'

'That's your theory?'

'You bet. Again, it would have been easy to do. Obviously – if it *was* her, I mean – she'd have gone to her brother's flat prepared. She was probably able to let herself in. So she's there, taking the paintings off the walls and stowing them away in her portfolio or suitcase or whatever, when in he comes, starts back, shouts, "What the fuck do you think you're doing?" and she turns round, bashes him with the poker or whatever, finishes packing up the goods and walks out, locks the door behind her, goes back home, no worries.'

'Wouldn't that take quite a bit of nerve?'

'Of course. But she was a clever woman. She could have planned it all, waited for the oppo, gone to do her research and then on to his unit. She hated him even more than she hated Miles. Let alone Sir frickin' bloody Gerald.' He grimaced. 'Look, I'm not saying she *did*, I'm just saying she *could*. And it would explain how the later . . . uh . . . deaths might have happened, wouldn't it?'

'I guess it would.' If you'd already got two murders under your belt, what were a few more, even if two of them were young boys? How would you feel about children who had been forced on you by incestuous rape? Would you, *could* you love them? Was this why Clio was so distant to her sons? 'You knew Gerald Palliser, of course.'

'Knew him, but didn't know him, if you see what I mean. Didn't *want* to know him, frankly. On the other hand, he gave me the commission for the chapel, paid me up front, let me have a free hand. He couldn't have been *all* bad.'

'I noticed your free hand,' I said drily.

He smiled. 'I've got to say I didn't realize that marrying his daughter was going to be part of the deal, or I'd have turned it down flat.' He sipped some more whisky. 'Probably.'

'Perhaps her brother's stuff was returned to the family by the police or the solicitors or something and the pictures were handed over to her.'

'Ah well, you see, that's just it. Nearly everything he owned went to his divorced wife and their two kids. So how come Clio gets the exact pictures she said he'd stolen from her?' Again he lifted his glass to his mouth. 'And I should add that when she was roused – and I don't mean sexually because we never went down that route – she had the world's worst temper.'

'I've heard that before.'

He put his glass down hard on the table between us and leaned forward. 'This is all just idle speculation, of course. No basis in fact whatsoever. *Nil nisi bonum* and all that.'

'Except that, as far as we know, she's not dead.'

'Mmm, yes. Obviously, I'm not exactly up to speed with things, living down under as I do. It's a bit strange that the Press Rottweilers haven't tracked her down.'

'I agree. Now, moving on, the chapel at Weston Lodge.'

'What about it?'

'According to the Palliser cousin who now owns the place, the carving you did above the lintel is Cronus, and not a Green Man.'

'Christ! It's all coming back to me now. Yes, she used to come down to that chapel and talk to me. I told her I was going to carve a Green Man, not something religious; she said it would be rather fun – that was her phrase, "rather fun" – to make the face look like her dad, and that I shouldn't carve a Green Man, it should be Cronus. Didn't mean much to me, I must say, until she explained. Bozo ate his own kids, didn't he?'

'That's right.'

'She said her father was thick as a plank and he'd never recognize himself, so I went ahead.'

'What about the symbols?'

'Symbols?'

'In the stained glass window in the chapel.'

'Remind me.'

'A crucifix. A white lamb. A jugful of coins. And . . . um . . . a scythe.'

Ferris closed his eyes, repeating the words I

261

had just spoken. 'I can't honestly remember. But they were probably references to the poor fucked-up woman who was briefly my wife. The lamb led to the slaughter. The crucifix, for her religion. The coins, for her oh-so-rich dad. And the scythe . . . hmm, don't know what that was for.'

'If you remember, Cronus sliced off his own father's private parts with a sickle.'

Ferris burst out laughing. 'That's right! I'd forgotten that. Was that before or after he chowed down on his kids?' He took a hefty swig of his drink. 'Jeez, what a set-up that place was. I bet Sir Gerald wasn't best pleased when he found out what I'd done.'

'According to the cousin I spoke with, he was furious, all for tearing it down and destroying it. Except someone pointed out that you were going to be big in the sculpture world – as indeed you are – and destroying it would not only be the act of a vandal, but also financially stupid.'

'Hang about.' Ferris sat up straighter. 'It's sort of coming back to me. I don't think that scythe thing had anything to do with Cronus.'

'I wondered if it was supposed to be Old Father Time. He has a scythe, doesn't he?'

'No, no. It was Death, creeping round in that hoodie of his and swishing his scythe about. Another of Clio's helpful suggestions.' He shivered, shook his head. 'Kind of creepy, isn't it? Prophetess of Doom.'

'Could be any or all of the above.'

'Too true. Sorry not to be more helpful.'

'On the contrary. I've learned a lot.'

* * *

And none of it very pleasant, I thought as I headed back to the office. I had now altered my perception of the Honourable Clio so completely that I actually wanted her to be innocent of the crime of murder. I wanted her to find some happiness, after all the horrors that had overwhelmed her, though even if she was still alive, it was probably far too late for her. Maybe all anyone could do for her now was to clear her name.

Walking up Bond Street, I thought about it. Perhaps she wouldn't even want that. Not only all the attendant publicity and press attention, but going to court to have the original verdict overturned, meeting with the police. She might simply prefer to live out her days in obscurity. I think I might have felt the same.

Chauncey's was buzzing when I turned in at the big double doors. A bunch of rather grand gold and silver balloons hung above the reception desk, and I could see into the big auction room where the usual chairs had been replaced with white-covered tables on which sat big silver punch bowls surrounded by bottles of wine and covered platters.

For a moment I couldn't think what was going on. Then I remembered we were supposed to be celebrating the opening of a branch in San Francisco. I hurried up to my office. Thank goodness I always kept a smart frock hanging on the back of the door and a set of make-up requirements in one of my drawers. I must appear to be making an effort, I thought. And I would have to phone Gavin. I picked up my phone and dialled his office.

'Darling,' I said, when he picked up, 'I'm afraid I'm going to be late home.' I started to explain but he cut across me.

'You can't be,' he said flatly.

'What do you mean?' He sounded so cold that I hardly recognized his voice.

'I mean that I booked us a table at Fiorentino's.'

'This is the first I've heard of it.'

'I told you about it the other day.'

'I'm sure you didn't because I would have said I couldn't make it. Not tonight.' I frowned. 'In fact, Gavin Vaughn, it was me who told you about this party tonight here, and you said *you* couldn't make it and that it was better for me to be unencumbered by hangers-on, since it was a work occasion.'

He was silent for a moment. 'I think you must be mixing me up with someone else,' he said eventually. He didn't sound as though he was joking.

I laughed. 'Don't be silly, darling. Who would I be mixing you up with?'

'How about that Scotsman, the one who used to be your sister's boyfriend?'

I gasped. 'Wh . . . *What*?'

'I know you have the occasional lunch with him.'

'How do you know that?' I could feel rage creeping up my body and heating my face. 'Have you been hacking into my email, or something?'

'I'm not going to dignify that question with an answer,' he said pompously.

'Gavin, I'm not going to put up with this,' I

264

said. 'You have absolutely no right to read my emails.'

He paused and took a deep breath. 'I know, darling, I know,' he said apologetically. 'Sorry, sorry, sorry. It was just that you were out one evening, and I was idling around because I'd left my PC at work, and, well, one thing led to another.'

'I'd really like to know how it led to my emails. How did you know my password in the first place?'

'You told me, don't you remember?' he said easily.

'No.' He was lying. I had done no such thing.

'That weekend we went down to Cornwall to see your friend Rosemary. I didn't have my PC with me so I had to use yours to check some urgent emails. You told me then.'

'The hell I did.' As soon as I'd put the phone down, I was going to change the password. 'And don't forget to cancel the table at Fiorentino's.' If he'd even booked it, which I doubted. I was learning that when it suited him, Gavin had a tenuous grasp of the truth. Curiously enough, this hadn't bothered me very much until now; I could be glib too.

It was nearly midnight when I got back to my flat. There were no lights on, only the muted blue glow of the television. And Gavin, asleep on the sofa. I crept across the sitting room, not wanting to wake him up, but he heard me and sat up.

'You're late,' he said, squinting at his watch.

'Yes.'

265

'What kept you?'

'It was a *party*, Gavin.'

He sat up straight and stretched. 'Of course.'

'Mind if I put the light on?'

'Go ahead.'

As I reached for the switch on the lamp beside him, he got to his feet. 'Darling,' he said hesitantly. 'I've done something absolutely awful.'

'What?'

'Oh God, I just don't know how it happened. But . . . that beautiful dish of yours, the one which was your mother's?'

I already knew what he was going to say. 'What about it?'

'It . . . I dropped it. Darling, I'm so so sorry. I managed to pick up all the pieces, and we could get one of those porcelain experts to put it together again. Good as new.'

'But it won't be the same, will it?' The distance between us was chilly.

He gave a kind of shrug. 'No, I suppose it won't.' He tried to take me in his arms, but I stepped back. He frowned. 'Chantal. Darling. Please forgive me.' He made a rueful face. 'I suppose I could argue that it's your fault, really.'

I was hanging up my coat, taking off my boots. 'How do you make that out?'

'Well, if you hadn't insisted on going to that party, instead of coming out to Fiorentino's with me, this wouldn't have happened.'

'No, I suppose it wouldn't.' I debated telling him that earlier I had rung Fiorentino from my office and they had no record of any booking for that evening in either of our names.

266

Lying rigid in bed, with Gavin asleep beside me, one of his big hands on my breast, I thought how strange it was that love could change so quickly: one moment round and shining and perfect, the next riddled with suspicion, dislike, even fear. *Love is not love which alters when it alteration finds*: that was all very well, but must surely depend on the alteration concerned. What had I – usually so circumspect – done in giving my heart so freely to a man I scarcely knew? How recklessly I had behaved. I'd been seduced by his charm, and by our shared history; I should have realized that something more solid should lie at the core of a relationship. I believe I still was. I felt he was my soulmate, whatever his flaws . . . and which of us is unflawed?

Sixteen

I increasingly looked forward to my meetings with Malcolm Macdonald. His quiet sense of authority, his inner calm, reminded me so much of Hamilton. I wished I felt more at ease with him than I did, but lurking in the background of any conversation we exchanged was the presence of my sister, so that it felt almost unnatural for me to be with him, when he should have been with her. I often found myself engaging in stilted discussion of something completely banal, or else reduced to silence, however companionable it might be. What made it worse was the compassion and kindness which spread across his face when this happened, as though he was perfectly aware of the implicit awkwardness of any relationship between us.

He was down in London again, he told me, as we sat in pale sunshine beneath chestnut trees bare of leaves, looking for a place to live. A two-bedroomed flat, he said, to accommodate visitors. His company was seconding him to their London branch for at least two years. He reached across the little marble-topped table which held our wine glasses and put his hand over mine in a gesture that was friendly and not intrusive.

'I hope I can see more of you then, Chantal.'

His look was tender, and I wanted to beg him

not to fall in love with me, as I suspected he was in the process of doing. I wanted to tell him I could never reciprocate his feelings, partly because now that I had found Gavin my life was already complete, and partly because Sabine's shadow would always be there between us, reminding both of us that we did not belong to each other and never could.

'Yes.' I smiled at him. 'I'd like that.'

'Maybe you could help me with a couple of things,' he said diffidently, pushing his glasses up his nose. 'If you've got time, of course.'

'I spend a lot of time on my own, Malcolm, so I'd be glad to help.'

'I'm looking for something unfurnished, so I'll have to make it into a home.'

'What about the possessions you already have? Books, favourite saucepans, pictures, that kind of thing?'

'I'm sending stuff down, of course. They're giving me a generous relocation allowance. But sometimes it's good to have a change, don't you think? To buy new things and so on. Get rid of the stuff you've lived with so long that you forget how shabby it is. Start afresh.'

I knew he wasn't just talking about soft furnishings. 'I do indeed. No wife, Malcolm?'

'No wife. No girlfriend, either.' The grooves in his cheeks lengthened. 'Oh, there have been relationships, but none of them particularly long-lasting. I don't seem to be capable of meeting the right person, not since Sabine.' His face drooped, then brightened. 'But when I do meet her, I'll know at once.'

I admired the way he didn't hesitate over my sister's name. 'So you're an optimist?'

'If you mean that I'm sure I'll find her, even at this late stage, then yes, I am.'

I wanted to tell him not to gaze at me like that. That I wasn't the one he was looking for. That whatever he might think, I was not the one he needed. 'When exactly will you be moving down?' I said.

'Soon. Just before Christmas, I hope.'

We looked away from each other without speaking. For both of us, Christmas had long been a word to avoid, a season to dread.

'Will you be spending the holiday with your father?' Malcolm asked.

'Yes.'

Gavin wanted us to spend Christmas with his mother; I had told him I couldn't since I'd already promised to go to Italy, adding that my father had been ill recently – which was true – and had particularly requested that I travel down to see him that year – which wasn't. Although I didn't like lying to Gavin, he often tried to curtail my independence, which I didn't care for, so I felt it was important to our relationship that I maintain a certain measure of autonomy. On top of that, I didn't think I could handle several days of Paula's non-stop smothering concern about her son. Lighten up, I wanted to say. It's a long time ago. He's a big boy now.

But who was I to be pointing any of this out (not that I had) when I myself had been so hung up on my own trauma? Paula would have been aware, just as much as Gavin and I were, of the significance of the time of year.

270

'I'd like to meet your father one day,' Malcolm said. 'Sabine often talked about him, and how proud she was of him.'

'I know he would love to meet you too,' I said. I meant it. Dad might have moved on, but he had by no means forgotten. The *contessa* was charming, intelligent and enthusiastic, all qualities that Dad appreciated, but I sensed that she could never mean as much to him as my little French mother had. And Malcolm would provide him with a link back to Sabine.

It felt odd to go furniture shopping with Malcolm, rather than with Gavin. He seemed to like my taste and went along with my suggestions without argument. I even found myself lending him bits and pieces from my own flat, particularly those that I had bought with Hamilton, in an effort to forestall further arguments with Gavin.

Another Sunday on my own: a brilliant day, unseasonably warm. As so often, Gavin was somewhere far away, and Malcolm was in Edinburgh, so I walked along the leafy Kensington avenues and strolled into Hyde Park, kicking at the piles of fallen leaves as I went. The sky was the kind of intense blue you only get in early winter; the Park was full of families making the most of the good weather. I went along to the Serpentine and found a bench from which I could watch the swans and mallards and squirrels scrabbling for the stale bread that little kids were throwing for them.

One of the nearby daddies was with a pair of adorable twin girls aged about five, both with

271

Asiatic features, although he himself looked as English as Windsor Castle.

'Look, Daddy, look,' one of them said.

'He's taking the bread right off our hands,' said the other.

'Can we take one home with us?' said the first.

'I don't think so,' their father said. 'The Queen wouldn't like that at all.'

'Why not?'

'Because all the birds here – all the birds in England actually – belong to her.'

'Couldn't she spare one, just for us?'

'It wouldn't be fair to ask her. She would be awfully sad to lose one.'

Daddy looked round, smiling, and I smiled back. He did a double-take. 'We've met, haven't we?' he said.

'Have we?'

'Aren't you . . . You're Chantal, aren't you? May I?' He gestured at the bench and sat down at my nod. 'You don't remember me, do you?'

'I'm afraid not.'

He gestured at his children. 'I'm putting in some significant daddy-time. We sort of met recently at that restaurant on the river.'

'Oh, yes.' I had placed him now. One of the less obnoxious of the men who had been on their way to Charlie Leeming's funeral.

He grimaced. 'I'm afraid the boys weren't behaving particularly well that day. Especially Barnesy. I suppose you could say we were drinking to forget – it's quite sobering when someone your own age dies.'

Tell me about it, I thought.

He put out a hand. 'I'm Rob Bradley, by the way.' He looked across the park at windows glinting in the sun and the tops of the trees lining the Mall. 'So where's your fiancé this morning?'

I said he was away. It didn't seem worthwhile enlightening him as to the true status of our relationship.

'And when's the wedding?'

I was evasive. 'Uh . . . we haven't settled on a date yet.'

'Have you known Metcalfe-Vaughn long?'

'Only about six months.' Looked at dispassionately, that seemed an awfully short time to make such a commitment. 'No, more than that,' I lied. 'More like a year.'

I don't think he believed me. 'I've known him for years,' he said. 'Played rugby with him all over south-east Asia and Australia. Singapore. The Hong Kong Sevens. Sydney. The financial world out there is very small, and you can't avoid bumping into people you know.'

'It was obvious that none of you liked him,' I said coldly.

'That's not quite true.' Bradley paused as one of his daughters ran up, asking if there was any more bread for the birds.

When she'd returned to the water's edge, he looked down at the asphalt beneath his feet, which was covered in breadcrumbs and duck-droppings. 'I often think about what that poor guy went through . . . what happened at his guardian's house . . . the two Palliser boys . . .' He shivered. 'God, what a frightful experience that must have been for a kid his age.'

273

'He still hasn't gotten over it.'

'I'm not surprised. I suppose they sent him to a psychiatrist.'

'If by "they" you mean his parents, yes. But they only suggested it when he was older.'

'What, some kind of anger-management course, was it?'

'Why on earth do you ask that?'

A leaf floated past Bradley's ear and he tried to catch it. 'Just, he used to have a bit of a temper, get himself into quite a state. He would be terribly apologetic afterwards. It was as if he just couldn't help himself.'

'I can honestly say that I've never seen Gavin anything but completely charming.' Again I lied: once or twice he had been considerably less so.

'That's a relief. I really shouldn't have said anything, damned cheek really, but after that strange business with his wife, I thought—'

'His *what*?'

'Hasn't he told you about Miki?'

I hated to admit that he hadn't. 'Not really,' I hedged. 'Just said there'd been . . . something. Someone, I should say.' I was finding it hard to get my head around this. Gavin had been married? Why hadn't he said anything? Especially when I had told him all about Hamilton.

'It was all pretty ghastly at the time, I can tell you,' Bradley was saying. 'The poor man was absolutely devoted to her, so you can imagine how devastated he was. And they were expecting their first child, too, which made it even worse.'

'How did she . . .' I coughed. 'Um . . . what exactly happened?'

'I seem to remember they returned an open verdict. She slipped off a cliff. Or jumped. No one was sure whether it was an accident or suicide.'

'Why would she want to commit suicide?'

'That's what wc all wondered. Whenever you saw them together they always seemed so happy. So much in love. It was really tragic . . . They were one of the top social couples out there in Singapore, life and soul of the party, always celebrating something or other, going out to dinner, Embassy functions, that sort of thing. Miki was a wonderful hostess, too. I've been to some super parties at their place.'

'What was she like?'

'Miki? She was one of those cute little Japanese girls, a real bundle of fun, rather like my own wife; in fact they were good friends, my wife was really cut up about her death. Hugely clever, of course, ran her own fashion business – doing very well indeed from what I heard – and thrilled to pieces to be having a baby, but determined that it wasn't going to cramp their social life.' Bradley laughed. 'My wife told them they hadn't got a clue. Amazing, isn't it? You can be out every night of the week, but once the first sprog comes along, that's it. Suddenly, rather than be out on the town, you'd much rather be home, staring into its crib and accepting that it's the most beautiful and amazing creature ever to be born.'

'And where did this . . . accident take place?'

'They were in Japan at the time, sightseeing at some well-known Lovers' Leap type beauty-spot with a marvellous view. According to Gavin, and to the witnesses, one minute she was there, the next she wasn't.' Bradley seemed embarrassed. 'Look, I do hope I haven't been telling tales out of school. I just assumed Gavin would have told you.'

'You'd think so, wouldn't you?'

'I can see how he might not want to upset you. A trauma like that – and the earlier one too. We didn't hold it against him too much when he got a bit worked up.'

'Worked up meaning what exactly?'

'Oh, you know . . . screaming at people. Throwing stuff around. Deliberately smashing other people's things if he was angry with them.'

'Yeah, well . . .'

Again Bradley stared out across the park. 'He was an only child. And because of what happened, his parents probably spoiled him. So he was used to everything going his way, couldn't handle it when it didn't.' He patted my knee in a fatherly fashion. 'But I've no doubt he's grown out of all that sort of thing by now.'

I nodded. My blood felt chilled at the edges, like milk left on a frosty doorstep. I didn't want to hear what he was saying. Partly because I didn't want to believe the subtext behind his words. But partly because I had already begun to sense – although I didn't want to admit it – a darkness at Gavin's core, something feral and uncontrolled. 'As I said, I've never seen the slightest sign in him.'

'Good, good.'

The younger of Bradley's girls had fallen over and instead of getting up was continuing to lie on the path, sobbing. 'I'd better go,' Bradley said.

'Marshal the troops. Find a café or an ice-cream seller.' He grinned at me. 'It's amazing how many ills an ice-cream can cure. Especially if it's got chocolate sprinkles on top.'

'I'll try to remember that.'

'It was nice to meet you again,' he said.

He was describing a Gavin I didn't know, I told myself. We were *happy* together. There was no flouncing or sulking. I loved him. I was sure he loved me. I knew that love could be quiet and still be passionate. And that passion can transmute into contentment, and love remain as strong. If – *when* – Gavin asked me to marry him I anticipated nothing more than a blissful life with him, a contented family, few if any money problems, successful children, all the usual uncomplicated middle-class desires. Unambitious, yes, but then I had never been ambitious. I was quite content to leave that to Gavin. There had been certain things I wanted, such as my career, and I had come by them relatively easily. Now Bradley had raised spectres I could not have envisioned.

Back at home, I spent part of the evening lying in a hot bath and examining the time Gavin and I had spent together, analysing the traces of bad temper or uncontrolled behaviour on his part, searching for flaws. Occasionally we had exchanged a sharp word or two, but we'd never quarrelled. True, he liked to tell me what to do, what to eat, what to wear, but I took no notice of that, seeing it as just one of his funny little ways. I had plenty of those myself.

I hoicked a toe round the hot-water tap and turned it on. We were two people who already

277

enjoyed each other's company, had a marvellous time in bed together, liked the same people, the same books, the same films. Together, we were each more than we were singly on our own – and wasn't that about the best definition of a good relationship you could ask for?

Nonetheless, the information I had so recently learned grew in me like a canker. Thanks to Rob Bradley, I had not only lost my peace of mind, but I was even starting to develop an unfocused sense of personal danger.

Meanwhile, my work load at Chauncey's was growing heavier. I was about to travel down to Wales to inspect a house outside Cardiff, in order to evaluate a number of paintings which the owners wished to sell. Then there was a catalogue to prepare for the sale of miniatures which I was supervising in the New Year, thanks to Desmond Forshawe's intervention. And on top of that, there was helping Malcolm Macdonald to set up his new flat, which was taking up most of my free time. I scarcely had a moment to do what I was best at: being dull.

Gavin telephoned from Papua New Guinea. 'How's it going, sweets?'

'Just fine, thank you.' Not as warmly as usual. I was more wary and hoped he didn't sense it.

'Are you missing me?'

'I think I must be, but honestly, darling, I've scarcely had time to. Up in the morning while it's still dark, home late, asleep as soon as my head touches the pillow.'

He made a disappointed noise, and I laughed.

'Of course I miss you. Horribly. Life's no fun without you.'

'Ditto, darling. Look, could you possibly go round to my place at the weekend? Water the plants, feed the cat, that sort of thing?'

'You haven't got a cat.'

'I know, but if I had, it would need feeding.'

'Idiot,' I said fondly.

'Also, could you pick up the mail? And check that there's nothing gone off in the fridge?'

'Shall I also stop by the employment agency and register myself as a maid-of-all-work?'

'Very amusing, darling.'

'*I* thought so. Hey, what happened to your char-student?'

'I had to let him go. He was mucking about with things, reading my books, actually playing my piano, if you can believe it.'

'Quentin is a music student, probably doesn't have a piano where he lives,' I said. 'Sounds pretty reasonable to me.'

'Not if he's going to leave pizza fingermarks on my piano keys.'

'Well, did he?'

'Not yet,' Gavin admitted.

'How do you know he even eats pizza, you old curmudgeon? Or if he does, that he would be eating in your place instead of his own?'

'I sound like a real grouch, don't I?' Gavin said cheerfully. 'But I bet it was only a matter of time. You know what students are like. Besides, I was paying him to clean the flat, not to lounge about playing Chopin all day.' He gave a little groan. 'God, I wish I was with you.'

'So do I. How much longer do you think they'll need you out there?'

'No more than week, I think.'

'Good. I can hardly wait to see you again.'

'Same here.'

'We seem to spend an awful lot of the time apart, sweetheart.'

'That'll change. Once we're properly together, I'll ask to be shifted to another department. There's not much point having the most super woman in the world and spending so much time away from her.'

'Oh, darling.' My heart melted. 'Kiss, kiss.'

Saturday morning, I drove to Gavin's flat in the Barbican. I'd been there many times and by now had my own key, even knew the couple next door, who'd invited us in for a drink not long ago. Gavin's cleaner, the student from the Royal Academy of Music had always done a pretty good job of keeping the place neat and tidy. When I let myself in, it was fairly obvious that no one had cleaned up since Gavin's departure: his breakfast things were still in the kitchen sink, covered in a disgusting green mould, and the milk in the fridge had long ago separated into curds and whey. As I emptied it down the sink, averting my nose, I asked myself, as I had done many times before, why Miss Muffet seemed to relish them so much.

The Sunday papers from two weeks ago were still strewn over Gavin's white leather sofa; the bed was unmade, the trash had not been emptied. There were lights blinking on his answering machine, and I stared at them for a moment, wondering whether listening to the messages was more or less the same invasion of privacy as opening someone else's mail, or reading their personal diary. I decided that it was.

I tidied up, changed the sheets on the bed, dropped the trash down the chute into the basement. Watered the herbs Gavin kept on the kitchen window-sill, washed-up, cleaned out the fridge. Threw out the dead roses in a vase on his piano, crimson ones which I'd brought the week before he left. *(Guess what, Gavin: I love you.)* Then I made a cup of instant coffee and sat down in the living room to drink it. It was a pleasant space, but a little small for two people to live comfortably together. My flat was much bigger, much more suited to a couple just starting out on married life, especially if children were to come along, although Gavin had expressed no enthusiasm at the prospect.

'Won't it cramp our style?' he'd said.

'I don't think I've got any style to cramp,' I said.

'Well, I certainly have. I'll go along with what you want, of course, but I can't say my heart leaps up at the thought of baby-sick all down the front of my suits. And I can tell you, the clients aren't going to be hugely impressed.'

'You could always take your suit off before you hold him or her.'

'Anyway, I prefer it when it's just the two of us.'

I had patted his arm. 'I shouldn't worry about it, sweetheart: at my age, the chances are fairly remote,' I said, jokingly.

281

'There is that, I suppose.'

'Thank you very much for making out that I'm some dried-up old crone too old to have babies!'

He had pulled me into his arms and kissed me. 'Have I ever at any point suggested in any way that you're too old to do anything? Have I? Have I?'

'No, Gavin, you never have.'

'Well, then.'

Well then was all very well, but it would have been nice if he'd been a bit more positive. My mind wandered to the future and what it might hold for us both, while my eyes moved idly among Gavin's possessions. That silver vase, badly in need of polishing, would look good on the sideboard in my small dining room; that hideous bowl would have to go; the ceramic candlesticks blended nicely with my sitting room curtains; the scene in bright colours which I knew he'd bought in Papua New Guinea could hang in our bedroom.

Our bedroom . . . but it wasn't *our* bedroom, it could never be. What was I doing, hypothetically moving Gavin and his things into the home which Hamilton and I had built up together? There was only one thing for it, and that was to sell up, buy another apartment, get rid of the things which Ham and I bought together with so much hope, give Brigid or his brother the furniture which he had inherited from his grandmother.

But I didn't want to. I couldn't just junk my former life. If Ham had been in the room with me, he'd have told me not to be so silly, the furniture was just polish and memories, nothing that should play too big a part in my future relationships. And he'd be right. Nonetheless, I had a feeling that Gavin wouldn't see it that way.

I stared at the books in the low white-painted bookshelves which stood all along one wall. A lot of cheap thrillers – aircraft reading, Gavin had told me; a set of illustrated Dickens; various books on money and business practice, on sport, on art; some dictionaries; books on PNG, Singapore, Hong Kong, Australia, South America. An eclectic reader, my Gavin. And a constant traveller, since he was always being sent to far-flung corners of the earth to negotiate big deals. Several of his art books were duplicated on my own bookcases: a book on Frida Kahlo, for example, another on Canaletto. And a book about the paintings housed in the Scottish National Gallery. I'd ordered the same book online from California as a Christmas present for Sabine; I'd selected the gift-wrapped option, and since I couldn't write in it myself, had asked them to enclose a card with a message I sent them. Now I sat back on the sofa with it, realizing how much less often I thought of Sabine these days. Happiness was a good a way to drive out grief. And I *was* happy, wasn't I? Of course I was.

Opening Gavin's copy, I flipped through it, enjoying the contents: Ham and I had often wandered through the rooms on the Mound, sharing our favourites with each other. How young I had been back then; how jaded I felt now. I turned to the title page – and stared in disbelief.

*To the one and only Sabine Françoise
Monroe, from her adoring little sister,
Chantal*

The words were written in someone else's hand-
writing, on a card which had been loosely stuck
to the first page. I read the inscription again. And
then once more. It was undoubtedly Sabine's
book, but its presence here made no sense at all;
I could not work out how it came to be in Gavin's
flat. She couldn't have lent it to him, because
she'd died before she could open it.

To the one and only Sabine . . .

Once more I read the inscription, while my
brain tried to compute how the book had ended
up in Gavin's flat. Had he seen it in a second-
hand bookshop – he liked to browse through such
places – and bought it for sentimental reasons,
long before he met me? But if that were the case,
how could it have ended up in this putative shop
in the first place? Why hadn't it been returned
to us in California after Sabine's death, along
with most of her other possessions?

Or – and this seemed the least likely possibility
– had Gavin himself taken it from under the tree?
But how could he have done that? And when?
My first thought was to ask Gavin next time he
telephoned from Port Moresby. Then, I don't
know why, it occurred to me that it might be a
good idea to keep my knowledge to myself. It
could have been a desire to find out a little more
before confronting him; it could have been fear
of what he might do if he found out that I knew
he had my sister's book. But on the other hand

– my more rational side entered the debate – there could be some perfectly logical reason for it, and it was not fair to find him guilty (but of what?) without giving him the chance to answer the charges (which were?).

I replaced the book on the shelf and scanned the other titles for ones which I knew Sabine had taken to England with her. I couldn't find any. There was a book on Howard Hodgkin which I had been meaning to buy for myself; it would be useful if my library and Gavin's complemented each other. I would have looked at it but time was moving on and I had arranged to meet Lorna and Nat somewhere for lunch. I popped the book into my bag and went to Gavin's front door, then stopped. He had a charming little bureau in his hall, all brass handles and piecrust edging, which he used as a place to store his more important papers.

I defy any woman who has just learned that her partner once had a wife to ignore a desk which might be full of helpful information. Letters. Photographs. Would I really read someone else's private mail? I'm afraid to say that in certain circumstances, I would. I *think* I would. So far, the opportunity had never come up, but . . . yes, I might.

I opened the bureau's drawers one by one, starting with the three along the bottom. In all three drawers, rectangular see-through button-down folders lay in ordered piles. I pulled them out. Stickers on each one told me they held cancelled bills, bank statements, advisements from Gavin's accountant, papers pertaining to the purchase of his flat, work reports. Everything seemed of the utmost boringness and not worth any kind of a search. The left-hand drawer above them contained some more see-through folders in different colours: one contained letters, another held a jumble of loose photographs.

Aha! Since they did not appear to be in any particular order, I emptied them out on to Gavin's dining room table and sifted through them. I don't know what I was looking for, or what I expected. Probably nothing. There was a number of photographs of school plays with Gavin in the centre, obviously in the lead part. There were many team photographs, again with Gavin sitting in the centre and holding a rugby ball on his knee, sometimes with the year painted on it in white. There were photographs of Gavin with his parents, on holiday in foreign- looking places, and standing outside a house which looked distinctly Antipodean, painted white with palms and banana trees all round and glimpses of red hills in the distance. There was Gavin in a swimming pool, grinning up at the photographer with his arms hooked over the edge. A sweaty Gavin in a red rugby shirt. And Gavin – this must have been what I was hoping to find – at his wedding.

On the back, someone had written *Gavin and Miki*. Miki was a small Japanese girl dressed up for the occasion in a white silk kimono, her doll-like features also painted white, with gold coins and silk ribbons decorating her elaborately coiffed hair. Gavin loomed tenderly over her. She was beautiful, with dark almond-shaped eyes and a rosebud mouth, and hardly taller than I was. He was obviously drawn to small women, perhaps because he was so large himself. There were many other photographs of them both: the two of them in evening dress getting into a car, Miki in a tiny red bikini, Miki and Gavin and a third guy jogging along beside the sea. Dozens more, showing the kind of life they had lived in Singapore. I wondered what could possibly have made Miki jump off a cliff to her death. Unless it really had been a tragic accident. She looked so happy, so proud of her husband.

I bundled the photographs up together and put them all back in the drawer.

I was late for Lorna and Nat, but they didn't mind, being too busy smiling at each other, holding hands and drinking an aperitif. We ordered, chatted of this and that, exchanged our news, not that any of us had much news to impart. We tended to live ordered lives, we did not crave excitement. Perhaps that was why I loved Lorna, who, despite her often melodramatic delivery, was at heart a homebody.

'I've got a question for you,' I said. Lorna was an enthusiastic *fashionista*, sometimes spending a month's wages on a must-have handbag or pair of shoes. 'Ever heard of a fashion designer called Miki?' I spelled it out for her.

'Heavens, yes. Lived in Japan, I think. I did once try to buy a skirt from them but decided that even for me it was too over the top, price-wise. Miki Masshi, she was called.'

'How come I never heard of her?'

'Because, sweetie, fashion isn't your thing.'

287

'Though you always look really nice,' blundered kind Nat, making Lorna's veiled insult worse.

'And why do you use the past tense?'

'Because that's precisely what she is: past.'

'Fashion-wise, or life-wise?' I asked, although I knew the answer.

'She jumped off a cliff, I think. Or slipped. Or fell. You must have read about it; there was a husband, far as I remember, who was arrested for pushing her off, but there were witnesses who claimed he was nowhere near her when she fell. Very sad.'

'I wonder who they were.'

Later, over coffee, Lorna pursed her mouth and looked serious.

'What's up? I asked.

'We're just not sure,' she said suddenly. She looked at Nat, who nodded encouragement. 'You know me, sweetie, always absolutely certain about everything, normally see the world in black and white. But . . .'

I looked from one to another in alarm. 'You're not having second thoughts, are you?'

'What, about us?' said Nat. He roared with laughter. 'Heavens, no.'

'It's not us, silly. It's *you*.' Lorna swallowed nervously. 'Look, it's none of our business and we have no right to say anything and feel free to tell us to butt out, but we feel – we both feel – that we just had to tell you that we . . . well, basically we don't really think that . . . um . . . that Gavin is quite . . . um . . . quite the right person for you.'

288

'I couldn't have put it better myself,' said Nat.

'Can you explain why not?' I said.

'It's just a feeling. Nothing concrete. But we both felt that there's something kinda . . . well, *weird* about him.' Lorna reached for Nat's hand and squeezed it.

'People have a right to be weird.'

'I know. But not *weird* weird, if you know what I mean.'

'Not really.' Why was I suddenly being warned off Gavin? What had he done to anyone?

'Thing is,' said Nat. 'After we met the other day, I rang some of the people that he and I had in common out in Singapore and Hong Kong and frankly, quite honestly . . . oh God, this is so difficult . . .'

'It's OK. I get the picture.' I tried to sound neutral, but in fact I was steaming mad. What right did people have to criticize my boyfriend, lover, future husband? 'There's no law that says all your friends have to like the person you choose.'

'But, honestly, Chantal, we felt that, as your good friends, we would be failing in our duty if we didn't say something,' said Nat. 'You're free to ignore us. You're free to hate us.'

'You're *not* free never to speak to us again,' Lorna said, her eyes wide with trepidation. 'And I can promise we didn't decide to tell you how we feel without discussing it endlessly with each other beforehand. It was not a lightly taken decision.'

'But the money-market guys overseas weren't exactly complimentary,' said Nat. 'I won't go

289

into details – at least, not unless you want me to – but trust me . . .' The two of them stared at each other and then at me, both of them biting their lips.

'Thank you,' I said. 'I really mean it. And don't worry, I shan't hold it against you.' But all three of us knew that I would. That we were unlikely to be friends again for a very long time.

Yet sadly, despite the anger I felt, I was beginning to realize that the ringing noise in my head was alarm-bells. And that they had been ringing for some time. The breaking of my Limoges dish was the first real sign I'd had that Gavin was considerably less than I had thought him to be. In my heart, I knew he had deliberately dropped the dish to punish me for attending the Chauncey's party when he'd suddenly decided he wanted to do something else. My throat was seizing up.

'*Ouf*!' I puffed out my cheeks and touched my napkin to my eyes, which had filled with tears. Love was fading; what hurt most was that I'd really thought that Gavin and I . . . We had so much in common. We laughed at the same things. And uniquely, we shared the same nightmare from the past. I had truly believed that I had found a replacement soulmate. Now, I was very far from sure.

'Chantal. Sweetie.' Lorna was at my side, trying to put an arm round me. 'I'm sorry. We shouldn't have said anything.'

'You should. You were quite right to tell me.' I tried for a laugh but didn't quite make it. 'All the agony aunts would say that you should, rather than keeping your feelings bottled up.' Those same agony aunts would add, *But only if you're prepared to risk losing your friend.*

Which didn't stop me from feeling forlorn and bereft and all those other lonely things.

We tried to resurrect the easiness that had been between us, but it was difficult. I was already envisaging having to change jobs, since after this bombshell, I didn't see how I would be able to face seeing Lorna every day. And wondering if I could still bear to be her bridesmaid on January the eighteenth.

After a while, I checked my watch and made *oh-goodness!* types of noises. 'Hey, I've got to get back,' I said, fooling no one, and left them sitting dejectedly together, their faces dismal.

What was happening to me? I had thought that my life was at last knitting together. Instead, it appeared to be unravelling at a rate of knots. And I seemed powerless to do anything about it.

Seventeen

I made a phone call on my return to my flat that Saturday afternoon. 'Brian? It's Chantal Frazer.'

'Hello, Chantal. How can I help?'

'Will you come and have lunch at my flat tomorrow?'

'That would be very nice.' He waited a heartbeat. Then, 'I'm assuming it's more than my blue eyes that you're anxious to see.'

'Quite right. But of course it's a pleasure anyway.'

'Should I bring anything?'

'Only your files on Weston Lodge.'

'How did I know that?' He chuckled. 'What time?'

I'd arranged to go to the cinema that evening with Malcolm. He seemed quieter than usual, anxious about something. Although I tried to draw him out, he didn't want to talk about whatever was bothering him. At least, until we were sitting across from each other in his new flat, on his new sofas. The place smelled of fresh paint and coffee; his sitting room was still full of packing cases waiting for their contents to be stowed away, though he'd managed to get his favourite coffee-maker out and a few pieces of crockery. He'd spent heedlessly, buying up half the contents of the household departments at John Lewis's, recklessly purchasing duvets, towels,

292

bedlinen, glassware, a dinner service. It had been fun. But tiring, as we both agreed.

'There's nothing more exhausting than spending a lot of money,' I said.

'Especially when it's someone else's cash.'

Now we sat drinking coffee, our feet up on the new coffee-table. 'Malcolm,' I said. 'What's wrong?'

He grimaced. 'Nothing, really.'

'It's getting late, and I'll have to go soon. But not until you tell me what you're worried about.'

'You could stay the night here, if you wanted to,' he said diffidently. 'You could christen one of the new duvets, the as-yet-untouched-by-human-hands sheets and so on.' He didn't look at me, and I saw how very much he wished I would. Not just that night, but all the nights of our future.

'Not tonight.' I was well aware that the phrase implied that there might be other nights when I *would* stay.

'All right. Look, Chantal, I hate to do this, I have no right at all, but . . .' He pushed his glasses up his nose, a gesture I had learned meant that he was unsure of himself. 'Sabine would have wanted me to.'

'Wanted you to do what?'

'Give you these.' He got up and went over to one of the as-yet-empty bookcases. On one shelf was a large Manila envelope. 'Take them home with you.' He took my hand and held it against his heart. 'Don't read them until you get home.'

Sunday, two fifteen. Brian and I were sitting on either side of my dining table. I'd roasted a chicken with potatoes and three other vegetables, made plenty of wine-flavoured gravy. I'd even made bread sauce – admittedly out of a packet – since I figured Brian would welcome a traditional home-made English Sunday lunch, followed by apple pie and a piece of really good Cheddar.

'Delicious,' he said, wiping his mouth. 'Haven't had a feast like that since my wife died.'

We cleared the table together, I made him a pot of tea and we sat down again. 'All right, Brian, let's get going. First of all, has your niggle become any clearer?'

He shook his head. 'It's stronger now. I'm completely convinced that I know the answer, if I could only work it out.'

'I have several niggles myself. And I also know that between us we ought to be able to identify what they are. So what I want you to do is go through the whole thing again, as you told me before. But this time I'm going to ask you questions.'

'Two heads are better than one,' he said, never a man to shy away from a cliché.

'Start from where you came through the front door. What did you see?'

'I've told you before, what I remember most clearly from first impressions is a man with twitching hands, a woman covered in blood, a fire burning, a Christmas tree.'

'Was the man bloodied as well?'

'No more than you might expect from a cursory inspection of his stepsons and your sister. He must have turned them over, checked a pulse, that sort of thing.'

'No funny smells, as though something had been thrown on the fire?'

'No. Anyway, we raked through the ashes the next day. There was nothing but wood and a few typewritten pages.'

'But didn't the police say that her manuscript had been shoved on the fire and been partially burned?'

'That's right.'

'OK: here's one of my niggles. How did the boys get hold of her manuscript in the first place?'

'Sneaked into her study and took it, I presume.'

'But she was *in* there, Brian. Working. She didn't come out until much later. So how could anyone have snuck in without her noticing?'

'Hmmm. I never thought of that.'

Frankly, in my opinion, the investigating officers at the time didn't seem to have thought of much. 'Did you actually see the manuscript, charred or not?'

'There were papers on her desk. I don't remember them being burned.' He riffled through his files and studied the report. 'Nope. Doesn't say anything here.'

'Where did the description of a burned manuscript come from in the first place?'

'Just a minute . . . The inspector mentions it here: several pages of typescript were found on or in the hearth. Upon examination, these proved to be part of Mrs Clio Redmayne's work-in-progress.'

'Did Gavin Vaughn mention the manuscript?'

'Not as far as I'm aware.'

'It's perfectly possible she burned them herself.

Academic writers do chuck stuff out if they're revising their work; I know that from my father. And what handier than a nice big log fire outside her room in the hall? It's perfectly possible that she came out with a sheaf of papers and threw them into the fire, then looked up and saw the deliberate damage to the Balthus painting.'

'Which wasn't even hers. No wonder she was furious.'

'All right, Brian. You've briefly emerged from your study, carrying pages which you're going to burn. You wait to make sure they don't fall out of the grate, and while waiting, you look over at the Balthus. Someone's written FUCK YOU on it, clearly visible. You are absolutely livid, since the picture doesn't even belong to you but to a friend. You know that the culprit has to be one or both of the boys. You race up the stairs and start shouting at them.'

'Do I?'

'Of course you do. You certainly don't go through the baize door to the kitchen, search around for a knife – it's your own kitchen, but you don't know where things are kept, since you don't spend much time there – and then go upstairs to begin indiscriminately slaughtering your sons.'

'I suppose I don't.'

'You scream at them. You threaten to stop their television privileges, you ground them. As a person who knows quite a lot about art, with a husband in the business, you're fully aware that the words can be cleaned off the canvas, so although you're furious, you know it's not the end of the world.'

'Then what do I do?'

'Brian, I'm perfectly prepared to believe that she never went upstairs at all. Not until several hours after the killings had taken place.'

'Who knifed them, then?'

'I honestly don't know at this point. I'm not even saying it wasn't Clio. Just that there's reasonable doubt. And since she never spoke a word from that day onwards, we don't have any idea what really happened. It was much easier for the police simply to seize on the most likely person, and she didn't offer any defence, refused even to have a defence lawyer, if I remember rightly.'

He nodded. 'Good point.'

'Moving on. Was there anything suspicious on the floor? I had a look at the photographs you brought . . . so what's that lying by the skirting board?'

He peered at it, then reached into his breast pocket and brought out a pair of glasses before looking more closely. 'I'd say it's a recorder. If you read the SOC report, it'll tell you.'

'Why was it there?'

'The third boy came back at about seven thirty. He was a pretty good pianist, so he sat down at the piano and one of the others played the recorder, or so he told us. He said they were practising carols, ready for Christmas Day. You can see right there, on the grand piano, that there's a carol-book open on the music holder. Perhaps one of the boys left the recorder there and it rolled off later.'

I looked more closely. *The Holly and the Ivy*,

I read. George, the youngest, would still have his soprano voice, and Gavin might have been singing alto, if his voice had broken. The scene was all too poignantly clear in my mind. 'What about the tree?' I asked.

'You can see for yourself: no problems there.'

'What about the presents?'

'*What* about them?'

I told him about the book which I'd sent Sabine as a Christmas present. We stared at the police photographs of the presents piled under the tree. There were not a great many of them yet – there were still forty-eight hours until Christmas Day – and I imagined that a lot more would have been put under the tree the night before. There was a big old-fashioned magnifying glass in the desk which had once belonged to Hamilton's grand-mother; I got up and brought it over to the table.

'Look,' I said. 'My present for my sister was wrapped in shiny red foil with silver ribbon, and in one of her letters, she specifically mentions that she put it under the tree when it arrived for her from California. I can't see anything wrapped in red there, can you?'

Stonor examined the photo with great care. Shook his head. Said, 'If it's there at all, it must have fallen behind the tree, because it's certainly not in front of it. And there aren't enough presents out there yet for it to be hidden under a pile of others.'

'So who would have taken it?'

'Certainly seems an odd thing for the murderer to steal. He or she would hardly want to make off with an art book, even if he or she knew exactly what you'd sent your sister.' He looked at me sadly. 'I know you want to exonerate Clio Palliser, but it seems to me that she's easily the most obvious person to have stolen it.'

'So in your eyes, as well as being a murderer, she's also a thief.'

'I didn't say that. But she's right there on the spot, she can see it's too big to be a novel, Sabine's studying art at the university, so it's pretty likely to be a book on art. Which was one of Clio's own interests.'

'That's ridiculous. She had plenty of money. Why would she steal someone else's art book? Especially when it's wrapped up so she doesn't even know what the package contains. And when would she have stolen it? After she'd killed everyone? She wouldn't have done it before because at some point I'd have asked my sister if she liked her present from me.'

'Well, it looks like someone stole it. And who else but her?'

'Something we should clarify to ourselves,' I said. 'These murders weren't premeditated. There has to have been a tipping factor of some kind – doesn't really matter what it was – which triggered them.'

'Very true.'

Which still didn't explain how the book had ended up on Gavin's bookshelf.

Outside the windows, grey clouds were pouring rain on the city, fat droplets drumming at the windows, darkening the room. I switched on lamps and the overhead lights so we could see more clearly. And while I was doing that, it came back to me. 'Didn't you say that Gavin Vaughn was allowed to pack up his things before the house was sealed?'

'That's right. Some of his belongings from their shared room. His presents from under the tree.'

I felt an enormous sense of relief. There was no sinister edge to the fact of Gavin having the book, just a simple mistake. So at least one small mystery appeared to have been solved. Gavin must have picked up my present for Sabine, along with his own. Perhaps he had even taken some of Edward's. All too easy to do, whether by design or by accident. The boy was traumatized, unable to think clearly, sobbing his heart out, according to the police report, dying to get away from the house and into the safety of his mother's arms. He must have just snatched at a few things . . . and probably been mortified when he discovered what he'd done.

'All right: carry on with your description of what happened that night.'

'The woman – Clio Palliser – simply refused to speak. The man – Harry Redmayne – was in such a nervous state he could hardly speak himself. But he did come upstairs with us and identify the bodies of George Palliser and Sabine Monroe. He said there were two other boys, so we started looking for them. It didn't take us too long to find the body of Edward Palliser, hidden in a cupboard under the back stairs which led down into the kitchen.'

'What about the third boy?'

'Neither hide nor hair. Later we went all through the house looking for him: cupboards, attics, under beds and so on, calling his name, telling him everything was OK, but we couldn't find him. It was pitch dark by then, and the whole house was a crime scene, so it was hard to organize a search party. Of course we went outside and shouted for him, but he couldn't have been anywhere close by or he would have heard us and answered. The poor kid must have been too terrified to do anything but stay where he was, I imagine.'

'Yes. I guess so. Anyway, moving on from when you first arrived at the house.'

'Like I said, we went upstairs . . . and found the two bodies. I'm not going to show you photographs of either of them.' He quickly turned over several shots, but not before I'd caught glimpses of a prone body, outflung arms, my sister's russet hair.

I gulped a bit, feeling my eyes moisten.

'Later we took shots of Sabine's room, both that night and the next day . . .' He handed me a couple. A nice room, the opposite end of the house from where I'd stayed on the special bank holiday weekend. There was pretty much the same view as I'd had: trees, fields, grazing sheep.

On the table by her bed I could actually make out the titles of some books, and there was a desk where she would have sat to write her letters to me. An open box of Tampax stood on the window sill: she must have been having her period. This was a detail I'd not known before; it brought her suddenly closer. A small kilted teddy-bear in a tam-o'-shanter holding a tiny red heart stood on top of a pile of papers: a present from Malcolm

301

Macdonald, I guessed. The same one my mother had been holding when she died.

More barely held-back tears. More gulping. Without looking at me, Brian put his hand over mine. Brushing my eyes, I stared intently at the photos but could see nothing that shouted significance at me. But why would there be anything? It had been a perfectly routine evening for her until she heard George screaming, came out into the passage outside her room, was struck down.

'Right,' Brian said, trying to sound brisk. 'There's nothing in these bathroom shots that would—'

'I want to see them. The ones after poor little George was taken away,' I added hastily.

'Yes.' He handed over a set of prints. A big old-fashioned bathroom, chequered floor, towels hanging on thick metal rails, a half-open linen cupboard containing folded laundry, more towels, Georgie's jeans and sweatshirt lying in a heap on the tiles. There was blood everywhere: the edge of the bathtub was smeared with it, the water was a dull crimson, blood had pooled on the wet floor and spread across to the boy's crumpled clothes.

'Then what?' I said.

'There was this trail of bloody footsteps leading to the door of the room where the older boys were. They'd been playing together but came out in the passage when they heard George yelling.' He rested his chin on his hand, looking down at the file in front of him. 'Can you imagine? It must have absolutely terrifying to see her coming towards them with a bloodied knife in her hand.

302

I imagine by then, having killed George and your sister, she must have looked like something out of a horror film. Anyway, they both took off towards the back stairs, and she went after them. You can see traces of blood on the wooden steps, though by then most of it would have been wiped off the soles of her shoes by the carpets along the corridor. Edward tried to hide in the cupboard where the brooms and mops were kept, while the third boy carried on to the kitchen, into the pantry and out through the gap into the paved area outside.'

Stonor passed over the relevant prints and again I studied them, without the slightest idea of what I was looking for. Edward's and Gavin's shared room looked like the bedroom of any couple of young teens. Two beds stood against either wall of the room. One was tidy, the duvet pulled up to the pillow and carefully straightened, the other with the bedding thrown carelessly back. I could guess which had been Gavin's since he was always meticulous about keeping things neat. Lying on the tidied bed was a carrying case which must once have held a camera. A big panda sat in one corner, with a school cap on its head and a pair of football boots tied together and strung round its neck. Model planes hung from the ceiling. A large globe stood in one corner. On a central work table, there was a microscope, a boxed chemistry set, another box with the lid off, holding the paraphernalia for performing conjuring tricks, and a couple more planes, half-finished.

Low bookshelves held what looked like pretty standard fare. With the magnifying glass I was

303

able to read most of the titles: *Treasure Island*, the William books, Enid Blyton, *Beano* and *Dandy* albums, the Narnia books, T.H. White, Rider Haggard, Roald Dahl . . . and dozens of others, most of which I'd read myself as a child. I could make out the tattered covers of Dr Seuss books, and a copy of *The Night Before Christmas* lay open on the floor, the photograph so sharp that I could easily make out the words on the page.

It was a boy's room, a child's room, innocent as milk, until the killer had destroyed it forever. Nausea curdled the pit of my stomach, and I clenched my teeth. But there was no stopping now. One way or another I had to get through this ordeal. 'What was Edward wearing when you found him?'

'Jeans. Checked shirt. Sweater. Trainers. More or less what you'd expect from a kid that age.'

'So, what next?'

'Well . . . here's a shot of the big old kitchen, as it was then. Since converted into ground floor bedrooms. No bloodied footprints – the murderer obviously gave up after realizing that the third boy had got away. I imagine she went back up the stairs, along the passage, down the front stairs and on to the chair by the fire.'

'Look,' I said. 'Let's keep this neutral, shall we?'

'I am trying,' he said.

'I'll say.'

'If it wasn't Clio, how did she get covered in blood?' he said.

'Haven't we been over this before? If she wasn't the killer, it seems fairly obvious to me

304

that at some point she must have come out of her room, gone upstairs to kiss the boys goodnight or whatever, found the bodies, gone into shock, held them against herself saying *oh no, oh no*, or words to that effect, gone back downstairs into the hall and sat there to wait for her husband to arrive home.'

'Wouldn't she have wondered where the third boy was?'

'She was so out of it most of the time, if she even registered that he wasn't there she probably assumed he was still having supper with his parents' friends.'

'Our problem really is that we only have one witness to what happened and he was so traumatized that he probably wasn't a very reliable source of information. And strictly speaking, he wasn't even a witness.'

'We came up with at least two other possible killers,' I said. 'Harry Redmayne. And Jenny Forshawe.'

'It can't have been Redmayne. I've gone over and over his alibi, interviewed everybody again, and there really isn't any way he could have been on the scene. As for Jennifer Forshawe, she *could* have done it, I suppose, but it seems incredibly unlikely. Too many questions to be answered, such as what did she do with her dogs while she was laying about her with a knife upstairs? There were no signs of any dogs at all, though I know we weren't looking for any. Would she really have gone haring up the stairs with a knife and killed everyone because her painting had been defaced?'

305

'Her own husband outlined the whole scenario and how it might have played out,' I said.

'I'll bet you he'd be horrified to think you'd taken him seriously.'

'The arguments against it being Clio are the same for her. She'd have known that even though it was a wicked bit of vandalism, the swear words on her picture would easily clean off. And why would she have a knife with her?'

'If you lived in the country, you'd never ask such a question. From clipping a trailing bramble to freeing a trapped animal, you never know when you'll need one, is the simple answer. Especially if you're walking through woodland.'

'Here's another reason why it was unlikely to have been Clio,' I said. 'The older boys hadn't even had their baths when the killings happened, but according to the staff at the house, she normally never emerged from her study until nine o'clock or after. Or so it said in the various reports I read at the time. And remember she was desperately trying to meet a deadline with her book. I just don't see her coming out as early as eight o'clock, which was when George was supposed to have started his bath. Especially since, according my sister, the boys were allowed to stay up pretty late during the holidays. The older ones didn't have to get into bed until half-past ten or even later. So Clio wouldn't be kissing anyone goodnight as early as eight or so.'

'If she ever did. From what we've heard, kissing wasn't high on the agenda.'

'Were you there when they found Gavin?'

'Yes. It was about four thirty in the morning.

Obviously not yet daylight but we had powerful torches. I was with a colleague, a uniform, so that the lad would know we genuinely were the good guys. We were calling his name, shouting that we were the police, and he suddenly emerged from this tumbledown sort of stone hut and stood staring at us. Very wary, very unsure that we were who we said we were.'

'What did he look like?'

'Half-frozen. Completely out of it. He was in his underwear, barefooted, feet all cut up.'

'What sort of underwear?'

'Vest and Y-fronts, in that thick white cotton stuff they used to wear back then. Winceyette, is it called?'

'That's something else, I think.' I couldn't repress the image of Gavin as he was now, bare-chested and sexy as hell in his grey Calvin Kleins. Not that I was about to share the thought with Stonor.

'He told us that he was undressed because he'd been getting ready for his turn in the bath when she showed up with the knife – the killer, that is.'

'What did he look like?'

'More or less what you'd expect. Shivering, scratches all over his arms and legs from running through the wood in the dark. Face and hands streaked with dirt.'

'Is there a picture in the file?'

'Yes.'

'Let's look at it.'

Stonor leafed through the file and found the picture he was looking for. An unmistakable Gavin, hunched and freezing in the filthy bit of sacking he'd wrapped round his shoulders and was holding over himself like a cloak. His hands were filthy, his fingernails caked with dirt, his hair full of leaves and twigs and more soil. In a second photograph, he was wearing a policeman's parka over his dirty underwear.

'Anything else?'

'He kept saying, "*Where is she? Where is she? Don't let her get me!*" Staring round as though he was expecting Clio to leap at him any moment with a knife in her hand. It was pitiful to see. Poor kid, we felt so sorry for him. The sergeant put his jacket round the boy's shoulders, and we half-carried him back to the house.'

'Apart from that, did anything else strike you about him?'

Stonor frowned. 'I don't think so.'

'No blood on him?'

'Only from the scratches. Mind you, his underclothes were so filthy that you couldn't have told whether there was blood or not. Why do you ask?'

'I'm just trying to cover all the bases. I wonder why he was in his underwear, when Edward was still fully dressed.'

'As I said, they were expecting to get into the bath.' Stonor stared out at the weather in the street below. 'You ask me, it's going to snow any minute now. I ought to get back before they stop the buses and the Underground.'

'Will you leave the file with me?'

'All right.' He sounded doubtful.

'Don't worry, I'll keep it safe. And I'm not going to give myself nightmares by looking at the . . . the awful ones.'

As I helped him into his parka and saw him to the door, I said, 'Don't forget your niggle, will you? If you can remember what it is, it could be the key to the whole thing.'

After Stonor had gone home, I spent the next couple of hours minutely studying his police notes, poring over photographs, rereading witness statements, drawing up a timetable as far as it was possible. I started at the beginning, when the police first entered the house. There was the tree, the presents. There were the bloody footprints leading across the hall to the chair where they found Clio Palliser sitting. Apart from the missing present from me to Sabine, I could see nothing odd or unexpected about the scene.

Using the photographs, I followed the same route as Stonor had taken that night. I went upstairs, zoomed along the passage, avoiding the bloodstains. I closely re-examined the crime-scene photos of Sabine's room. Nothing new presented itself. There was Sabine's handbag, the glasses she sometimes wore on the night-table beside the bed, a book lying open on its face (I couldn't see the cover but it was undoubtedly one of the thrillers she enjoyed), her checked cotton bathrobe across the foot of the bed. I checked out the bathroom photographs, trying not to envisage the actions which had resulted in those blood-spattered tiles. I moved down the passage and stood at the door of the boys' room. It still looked just as it had earlier, when Stonor showed me the photographs. I hadn't really expected anything to have changed, but confess

309

that I kind of hoped something would jump out at me, some revelation would make itself known. I flipped through the pages in Stonor's files and found Gavin's testimony. He'd stated that they were building something out of Lego when they heard George's screams, then Sabine's. As before, the two sides of the room differed, one neat, one boy-messy. The two of them were both, according to Gavin, just waiting for the call to get undressed and go to the bathroom when Clio Palliser had begun her murderous attack. He and Edward had come to the door of their room, taken in what was happening and raced away down the passage, with her in pursuit.

I looked again at the photographs of the bedroom. And then again. I knew instinctively that the clue was to be found somewhere in there. I reread Gavin's testimony. I reread the police statements. I spread the photographs of the room out in a comprehensive display and once again examined them closely. The answer I wanted was staring me in the face, if only I could decipher it. I flipped to the photo of poor frozen half-naked Gavin emerging from the tumbledown stone hut. I went back to the boys' room. Finally, I looked up. There was a smile on my face.

I pulled out my cellphone and dialled Brian Stonor. 'Worked it out yet?' I said.

'Worked what out?'

'The niggle.'

'It hasn't popped fully formed into my head, if that's what you mean.'

'I know what was bothering you,' I said. And proceeded to tell him.

He was silent while he thought it through. Then he erupted. 'Oh my God! You know, I think you may be right!' He sounded almost orgasmic. 'Oh my heavens . . . That's it, that's the answer, has to be!'

When I offered corroborating evidence, he said, 'We weren't in full possession of the facts at the time. Even so, why on earth didn't we spot it sooner?'

When Gavin rang me later, I was lying on the sofa, snoring my lunch off. Not a pretty sight, I'd be the first to agree, mouth half-open, drool on the cushions. I was glad that he wasn't there in person.

'Hello, my little munchkin,' he said. 'How's things?'

'Things is good.'

'Did you feed my cat?'

'Absolutely. And delivered her eight kittens. Also changed the sheets, did some laundry, washed-up, cleaned out the fridge, watered the plants, threw away the old newspapers, vacuumed the carpets . . .'

'You're an angel.'

'I know,' I said. Should I say it? Yes, I decided. Nothing to be lost and with any luck a puzzle sorted. 'I got a bit of a surprise, actually.'

'Oh?' His tone was guarded.

'Yes.' I mustered up some nonchalance. 'You've got a book I recognized on your shelves.'

'You know we have many books in common, darling. What was special about that one?'

'It happens to have belonged to my sister.'

'I told you, she often lent me books,' he said easily. 'It must have been packed up with my other things by mistake.'

'Except that this one was the present I had sent her from California for Christmas. It was under the tree, waiting for Christmas Day. It hadn't been opened when she died.'

There was a pause before he said, 'Are you accusing me of something, Chantal?'

'No, but—'

'But what, exactly?'

'I don't understand how you got hold of it.'

'I already said, it must have got mixed up with my stuff when they were packing everything up.' He sounded impatient.

'I suppose so.'

'You sound as if you don't believe me.'

'Of course I believe you, Gavin.'

'I'm not clear why you were rooting round among my possessions in the first place.'

'Don't be so anal,' I said. 'For a start, I wasn't rooting. I made a cup of coffee and sat down for a few seconds, after all my hard work. That's when I noticed the book. That was before I cleaned all the windows and just after I'd painted the entire flat from top to bottom. I do hope you don't mind me taking a break.'

'Sorry if I sounded annoyed, darling.' The friendliness was back in his voice. 'I'm a bit stressed over here. Work's not going as smoothly as we'd all hoped.'

'I suppose it means you'll be away longer than you planned.'

''Fraid so.'

Eighteen

The light was already beginning to fade when Stonor and I arrived the next day, although it was barely quarter-past three. Stonor pulled the car into a lay-by and parked. We stuffed gloves in our pockets and hats on our heads, laced up our boots, then struck off the road and down into the woods between Weston Lodge and Byfield Hall. The sky was grim with snow-heavy clouds: every now and then a handful of flakes came drifting down. 'You've got a torch, haven't you?' I asked.

'Of course.' He patted a pocket. 'Plus some spare bulbs, just in case.'

'Do you think we'll find anything?'

'After what you've told me, I'm a hundred per cent certain that we will.'

I took his hand in mine, held it tightly. 'I feel like a Judas,' I said.

'Don't, Chantal. Do *not* think that. The man is no more than vermin, a dangerous wild animal who will kill and kill again. You don't think that your sister and those boys were his last victims, do you?'

'Well, unless we find some evidence to prove that he was responsible for the deaths here at Weston Lodge – and make sure that he's put away for life – he's going to run around free to do whatever he wants to whomsoever he wants.'

'Maybe we should have told David Charteris

313

we'd be here. Someone. Anyone.' Even with Stonor at my side, I was uneasy, remembering my first walk through these woods, the sense I'd had of some sinister element stalking me. It had been daylight then, bright sunshine reaching through the leaf-cover. Now it was darkening, the black-trunked trees crowding in on us, branches clacking in the sullen wind. 'Why didn't we?'

'Because we're not going to be very long,' Stonor soothed. 'It's an in-and-out job: we know exactly what we're looking for, we find it, we go up to the house or drive home again.' He put an arm round my shoulders and pulled me closer. 'Cheer up, Chantal. We even know more or less where it is. There's no need to get anyone else involved, or alarmed.'

'But suppose something happens?' I was beginning to feel a chill between my shoulder-blades, a whisper of fear.

'What could happen? He's miles away. He can't hurt you. Trust me.'

We reached the little hut, still as tumbledown as it had been in the spring, but surrounded now by dead yellow grass and the withered stems of nettle and willowherb. Dull leaves of ivy sprawled over what remained of the stone walls and up over the few slates which still clung to the brittle timbers of the roof. Elder and bramble crowded the doorway.

Stonor pulled a rubberized torch from the pocket of his padded jacket and went inside, treading across broken pieces of tile, kicking a dead pigeon to one side as he advanced on the rusting piece of machinery which stood to one

314

side of the earthen floor. I stood at the entrance space, watching him as he aimed his torch, examining the ground around it. Behind me, tree branches creaked in the cold wind, and evergreens rustled. Something was moving about amongst the foliage: a bird foraging in the dry leaves, some animal searching for prey.

'Here we are,' Stonor said. He knelt on the ground to look closer at the floor of the hut.

'See anything?'

'Not really.' He shone the torch round the space. 'He testified that he crawled into the piece of machinery to keep warm and pulled up some old sacking to cover himself, didn't he?'

'That's right.'

'I can't see anything. At least, nothing which might – hey! Just a moment. What's this? I think I might have found . . . Where's my trowel?'

He started rooting round in the pockets of his padded jacket. At the same time, an arm clamped round my neck and a big hand covered my mouth. I was yanked backwards and off-balance. My lips were crushed hard against my teeth, so hard that I was afraid some of them would come loose and lodge themselves in my throat. All I could do was make faint whimpery noises but they weren't loud enough for Stonor to hear. I was held in an iron-solid grip and silently pulled away from the hut further into the woods, my heels dragging through the leaves. Then I was flung hard down on my face; someone knelt heavily on my back, crushing me into the ground, and my arms were wrenched viciously backwards and fastened with the sort of plastic tie that people use to secure

315

their suitcases. My ankles too. I lay there terrified, immobilized. I opened my mouth to scream, but before I could do so, my face was jammed down even further into the mud of the forest floor. A brutal hand grabbed my hair and turned my face sideways, at the same time shovelling handfuls of leaves and wet earth into my mouth until I could hardly breathe. Then I was turned over on to my side.

The whole operation couldn't have taken more than half a minute. Lying immobilized and gagged, I could only watch helplessly as my captor moved silently back to the shed. He must have jumped on to Stonor's back and knocked him flat before he even realized someone was behind him, someone who was not me. I heard the 'ouf' of expelled air as he collapsed on to the floor of the hut under the weight of his attacker. It was only a few seconds later that he appeared in the doorway of the hut, hands caught behind him, a knife at his throat. He was forced over to where I lay, pushed to his knees and then to the ground, where he was ordered to lie prone, then he too had his ankles trussed with a plastic tie.

The situation was so absurdly over the top that at first I didn't really feel panicky. It felt more like a play or a film than real life. This sort of thing didn't happen outside a thriller, or off-screen. Not to average citizens such as Stonor and me.

I had managed by now to spit out most of the mud and leaves but my mouth was rough with dirt and leaf-mould. I already knew who was responsible for this. I knew his smell, his feel, the touch and taste of his body. I had lain in his

316

arms and thought that this was all the ecstasy I would ever need.

I had forgotten how strong he was. Without much effort he dragged us both further into the woods, towards a smooth-trunked beech which stood beside the track. First me, then Stonor. In turn, he lashed us against it, sitting up, shoulder to shoulder; he must have come prepared with rope and tape, the plastic ties, the brand-new, shiny-bladed axe he was now hefting from one hand to the other as he stood observing us.

'This is going to be such fun,' he said.

'What is?' said Stonor. I could feel the tips of his fingers against mine.

'Why, punishing you both, of course.'

'Punishing us? What for?' I asked.

'Oh, Chantal, Chantal,' he chided. 'Surely you know by now that I can't stand people using my things. Damaging them. That's what happened with Georgie, all those years ago. I came home from having supper with the Archers, and when I went up to our bedroom, bloody Edward had let bloody Georgie muck about with my brand-new Nikon, which he'd then dropped on the floor and broken.'

'Bad luck,' I said. 'They certainly got what they deserved. Unlike my sister.'

'Come on,' he said. 'Be reasonable. She knew I'd killed Georgie. What else could I do? Besides, she kept treating me like the other two, as though I was just a little boy.'

'Resisting your advances, you mean.'

He blinked. 'If you want to put it like that.'

'You can't seriously think you can kill us both and get away with it, do you?' Stonor said.

317

Between us, his fingers were working against the plastic tie round his wrists.

'I got away with the others,' Gavin said. 'All this time. I suppose I was lucky that poor old Clio chose to keep her mouth shut.'

'What would you have done if she hadn't?' asked Stonor.

Gavin shrugged. 'Her word against mine. I think they'd have believed me over her. After all, the woman was known to be as nutty as a fruit-cake. And I had spent most of the night in the shed, freezing to death.'

'Most of it? Not all?'

'God, no. She didn't even come out of her study for about two hours – I knew she wouldn't because she never did. I had plenty of time to sort a few things out.'

'Like steal the Christmas present I'd sent my sister?'

He looked shamefaced. 'I shouldn't have done that. Thing is, I knew it was a book on art, and she'd lent me books before, so I didn't really think anyone would mind – if they ever knew.'

'*I* mind,' I said. 'I mind very much.'

He shrugged again. 'There you go.'

'I'd also like to say that I think you are vicious, evil and completely insane.' I had nothing to lose by angering him: we were at his mercy and he could do what he liked to us. 'It turns my stomach that I could ever have loved you. Slept with you. Fancied that we might make a life together.'

The expression in his eyes made me shiver. 'Funny,' he said. 'That's pretty much how I feel myself.'

'Do you honestly think you'll get away with this?' said Stonor. He pressed his fingertips against mine; they were looser this time.

Daylight had almost disappeared, but the snow, now falling more thickly than before, gave a moonlight-glow to the woods. In the distance, near the entrance to the woods, I thought I could see two black-clad shapes. Were they trees, or people?

'I always have before,' Gavin said. 'Besides, they'll never find you. Not until it's far too late. If at all.'

'If we disappear,' I said, 'why wouldn't they search for us?'

'I thought I'd use the well,' he said.

'Wouldn't they look down there?'

'Not after I tell them that I saw you both drive away. I shall play the wronged lover. I shall cry a bit. I'll say I came back early from Port Moresby, because I already suspected you of deceiving me with that Scotsman. That I discovered you were also having it off with the policeman. That I followed you both here, we argued, you two left. They'll believe me. People always do. That's why I'm so good at my job.'

I couldn't tell if the two distant shapes had moved or not. Or even if they had been there in the first place. The light was deceptive, bright and yet imprecise.

'Don't!' I screamed suddenly, for the benefit of the possible watchers. 'Please don't kill us, please don't, Gavin. We've done nothing wrong.'

Gavin turned his mad eyes on me. 'Shut the fuck up, you sodding faithless bitch. You're worse than

319

your fucking sister. And when I say fucking . . .'
He grinned. Nodded. Said, 'Oh, yes, she was a
hot little number indeed, especially for a randy
thirteen-year-old like I was back then.'

I knew he was deliberately winding us up. I'd
read the letters from my sister which Malcolm had
given me, saying that the third boy, Gavin Metcalfe-
Vaughn, was constantly coming on to her, that
he'd appeared in her bedroom several times and
tried to get into bed with her, that he was so much
bigger than she was, that she was afraid he might
rape her. The phrase *my blood began to boil*
seemed literally true at that moment; I could feel
the heat running along my veins, seeping through
my skin. It would not have surprised me if there
were scorch-marks up and down my limbs. If I
had had a gun in my hand at that moment, I would
have had no compunction whatsoever in shooting
him there and then. Straight through the testicles,
if I could manage it.

'What about my car?' Stonor was saying.

'Yes,' I added. 'We both have jobs, family . . .
If we go missing, they'll search for us.'

'Don't you worry your little red head about the
car,' Gavin said. 'I'll be able to dispose of it and
no one the wiser.'

Looking at him, this brilliant, unstable psychopath, with his nice face and good hands (how
wrong my mother had been, maintaining that
good hands meant a good man, and how foolish
such generalizations were, and how so much
more foolish I had been to believe her), I thought
of poor Miki Masshi, carrying this monster's
child. I thought of Paula Metcalfe-Vaughn, that

320

harried expression on her face, the tortured way her eyes rested on her son. Did she know what he was? What he had done? The trouble with being a mother was that even if she knew her son was a murderer, it wouldn't necessarily stop her loving him, or worrying about him. Hoping against hope that he wouldn't do it again.

I thought of the dilemmas posed: knowing how dangerous he was, do you turn him in? Could you do that when you had given birth to him, seen him through babyhood, childhood, adolescence? Or would you try to watch his every move, try to forestall him, warn people off him? I thought of the damage he had caused, the lives he had taken, the lives he had ruined. I determined that if Stonor and I got safely out of this, I would finally lay to rest what was left of my sister's ghost and move out of the shadows into the sunshine. I had been happy with Hamilton; I could be happy again with Malcolm, I thought.

But it looked as though I was not destined to survive. I looked beyond Gavin, but the cold was making my eyes water, and I now had no idea whether what I thought I'd seen had been anything more than winter-bare trunks. After all, who would be out in this kind of weather, at this time of day? Jennifer Forshawe had been one, but I did not imagine that Desmond was likely to be tottering through the trees towards us, and even if he were, he was far too frail to take on a maniac like Gavin. One tiny corner of my mind hoped he never discovered that I had briefly fingered him for the Weston Lodge killings.

Gavin was coming closer towards the tree to

which we were tied, the axe-blade catching what little light was left as he swung it back and forth.

'I promise this will hurt,' he said. 'Like it hurt poor little Georgie and the lovely Sabine. I wish I'd had longer to deal with bloody Edward – if he hadn't virtually given my camera to his brother to play with, nothing would have happened – but I needed to get away before Madame finally came out of her study. Not that she would have heard any of the screams and shouting, in her sound-proofed space.' He looked from one to the other of us. 'Is that bizarre, or what? A mother who shuts herself away from her children like that? Barely comes up to say goodnight? We didn't see her at breakfast, or dinner. Sometimes at lunch, but for the most part she had a tray in her room.'

It *was* bizarre. The Hon Clio's indifference to her sons had caused the death of two boys and my sister. If she'd come out of her room earlier, instead of leaving her maternal responsibilities to Sabine, they might all have been saved. And in that sense, she was culpable; perhaps, after all, she fully deserved her incarceration in Broadmoor.

Gavin began dancing round the tree, taking playful jabs towards us with the axe. He didn't make contact with our flesh: I could tell this was by way of being a preliminary warm-up for him, the foreplay to the act, a means of heightening the tension for us all. I suspected that he was getting a sexual thrill out of the thought of sliced flesh and gushing blood. Each time the axe-blade came near me, I cringed, knowing that eventually he would begin to carve us to pieces. Slowly. Taking his time. Enjoying our agonies. I could feel screams of terror building up in my chest; I'm not brave, I'm not heroic: I would scream and scream, even though I would know that nobody could possibly hear me.

But in all the thrillers I'd ever read – which was a great many – the mantra seemed to be that when faced with a homicidal maniac, you should keep them talking.

'How did you know we were here?' Stonor said.

'I followed you, of course. I've been keeping an eye on you for days. I told this fucking faithless cunt here that I was going to Papua New Guinea, and went to stay in a hotel, keeping a close eye on developments in South Kensington. And sure enough, a car containing both of you left this morning, with me close behind.'

'What did you think you were going to find?'

'Proof that the two of you were cheating on me. Well, let me tell you, that never happens, not without immediate retribution. The last person who – tell you what, sweetheart,' he said, smiling at me while he rested the axe lightly against his thigh, 'I think I'll do him first.' He jerked his head at Stonor. 'Take it nice and slow, nice and painful. You can watch . . . You should enjoy that.'

'Why are you doing this?' I said.

'I told you: I don't like people messing with my stuff.'

'Your *stuff*?' I couldn't hear even the faintest tremor in Stonor's voice.

'Yeah. Her.' He approached Stonor and, using the flat of his boot, kicked him as hard as he could in the face. 'She's mine. Not yours. Not anyone else's. *Mine.*' He kicked Stonor again, drawing blood. I heard the squash and crack as the ex-policeman's nose was broken.

'I'm *not* yours,' I said, trying to keep my voice steady. 'I'm not anyone's. So you can stop kicking him.'

'Would you rather I kicked *you*?' He moved towards me, punched me in the face, stamped hard on my knee and then kicked me in the stomach. Jesus! The pain was so huge that I screamed at the top of my voice before slumping forwards, only the bonds around my chest keeping me upright against the trunk of tree. My head whirled like a fairground attraction, coloured lights shooting off and on, each spark a thrust of pain. Oh God, I prayed. Let it be quick. Let me pass out as soon as possible.

'Don't take him on, darling,' Stonor said. I realized he was trying to make Gavin think we really were lovers.

'Darling?' said Gavin, his voice rising. 'Darling, is it? I'll show you whose fucking darling she is.' He ran towards us, spinning the axe as though it were a straw in his big hands. He lifted it high in the air, and I closed my eyes, thinking of Kathy Bates sledge-hammering James Caan's ankles in *Misery*. This would be much worse. We were in the hands of a sadistic psychopath. I heard the thump of the axe-blade against flesh and Stonor's involuntary shriek of pain. I could see the gleam of white flesh against his slashed trouser-leg and even the welling of blood, black in the faint darkness.

'You're a maniac,' I said rapidly. 'You are stark raving mad. You should be in an institution. Or better still, hanging from the gallows. Or being electrocuted by—'

It was Gavin's turn to scream. 'Shut the fuck up!' he shrieked. 'Fucking shut up, you sleazy cunt.'

I'd read somewhere that while psychopaths generally have no empathy with their fellow human beings, are cold-hearted, ego-centric and manipulative, they take particular exception to being called mad. Was it worth antagonizing him further by repeating it, would it buy us any more time? Or would it simply make him even more cruel in his dispatch of us?

He stood in front of Stonor and lifted the axe once again. 'I want her to watch this, Mr Stonor. Now, where shall I start? An arm? A hand? A foot?'

Was this craziness what Sabine had faced?

'You know,' Stonor said conversationally, 'you're rather overacting the part of the crazy psychopathic killer. All we need now is a fiendish laugh.' His voice was fainter than usual, husky with pain.

'Thank you,' Gavin said. 'I've often been complimented on my acting talents.'

Behind him, I could still see along the track which led to the end of the woods and this time, despite the uncertain light, I was almost certain that two of the trees had moved closer. Someone was in the woods with us. I had about three seconds to convey to them that we were facing mortal danger. The man who had committed at least three murders was about to commit two more.

'Help!' I shouted. 'Help us!' I nudged Stonor. 'Quickly! He's going to kill us! He's got an axe.'

'Help!' shouted Stonor. 'Help!'

But the two shapes did not stir, and no one came running to our aid. They were just trees, after all. I slumped against the bonds which held me against the trunk of the beech.

'Scream as much as you like!' Gavin laughed. 'No one can hear you. We're surprisingly far away from any of the nearby houses. And in any case, old Dessie Forshawe is as deaf as a post. Take him out of the equation, and there's no one else within miles. Except for the shirt-lifters at the Lodge, and they're too busy poncing around being nice to their so-called guests to hear anything going on outside.'

Tears filled my eyes. My bravado and disbelief at the surreal situation we were in melted away, leaving me paralysed and despairing. My mouth was dry with terror, and one of my legs shook uncontrollably. This was it: I was about to die. I knew there was no point in pleading with Gavin, or begging him to spare our lives. We were only alive and still undamaged because of his over-inflated ego, his arrogance and conceit, his desire to let us know how clever he was. Nor did the irony of my situation escape me: I had always followed so closely in my sister's footsteps, instead of making my own history, and now I was to die a similar death to hers, at the hands of the same deranged maniac.

I reached again for Stonor's hand and was surprised at how much of it I was able to grasp. The plastic ties were softening and stretching

326

from the heat of our bodies. We'd be able to get free of them any moment. And much good it would do us, hobbled as we were.

Now Gavin was standing over us. 'You know, for once in my life I really don't where to start.' He flicked the axe first towards me, then towards Stonor. I hunched into myself as much as I could, making myself small. It was now so dark that I couldn't actually see more than the shape of his face, the two dark circles of his eyes.

He lifted the axe. He faced Stonor. 'Pity it's so dark,' he said. 'She won't be able to see you suffering.' A thought struck him. 'Tell you what, though. We could throw some light on the proceedings. You had a torch, didn't you? Must still be in the hut.' He started to move fast towards the tumbledown structure. 'Don't go 'way, now!' he called over his shoulder.

But that's exactly what we did. Suddenly, out of the dark, a knife slit the bonds round my chest and ankles, while at the same time someone did the same for Stonor.

'Come on, you two,' a voice whispered. 'It'll take him a while to locate that torch.'

'Get moving,' said a second voice. 'Quick!'

We were dragged to our feet, and all four of us ran or stumbled down the track to where the woods opened out. Now I could see the lights of Weston Lodge through the trees and, between them and us, the round shape of the well. I shuddered with horror. Gavin would have tossed our bodies down there without a thought, replaced the lid, and gone away, back to his everyday life.

'What the fuck . . .?' There was a furious yell

327

behind us as Gavin found that we had got away.

I glanced over my shoulder and could see the thin beam of a torch. Life was returning to my legs now. Beside me, Stonor was gasping. 'I don't know how much further I can manage,' he said weakly.

'Not far now. Put your arm round my shoulders.' I recognized Trevor Barnard's reassuring voice. 'I've got you.'

And then suddenly, almost, it seemed, at my shoulder, I heard a mad voice, whispering, whispering. *'You can't get away, you can run but you can't hide . . . I'll find you in the end, and when I do . . .'*

They were almost the very words which my sister's killer was supposed to have whispered as she struck down her boys and my sister.

'Come on,' Barnard said, his voice urgent. 'Quickly.'

We were at the well now. To the right of us, someone said, 'Over here. This way. Quickly, now.'

Stonor and I veered to the right, while Barnard raced to the far side of the well-mouth. I could faintly see him standing there and hear Gavin labouring and cursing along the path we'd just travelled, only feet behind, flashing his torch on the ground and then upwards, trying to find us.

'You won't get away,' he was screaming.

Someone spoke into my ear. 'I rather think you will, you know.' It was a voice I'd never heard, but I had a strong suspicion whose it was.

'Thank you,' I said. Tears filled my eyes. 'Thank you very much.'

'I'm sorry. I'm so very sorry.' It was the same voice. Arms went around me and held me tight.

'All right, son.' I recognized Trevor Barnard's voice. 'Put the axe down and come over here. The game's finally up.' Faintly against the night-glow of snow and lights from the Lodge, I could see his tall figure.

'Not yet!' Gavin snarled. It was as though an animal was speaking: a wolf, perhaps, or a rabid dog.

Hidden among the cold trees, snow falling on my head, my face, into my eyes, I saw him leap forward, screaming incomprehensibly, the sounds of pure uncontrollable rage and hatred. He ran fast towards Barnard, the axe lifted high above his head.

Then, all of a sudden, he was gone. A long-drawn-out shriek, this time of terror, a couple of thumps, a hollow splash. Someone had removed the cover of the well; Gavin had tripped over the edge and disappeared into its depths.

There was complete silence for a moment, apart from the hiss of snow landing on wet branches and the faint clicking of holly leaves rubbing together.

'You can come out now,' Barnard called. One by one, we emerged from hiding: Stonor, me and a plump white-haired woman. Even before Barnard flashed his torch at her, I knew there was only one person it could be.

Barnard put his arm round her. 'It worked!' he said triumphantly. 'Well done, love.' He turned to us. 'It was all her idea. She said she was sure we could lure him towards me and in the dark-ness he wouldn't see the well and would trip head first into it.'

'Clever.'

'This is Clio,' he said proudly.

'I rather guessed it must be,' said Stonor.

'I'm very glad to meet you at last,' I said.

'What are we going to do about Sonny Jim down there?' asked Barnard.

'What are the choices?' I said.

'Only two, as I see it. Either we put the lid back over the well and forget about him forever, which is the option I personally favour. Or we organize a party to get him out of there and see that he faces justice after all these years.'

'I'm with you on the first option,' I said. 'But . . .' It would have been so easy, and a fitting end, but I could not add my endorsement. I had loved this man. Slept with him. Imagined a future with him. I knew he had killed my sister as well as Clio's sons, in cold blood, and not felt a shred of remorse. There was his wife, too, another probable victim, and who knew who else? And I had no doubt that given time he would have hacked both me and Stonor to death, and enjoyed doing it. Nonetheless, he was a fellow human being and deserved something, though it was difficult to say what.

'Me too. That . . . that . . . spiteful evil manipulative *devil*.' Stonor could hardly get the words out.

'The only reason I don't want to leave him down there,' said Barnard, 'is because I want to clear Clio's name. She spent nearly twenty years locked away for something she didn't do, and she deserves to be able to hold up her head at last, instead of skulking her life away.'

330

'I don't skulk,' protested Clio, and there was the hint of a dimple beside her mouth. She wore a white knitted hat which covered most of her hair, a thick white padded ski-jacket. Melted snow gleamed on her shoulders, and snowflakes sparkled in her hair. She was the palest person I had ever seen. A snow-woman. An Ice Queen.

'We'll get him out,' Barnard said. 'But not just yet. I'm going to put the lid on. Let him think that we're going to leave him there.' He and I dragged the wooden lid over the opening with considerable difficulty. Furious yells and threats could be heard from the bottom of the well, followed by desperate pleas not to be left there. No one took any notice.

'Mr Stonor needs medical attention,' I said.

'Why don't we go down to the Lodge and, as a matter of extreme non-urgency, organize a rescue party for this bastard,' said Barnard. 'Have some dinner or something.'

'How many people know who you are?' I asked Clio as we set off towards the Lodge. 'Or where you are?'

'Very few. We felt it safer to keep it quiet.'

'Safer?'

'Trevor was convinced that if Gavin knew I was alive and free, he would come after me. I'm the only one who really knew that he was responsible for the deaths of my poor children. If I'd been a better mother, more engaged . . .'

'There are several people who suspected that it wasn't you,' I said. 'Does David Charteris know you're here?'

'No. My solicitor arranged all the details to do

331

with the sale of the Lodge. All I had to do was sign the papers. But Lord Forshawe knows.'

'He tried to convince me that his wife had been responsible for . . . for what happened.'

'Typical of Desmond.' Clio laughed, a bright sound among the dark masses of holly bushes and laurels which lined the path down to the house. 'Jenny was more than capable of it, I can assure you. A genuinely fearsome woman, she was.'

Through the still uncurtained windows of the Lodge, we could see people sitting in the bar with drinks in their hands, the dining room already lit with thick church candles, lights in the smaller salon and people laughing in front of a blazing fire. It all seemed so normal, compared to what had taken place only minutes earlier. I thought of Gavin down there in the darkness of the well, glowing in the wet shadows like a giant pus-filled insect.

He'd be pulled out, arrested, put in prison until his trial, and then, with any luck, would spend the rest of his life behind bars.

'Why are you out in the woods at this time anyway?' I asked as we slid down the slope to the side door of the Lodge.

'That's when we usually go for a walk,' Clio Palliser said. She had an unusually clear voice, uninflected and even. 'We don't want people to know I'm here.' She raised a hand and brushed a strand of snow-wet hair from her face. 'Not that I look anything like I used to do.'

'There's always someone who'll recognize you,' I said.

'Of course. I just didn't want to cause any more

trouble for Trevor than I had to. He's been so amazingly good to me.' Clio led us towards one of the side doors and pushed at it. It squeaked open, scraping an entrance way of red and black tiles. The four of us walked along a passage lined with shelves full of catering packs of flour and sugar, lentils and paper towels, jars of expensive jams and boxes of detergent. Clio opened a door at the end, and we were in the body of the hotel. To the right was a door at which she knocked. A voice called to us to come in, and the four of us entered.

David Charteris was sitting in an armchair on one side of a log fire, while opposite him sat Omar, his partner. He rose to his feet and stared at us all, a look of puzzlement on his face.

'Trevor,' he said. 'And – um – Mrs Frazer? Mr Stonor.' He looked at the blood pouring down Stonor's leg. 'Oh my God . . . Can I help?' His gaze fell on Clio. He stiffened. For a moment he was silent. Then he said uncertainly, 'Clio?'

'She didn't do it,' Barnard said quickly. 'It wasn't—'

'Shh,' Clio said.

'Is it really you?' David came forward and wrapped his arms round her. 'Clio,' he said softly. 'Oh my dear.' His voice broke and tears filled his eyes. 'We have so wondered where you were, what you were doing.'

The room broke into a babble of sound as introductions were made and explanations were given. David opened a small fridge concealed by wooden panelling and brought out a bottle of expensive champagne. Omar found glasses.

David offered a toast. 'Welcome home,' he said.

Clio shook her head. 'This was never my home. Not after my mother died. It was my hell.' Even overweight and white-haired, she was still very beautiful. She carried herself with dignity, and I wondered how she had endured the years in Broadmoor without breaking. Her Catholic faith, perhaps. Her inbuilt sense that sin must be atoned for, and that her sins of omission had led to the deaths of her sons and of my sister.

How had Maggie Fields described her? Like a dragonfly on speed. I doubted she would ever return to that frenetic sense of activity, but now that we knew the whole story, maybe she could at least return to some of the lively happiness she'd known up at Oxford.

While Omar pulled a first-aid kit from a drawer and started to deal efficiently with Stonor's wound, David Charteris had moved over to a desk standing in the middle of the room. He dialled a number and, turning away from us, said something we couldn't hear.

Minutes later, there was a tap on the door, and Maggie came in. 'You said there was someone here I should meet,' she said looking from one to another of us. 'I don't . . .' She stopped. Widened her eyes. Held out her arms, screaming, 'Clio! Clio Palliser! Ohmigod, this is incredible. Where – how – what are you *doing* here?' Then she was crushing her friend in her arms.

'More to the point, what are *you* doing here?' Clio had removed her hat and jacket. In the light, she seemed paler than ever, her hair white, her face almost bloodless.

Maggie explained, clutching at Clio's sleeve as though afraid to let her go in case she disappeared again, as she had so many years ago. 'This is fan*tas*tic!' she kept saying. 'Unbelievable!'

Omar was holding a bewildered hand up to his head. 'I'm lost,' he said. 'Will someone please tell me what the *hell* is going on?'

Nobody took much notice. 'But how did you . . .?'

'How were they . . .?'

'I don't understand who exactly . . .'

'Yes, but *why* did you . . .?'

There was a jumble of explanations, until Clio held up hand. 'Please be quiet,' she said. It was easy to see the person she might have been if circumstance hadn't got in the way. 'First of all, don't mourn for my wasted years. I deserved them. Due to the situation surrounding the birth of my sons – of which I'm sure most of you are by now aware or have guessed at – I never loved them sufficiently. They were such beautiful boys, and I neglected them in almost every way possible.' Tears came into her eyes and slowly fell down her pale cheeks. 'Oh dear. Those poor defenceless children. How much better they deserved than me.'

Barnard tried to put his arm round her shoulders, but she edged away. 'No, let me speak.' Again she held up her hand. 'I'm not worthy of pity . . . and I've paid for my indifference. You wouldn't believe how many tears I've shed over the two of them. I accepted my punishment, and I let the real killer get away with it, which was almost as irresponsible of me as the way I treated my sons.'

It was more or less exactly the scenario I had

envisaged when I wondered why Clio had gone to Broadmoor without protest.

'Talking of killers,' Stonor said. His leg had been bandaged and was now resting on a foot-stool. He had a glass of champagne in his hand and looked extremely comfortable. He looked at Trevor Barnard and raised enquiring eyebrows.

'The hell with him,' Barnard said. He smiled across the room at Clio. Her dimples deepened as she looked back at him. 'It's nice and wet down the well, not to mention cold and dark. Let the bastard stew.'

David Charteris had been busying himself opening another bottle of champagne and refilling glasses. Now he said, 'I'm like Omar, slightly lost. Do I gather that someone is languishing at the bottom of our well?'

'That's right.'

'And who is this unfortunate person?'

'The real killer from twenty-three years ago,' I said.

'And he is?'

'Gavin Metcalfe-Vaughn. The third boy.'

'What? But he was just a kid.'

'A large kid,' I said. 'A bullying kid. A murderous kid.'

'The one that got away?' said Maggie.

'Not any longer,' I said.

David raised his glass. 'A toast,' he said. 'To all of us, though I don't pretend to have the slightest inkling of what's going on here. I always knew it wasn't you, Clio. I even guessed where you might be when you . . . when you came out of prison, but I wasn't going to interrupt your privacy. But how could this third boy have been the one to— He was only thirteen, wasn't he?'

'He was. But big with it.'

'The two other boys weren't big for their age,' I said. 'And my sister Sabine was tiny, like me. He didn't have any problem disposing of all three of them.'

'But *why*?' David looked from one to another of us.

'Because of his camera,' I said.

David raised his eyebrows. 'Oh well. I suppose one day someone will tell me what exactly happened. Meanwhile, cheers!'

I thought of Gavin, the handsome charming monster, down there in the well. Someone had said the water was four feet deep, so he would be in no danger of drowning. But he would be freezing cold, soaking wet and, with any luck, totally terrified that we were planning to leave him down there until he starved or froze to death. I wish I could say I felt even the tiniest qualm.

I asked the question that had been bothering me for some days. 'Mrs Palliser, Clio, did you know who the killer was right from the start?'

'I didn't *know*. But it was fairly obvious that it had to be Gavin. Who else could have done it? He'd lived with us off and on for years, ever since he was eight. Back then I was pretty unstable myself, but the tantrums he used to throw were absolutely extraordinary, and his violent tendencies were getting more and more marked. Edward and Georgie whinged about it several times and so did the staff, but I took no notice. I was a close friend of his mother's, you see.

Paula and I were at school together. I didn't want to rock the boat. Add to that the fact that he was the most convincing liar imaginable.'

'And strong for his age, too.'

'The boys used to complain that he hurt them, but if I picked him up on it, he always apologized profusely, said he was terribly sorry, didn't mean to. And again –' her mouth twisted – 'I did nothing. Always too interested in my own affairs to be concerned about theirs. Even when your sister came to me, I . . . I'm so sorry, so ashamed, but once again I did nothing.'

'In other words, he was a catastrophe waiting to happen,' Maggie Fields said.

'That's right.'

Barnard said, 'I suppose we'd better get the police over here, to get that bastard out of the well.'

'When you get him out,' I said, 'make sure someone checks to see what else is down there.'

Later, the story was pieced together, as it should have been from at the beginning. Twenty-three years ago, big Gavin Metcalfe-Vaughn had been brought home after having supper with the Archers. He'd sat down at the piano – he was a talented player – and hearing him downstairs, the other boys had joined him, Edward with his recorder. They'd played carols for a while, then Gavin had gone into jazz, then Beatles songs. Sabine had come down too, and they had danced the Twist and the Charleston, some funky dance-steps from the US. Although Clio wasn't far away, she had heard nothing in her soundproofed study.

Finally, Sabine had called a halt, said she was going upstairs, and they must too; George would be first in the bath, followed by the other two who were to come when she called them.

Gavin and Edward had gone to their bedroom, where Gavin had discovered that during the afternoon Georgie had somehow managed to jam the new and expensive camera which Gavin's mother had recently sent him. In an uncontrollable rage, he'd taken his Swiss army knife and run down the passage to the bathroom where he had stabbed George over and over again, ending up by slitting his throat. Edward had screamed at him to stop, at which point my sister had come out of her room, demanding to know what was going on. By now manic with fury, Gavin had turned on her and then on Edward, who was yelling for his mother, to no avail since she couldn't hear him. Having left Sabine on the floor of the passage, either dead or dying, Gavin had chased Edward down the back stairs to the kitchen and killed him too.

Like all psychopaths, he was cold-hearted and efficient. He knew he would have to dream up a scenario where he was the victim, not the perpetrator. He went back to his bedroom, found a small torch and a bar of chocolate, then went downstairs and squeezed through the hole at the back of the cold-pantry to the outside. He would have liked to linger in the warm house, but dared not. He found his way to the chapel and waited there in the relative warmth until he heard the police sirens, then he ran to the well, pushed back the lid, stripped off his blood-soaked day clothes and shoes, dropped them down the well, along with the knife, tugged the lid back into place, and made barefooted for the tumbledown hut from which he'd emerged, wincing with every step. Just as I had expected, what was left of his clothes was found at the bottom of the well. By smearing himself with dirt and leaf-mould from the woods, he had successfully concealed whatever blood had soaked through his shirt to his underwear, and at the time, no one had thought to submit them to forensic examination.

In the hut, buried beneath the soil under the rusting piece of machinery, they found his black Maglite torch and even a scrap of foil wrapping from the chocolate bar he'd taken with him to help him get through the long cold night which lay ahead. He had spent an hour or two with a stick, scraping away at the hard earth floor so he could bury the torch. No one would buy his story if they found he'd taken a torch with him.

Staring at the photographs of his bedroom, I had realized two things. Firstly, if Gavin had taken off his clothes, they would have been neatly folded at the end of his bed. But like Edward he was still fully dressed, so his bloodied cords and sweater somehow had to be disposed of, and the well was the perfect place to hide them.

Secondly, and perhaps less convincing as an indication of his guilt, there was no sign of the Lego construction that Gavin swore he and Edward had been working on when Clio Palliser was supposed to have come up the stairs. It could be argued – indeed later, Gavin's defence counsel maintained unsuccessfully that this was the case – that the boy had been too traumatized to remember exactly what had happened. But he'd had years to get it right, and arrogantly he still insisted on the Lego, even though there was nothing to support his claim. In the photographs of the boys' bedroom, the table had been littered with balsa wood and small plastic parts: Stonor's files confirmed that this had indeed been the case. A laundry basket full of Lego pieces was stashed under Edward's bed and did not appear to have been brought out for some time, judging by the dust on it – something I surmised, and then checked with Stonor.

You might wonder at what point I had changed from lover and friend to avenging angel; I think it was the moment when I opened the letter from Sabine which she had sent to Malcolm, and which he had passed on to me.

I seriously think he's going to rape me one night, she'd written. *I've twice complained to the Hon Clio, but she just nods vaguely and does nothing. He's so big, Malc: I wouldn't stand a chance against him.*

Another time she'd written: *I've taken to shoving the desk up against the door before I get into bed. I don't think it would stop him, but it would at least give me some warning. Last night I actually brought up a pepper-shaker which I keep open by the bed, just in case!*

Can you imagine? And no, I can't tell my family: they'd worry themselves sick . . .

If only I had known. But like everyone else, I was completely taken in by his plausibility, his charm.

* * *

341

There was one last repercussion. I was sitting in my South Kensington flat one Saturday morning, several weeks after Gavin had been consigned to Broadmoor – and no one involved in the case had missed the irony of that – when the intercom buzzed. It was Gavin's mother, wondering if she could have a few words, as she put it. And while I hesitated, she went on, 'I would quite understand if you would rather I didn't.'

I was free of Gavin, but she was not. It would be kind to allow the poor woman a chance to talk. 'Come on up,' I said.

She was nervous and sweating. She'd lost a lot of weight; her skin had an unhealthy colour. I brought her a cup of tea while she fanned herself with a magazine from my coffee-table.

'How are you?' It was hard for me to sound warm and concerned, since I felt neither.

Her eyes were slightly unfocused, and her hands shook as she lifted her cup to sip at the tea. 'I'm fine. Yes, just fine. Doing well. Getting on with life, you know?'

'Indeed I do.' I sat down opposite her. 'Now what can I do for you?'

'I just wanted to explain,' she said.

'Explain what?'

'About . . . about Gavin.'

'*What* about him?'

'Why he was like he was – is.' She fumbled with the bag beside her on the sofa and took out a small bottle of pills. She poured out two and swallowed them with a gulp of tea. 'He was our only child, you see. He never wanted for anything. Because he was so precious, we gave him everything he asked for. That's not a good way for a child. If nobody ever says no to them, they get to thinking they're entitled. They get angry, they can't see why they can't have something when they always have before. And then he grew so fast, he got so big.'

The gap between the last two sentences was full of implications which I didn't want to explore. Had Gavin lifted a hand to his mother? She wasn't very tall. Like me. Like, I guessed, his first wife . . . What was her name? Sammy? No. Miki. Did he deliberately target small women, ones he could easily bully? The letters from Sabine which Malcolm had shown me still made me furious on my sister's behalf. He'd only been thirteen then. I trembled for that poor little Asian girl, in her bright kimonos. Had he beaten her? Was that why she went over the cliff? Would he have beaten me if we'd ended up as husband and wife?

'He was a rugby player,' his mother went on, as though that somehow excused his behaviour.

It didn't seem worth pointing out that, on the whole, other rugby players, far more well-known than Gavin ever was, did not appear to be physically abusing their girlfriends.

'I'm buying a little cottage near Gavin,' she said. 'I'll be able to see him quite often.' She nodded at me. 'He's getting together a rugby team, you see,' she said brightly.

There was something disconnected about her sentences; I began to wonder whether she too had mental problems. She leaned forward for her cup of tea and somehow managed to knock the contents to the floor. 'I'm sorry,' she said. 'I'm

343

so sorry, so very sorry . . .' She looked at me. 'Don't worry, I'll clear it up if you just show me where . . .'

'Stay where you are,' I said firmly. 'I'll get a cloth.'

I went out to the kitchen and came back with something to wipe up the mess while she dithered, murmuring, 'Oh dear, oh dear, I'm so sorry.'

Kneeling down, I began to mop up the spilled tea. Out of the corner of my eye, I saw her reach into her bag again. More pills? No wonder she seemed slightly out of it. I was about to finish cleaning up when I saw her raise her arm. Something flashed.

'You little bitch,' she snarled, her face twisted with hate. 'You sent my son to prison, you accused him of things he would never have dreamed of doing, he's not like that, you've ruined my life, he's lovely, he's kind, he's . . .'

He was all those things. He was also a cold-blooded killer, a clever manipulator who for twenty-three years had persuaded people to believe a version of events which had nothing to do with the truth. Why had it not occurred to someone to doubt his description of what had gone down that bloody evening? He was the only witness . . . and everyone involved with the case had played straight into his hands.

Now, I fell backwards, screaming Malcolm's name, while I scrambled awkwardly away from her, still on my back, using my elbows to get out of her range. She slashed at me again, cutting straight through the sleeve of my shirt and sweater.

'*Malcolm!*'

She raised her arm again, saying, 'I've already lost my husband, now you've made sure I've lost my son as well, I'll kill you for that, someone like you doesn't deserve to live, doesn't deserve to have a life when my boy has been put away for the rest of his.'

As her arm descended again, Malcolm burst out of the kitchen and grabbed her as she tried to plunge the knife into my body. 'That's enough,' he said authoritatively. 'That's quite enough now. No more.'

'But you don't understand,' she said rapidly, the words tumbling from her mouth. 'If it wasn't for her, my son wouldn't be locked up.'

'Don't you think it's fair that he should be?' I said. I was still on the floor, my knees trembling too much for me to get to my feet. Blood was running down my arm, staining my clothes. 'After what he did to my sister, to those boys. To Miki . . .'

'He had nothing to do with Miki falling like that,' she said furiously. 'He told me. He said it wasn't his fault at all, nothing to do with him.'

'I don't suppose any of it's ever been his fault,' I said.

'If you mean his father, that was nothing to do with him either, Gavin was away at school when that happened, not his fault at all. Any more than George Palliser was. He was a nice little lad, George, I was always very fond of the two boys. If he hadn't broken Gavin's brand-new camera . . .'

'What did Miki do?'

'Only got herself pregnant, didn't she? He told

her and told her he didn't want children, but would she listen?' She appealed to Malcolm and me. 'Well, what would you have done?'

I had called the police while she was talking. Now I heard the sirens as they came down the road and stopped outside my building. When the police buzzed my bell, I let them in, while Paula went on convulsively talking. 'Same thing with that guy in Singapore, it was an accident but they said it was Gavin's fault, which of course it wasn't, but people always seem to blame him for everything, every little thing as though he was some kind of a . . .'

She was still talking as they led her away and down the stairs. Someone remained behind and took statements from us. I explained that I'd asked Malcolm to stay in the kitchen, just in case. After all, Paula and I had nothing in common, nothing to say to each other; I'd last seen her at Gavin's trial and had never expected to see her again. So why had she come? I had been fairly sure her arrival at my front door had not been intended as a social visit.

When everyone had gone, and the flat was quiet again, Malcolm and I fell into each other's arms. 'Please, God,' I said. 'Please let there not be any more of this. It's been going on for so long, and now I just want rid of it. I want to be free of it all.'

'It's over,' Malcolm said. 'Trust me.'

And I did.

Epilogue

Two years later

Malcolm and I went over to Rome for Christmas. Each day it was warm enough at noon for the four of us to sit out on the balcony with a glass of wine and smile at each other. We ate out, in a number of small restaurants lit by candlelight and full of laughter. One evening, Dad poured champagne into crystal flutes which I recognized as having belonged to my French grandmother.

'Two announcements to make, guys,' he said. 'First of all, I've finally persuaded Ingrid, my wonderful companion, to let me make an honest woman of her . . . and believe me, it was a hard sell.'

'I am very independent, Allessandro.'

'And will continue to be, *cara*. The other thing I very much want to say is this: life is like a river, it constantly flows onward, and there's little you can do to change it. Sometimes it hits rocks or falls over cliffs and then there's sadness and pain. And sometimes it just runs smoothly between banks full of flowers. Please forgive the homespun and unoriginal sentiments: they are nonetheless deeply felt, and I am joyful beyond words to see my dearest daughter happy again, after more vicissitudes than most people have had to endure at her tender age.'

'What is "vicissitudes", *caro*?' murmured the *contessa*.

'I'll explain in a moment. But first, let's drink to all that is lovely in our lives and try not to remember those things which have not been.'

Malcolm put his arm round my shoulders, and I knew with certainty that I was a woman not made for glamour and excitement, for obsession and madness, for fire and frenzy. I knew, too, that for the rest of my life I would sometimes wake sweating in the middle of the night, seeing again that axe-blade, listening to Gavin's demented words, wondering what malign influences had shaped him. And that I would turn to my husband, and he would soothe me, assure me in his soft Scottish accent, that everything was fine, there was no more danger, no more heartache. That there never would be.

And the words 'quiet' and 'comforting' had never seemed more beautiful.